DIEMENS

DIEMENS

Guy Salvidge

Published by Forty South Publishing Pty Ltd
Hobart, Tasmania
fortysouth.com.au

Printed by McPherson's Printing Group
Melbourne, Victoria
mcphersonsprinting.com.au

Cover image: 'Seal shooting in Bass's Straits',
Engraving from *Illustrated Australian News*, May 4, 1881
Courtesy of State Library Victoria

CONTENTS

NEW YEAR ISLAND

◆

1802

THIRTEEN MONTHS WE sealers have been trapped on the edge of the world – on an island off an island off an island. Our haven goes by the name of New Year, but it is hardly an apt moniker for while it is December, of warmer weather there is naught but rumour. Day upon day and week upon week, the fog rolls in and cloaks wretched men in a spectral gloom.

Fifteen turns around that coy sun I may be, but I can silence the roar of the bull sea elephant same as any man. The bull lays triumphant in repose on the grey sand beach where this past season he enjoyed the favours of the cows in his screeching harem. It does not occur to him that his breeding ground is mine for killing. The beast comes crawling with his stenchy breath and yellow fangs but fortunately on land he is no more than an enormous bladder filled with jelly. I strike! Driving the point of my lance into his rippling chest, piercing his heart, and when he stills I commence the butchering. With each slice I whisper *you are oil, you are oil, you are oil.*

I am George Baggs, wrenched from the cradle of my birthing and flung across the sea to this infernal place at the mercy of a pitiless wind. Here I huddle, my gaze ever eastward to Seals Bay on the parent isle, which in turn is named after

Governor King. I have heard that Van Diemen's Land seethes with natives but there are none on King Island, so the emus and kangaroos are docile prey, never having known any predator. This is a place where the western winds howl ceaselessly and rain pours down in sheets from the maw of a black sky. Where slumbering elephants appear as boulders and only turn back from stone as I draw near with lance and club in hand. Where we have found ourselves consigned by Captain Campbell to a life of boiling down sea elephants while we await his return.

A hard life, yet I have known harder still. I spent my first twelve years in England in Dunstable Town with scraps of mouldy bread for my supper. Ma with eight bairns, each one scrawnier than the last, and the only talking Pa did was with his belt. I was the eldest and destined for the flour mill, but I ran away to London with a vow to sire nowt on a woman unless I knew how the littluns were expected to eat. I was living on my wits but the River Police did not take kindly to us mudlarks and we were hauled off to Newgate Prison one and all. No worse there than portside and at least we were fed. I saw many a hanging at Execution Dock and I might have been fitted for the noose myself but for my tender years. I was pardoned to serve His Majesty by sea and sent aboard *Harrington* to work for Messrs Chace, Chinnery & Co in their southerly trading ventures.

I saw the ports of Madras, Calcutta and Sydney but I was ill-fated to tarry long at Port Jackson for Governor King would not consent to the landing of four thousand gallons of Bengal rum from *Harrington's* hold. Well might he not for the colony was awash with spiritous liquor already. No sooner had the Governor ordered us gone than wily old Campbell struck a deal transferring the rum to a departing brig, leaving *Harrington* free to undertake a sealing venture. The captain landed twelve souls on New Year Island to commence boiling down the blubber of sea elephants and meanwhile he went further afield to prosecute his various pursuits. Campbell said the island 'twas an oyster fit for shucking and we have been shucking ever since.

Now though, every oil barrel stands filled to the brim and there is little to do except warm ourselves by the fireside or scan the wet horizon for a sail. As I am the youngest man here, my days are oft given over to the latter. The oiling beach is unfit for observation and so I must traipse overland to the north shore and my rude shelter. The ground is boggy and overgrown with tangled thickets but I have worn in a track. My shelter is a gully's cleft and protected from the sou'west gale or else I should freeze to death here. There is no dry place on New Year except inside the biggest hut but Poseidon's own tempest must be blowing before those ruffians will admit me.

From my lookout, I can espy the rocky point of King Island's northern cape and it is from this direction that *Harrington* will come if it ever does. On the rare times when the sea is becalmed a hush comes over the world and my heart fills like a bellows. If it is possible to be further from the centre of things then my imagination will not allow it and yet here I am spared a life of tumult and the daily scrabble for bread. Not a day goes by without meat passing my lips. Better, in truth, that *Harrington* does not come for when it does it will bring the whole world tumbling after.

The sea today is not calm but instead a grey seething mass. The wind is more west than sou'west and it is a safe bet another storm is brewing. Our shore leader, Percival Grant, says that at this latitude the wind sweeps the world without ever touching land except here. He cannot say from whence this ill-wind springs for the west is the kingdom of nothing, and yet all Europe's ships must cross this void en route to the Antipodes. If I perceive a sail in the west it will be a ship bound for Sydney and with a captain foolhardy enough to try Bass Strait.

Many a grim morn I have spent at my vantage and it seems this is destined for another, the wind thinking to whip into a gale. As the first squall lashes me, I hear the barking of black fur seals at play on the ledges below. I shuffle around to take best advantage of the bough and draw my knees up to my chest. The wind swirls and raves and there is no escaping it nor the rain and so I jam my head between my knees and imagine myself a seal. There is a core of warmth within me that no blast of icy rain can penetrate and I fear nothing of the cascading water. Let it wash me out to sea and if it does I shall live as seals do. I will snort and rollick and never go hungry for the deep teems with fish and squid and crabs. Come breeding season, I will haul myself ashore to find a mate and bare my teeth at any who would deprive me of her favour. I shall bask in the sun until one day I will catch a whiff of an unpleasant stink and when I look up it will be myself, George Baggs, standing there in sealskin rags. The club comes crashing down upon my snout –

When I open my eyes, the rain has abated but I am still me, still shivering wet at the foot of a tree. I get to my feet to flee the bog and look out over the bay. It will rain again momentarily.

I am seeing but not registering and my mind screams *A sail! There is a sail!*

Not *Harrington* or anything of that order but a longboat labouring between our isle and King. It will do well to shelter in our lee for the rain is thundering again. I dash back to camp, the only thought in my head not for the fate of those sailors but because with news like this then surely – *surely* – I will be permitted to stand by the fire as I tell it.

◆

THEY ARE Frenchmen, four in number and allegedly the vanguard of a larger party encamped at Sea Elephant Bay on the far side of King. This is cause for alarm owing to the state of war between Britain and France, for does this not make them invaders? Supposedly it does not for theirs, they say, is a scientific endeavour. The Frenchmen are frozen half to death, their skin festooned with lesions and scurvy sores, and they are as thankful for a place at the fireside as I. Only the sortie's leader, Pierre Faure, speaks tolerable English. We listen as he delivers the news of peace:

'Our two nations ceased hostilities on March 27th as per the terms of the Treaty of Amiens and it is a very good thing. Commodore Baudin had the pleasure of dining with your Governor King many times during our recent sojourn at Port Jackson and now they are the best of friends.'

The sealers want to know if Faure has proof of the treaty – a paper.

'Ah no, although such a paper surely exists on our corvette, *La Géographe*. I am simply a surveyor sent to circumnavigate King Island and thereby to furnish the Commodore with a map. I had been informed about Englishmen on New Year Island but I would not have called upon you if not for this wretched storm. Your weather is terrible, no?'

As Faure speaks, his utterances compete with the raving wind. He is as slender as I although perhaps a decade older, a twig of a man amid the rough-cut sealers. He introduces one of his colleagues as Midshipman Charles Baudin – no relation to the Commodore – while the other two remain anonymous. The Frenchmen are given meat and drink and some of the sealers begin to drift away. Faure declares our kangaroo steaks the finest he has tasted but on the quality of our rum he remains tactfully silent.

Once he has eaten, he resumes speaking:

'There is a British schooner, *Cumberland*, at Sea Elephant Bay. Its master is a Lieutenant Robbins, and aboard is your surveyor Grimes. Your great cartographer Flinders neglected to chart these isles as part of his survey and yet they are all said to belong to the British by the Declaration of Taking of Possession. Every parcel of land east of the 135th meridian is covered under this declaration, even the isles of New Zealand! The scale of your acquisition is stupendous, no? You might as easily cast a net over the whole world and call it New Holland, although I think Governor King prefers the name Monsieur Flinders has given it, Australia.'

Faure pauses to hear our response, but he can see by our silence that we are unfamiliar with this strange-sounding term. He carries on:

'Forgive me if it has fallen to a Frenchman to inform you but this is my point entirely. The modest means of your infant colony are grossly outstripped by the territorial ambitions of your government. Your lawmakers in Whitehall issue a decree claiming sovereignty over a vast swathe of the globe and they do so in perfect ignorance of what it is over which they lay claim. It is left to men like myself to risk their lives describing to the British what it is they have taken. You have been here many months, I believe?'

Silence. None will speak.

'If my words have given cause for embarrassment then I offer my humblest apologies.'

'We've been here since November 1801,' I say.

'And what is your name, young man?'

I tell him.

'Then I offer you my thanks, George Baggs. A year is a long time to be left in such a frightful place.'

'Have you news of *Harrington*?'

'*Harrington*, the brig captained by William Campbell?' Faure frowns. 'I believe it was latterly anchored at Port Jackson.' He turns to his colleagues and speaks in their native tongue. Now Baudin is interjecting. Despite the fact I cannot understand a word, I hang on every one. Finally Faure explains what is being said.

'*Harrington* was indeed at Port Jackson during our recent sojourn, but Citizen Baudin informs me she sailed some days before we did.'

'Was she bound for King Island?' I ask.

Faure asks this of Baudin and the latter shakes his head. I catch the word *Peru*.

Faure's frown deepens. 'It is Monsieur Baudin's belief that *Harrington*'s destination is the port of Peru. If true, and I have no reason to think otherwise, then I am afraid it will be many months before your Captain Campbell sees fit to grace you with his presence.'

But what about the oil?

Barrel upon barrel of it, nearly odourless and said to burn longer than any other. For thirteen months we have toiled, our arms atremble and our nostrils filled with the stench of blood and offal. Sea elephants beyond counting have fallen before our lances and our knives, the trypots piled high with melting blubber. All the while we had imagined our labour worthwhile and our lives meaningful, and now we find it is a lie.

Perhaps in sympathy with my lament, the day has turned still fouler. The sou'west gusts are surging and they bring forth a rolling thunder. The worst accidents are to be feared by venturing into a sea as loathsome as this, and thus the Frenchmen are offered the use of the smallest and draftiest hut for as long as they should require it. As this is where I sleep, it falls to me to lead the way. A thick fog lies draped across the beach, rendering further efforts at observation pointless, and thus I am spared a return to my lookout. As I admit the swirling day into the hut I notice it is but a pitiful shanty. The Frenchmen go about selecting cots and I tell them that it doesn't matter which smells the worst, the one nearest the fire is always the one to be had.

'Tell me, George,' Faure says, 'who is your leader?'

'That'd be Grant with the hook nose.'

'And yet this Grant uttered not a single word?'

'He'll speak when he's ready and not before.'

'I do not envy you, George. How is it that a boy of such fine intelligence has ended up amidst such people?'

I explain that I am indentured to Captain Campbell until I am eighteen, an age I will not attain until June 1805. Until then I must serve Campbell aboard *Harrington* or any place he might choose to set me down.

'Your Captain Campbell is a privateer and a drunkard.'

I tell Faure that Campbell has a liking for the lash but that he is no worse a drunkard than any other. I know nothing of the man's dealings beyond the fact it was his intention to land four thousand barrels of rum and was prevented from doing so. Now he is a sealing master and no orphan in that.

'It all comes down to seals,' Faure says, 'From the black seal you take its fur and from the elephant its oil, and you'll go on until there isn't a single one left on these shores.'

I tell Faure it is a matter for the captain. I am but a servant and one labouring under sentence.

'Forgive me, George, for it is your government I would pass judgement on. Your hands are tied as you rightly say, but perhaps there is another way beyond blind obedience?'

'Then what is it, Monsieur Faure?'

'If you will address me as Pierre then perhaps I shall tell you.'

'Pierre.'

'First, I shall tell you how our paths have come to cross. Two years we have been at sea aboard *La Géographe* and *Le Naturaliste,* and in that time we have crossed the globe and seen many of its native peoples. New Holland is a vast and wondrous land and for days beyond counting I was engaged in charting its coastlines. It has been an honour and a privilege to prepare such charts.

'Our journey took us south to Van Diemen's Land and we were awed by the beauty of the landscape and the goodwill of its native people. It is a land strongly reminiscent of Europe and yet it has never known Europe's wars. We spent the months of your southern summer exploring the D'Entrecasteaux Channel and the many other rivers and islands there.

'Those of us aboard *La Géographe* lost contact with *Le Naturaliste* and for several months we knew nothing of the latter's fate. We sailed north to chart the southern coastline of New Holland, and there we were astonished to discover your navigator Flinders and his ship *Investigator* at a place he has dubbed Encounter Bay.

'With the weather worsening, we made our return to Van Diemen's Land despite the parlous condition of many of our sailors. It had been Commodore Baudin's intention to further refine our charts but by now he too had fallen ill from scurvy. We were months from port, our provisions scant and with more sailors sickening by the day. There were repairs to be made and missives to be sent and so we set sail for Port Jackson.

'By this time, I was myself debilitated and barely able to raise my head from my bunk. When we finally reached port, winter was upon us. Our spirits were revived by seeing *Le Naturaliste* safe at anchor alongside *Investigator,* and we were further encouraged to hear that our nations had resumed their peace. Governor King proved a most magnanimous host and our sick were received at the military hospital.

'We knew we would soon be saying goodbye to our friends aboard *Le Naturaliste,* for Captain Hamelin's mind was set on an immediate return to France. The little fleet sailed for the island bearing the name of our good friend the Governor. The weather, however, was in no way befitting of the season. Shortly after our arrival, imagine our astonishment upon sighting another sail inbound from Port Jackson! And yet our eyes did not deceive us, for it was yet another ship, *Cumberland*. A dinghy appeared alongside *La Géographe* and the British sailors were welcomed aboard, foremost among them Lieutenant Robbins and Surveyor Grimes. They had a letter from Governor King warning us not to lay claim to Van Diemen's Land in the name of the French Republic for it was already spoken for by the British.

'Our scientists set up their tents on the shore and there they dined with the British. *Cumberland* had been dispatched with such undue haste that it was soon found wanting of several necessary rudiments. Commodore Baudin said it would be his pleasure to furnish the British with all they needed. By that evening, the weather had deteriorated to the extent that the Commodore ordered *La Géographe* to sea to ride out the storm. Upon our return the following morning, we were surprised to find that *Cumberland* had elected to remain on shore, and soon enough came a request from Lieutenant Robbins for assistance in repairing an anchor. The Commodore led a party ashore and we were further surprised to discover the British flag hanging from a tree beside our tents. A British soldier had been left parading and when the wind picked up it was observed that the British colours had been set to fly upside down.

'What mockery was this? Had Lieutenant Robbins truly placed the flag in this fashion to convey the majesty of the British Empire, or was this also a misunderstanding? Perhaps, as the Commodore would have it, it was merely a flag used for straining water that had been hung out to dry. Upon inquiry we were informed that a special ceremony had been conducted and that by the terms of the 1788 Declaration, King Island and the entirety of Van Diemen's Land were said to belong to the British.

'This is the essence of our dealings with your government, George. One day the Governor calls us his friend, the next he sends his emissary with a letter warding us away. One day Lieutenant Robbins asks for assistance in repairing his vessel, the next he flies your nation's colours above our tents. I make maps, George, this and nothing more. I tell myself it is a noble endeavour and one for the glory of science, but in my heart I know I am an agent of the French Republic. It is not my place to ask for what purpose my maps might be used. Please do not imagine me foolish enough to think drawing maps any nobler a pastime than slaying defenceless creatures for their blubber. At least you must stare death down at the point of your lance, whereas the mapmaker is safely tucked up in his bed long before his map is put to use.'

Faure rises from his cot and picks up a lamp hanging from a hook. 'It is a superior oil, no?' he says. He holds the lamp out to me, shadows flickering across his face. 'How long does it burn?'

I take the lamp from him. 'A sixth of a pint will keep a wick alight twelve hours.'

'And there's no odour. No rancid taste when used in cooking.'

'No.'

'Such an oil must have great value.'

'They tell us it is worth six shillings and sixpence a gallon.'

'And how many gallons has your party procured?'

'I think ten thousand.'

'Ten thousand gallons! That is ... three thousand pounds worth! And what is your share of this immense fortune?'

'Nothing.'

'Not a single penny?'

'No.'

'You see? Here you labour a year of your life. You spend your days killing sea elephants, cutting blubber and peeling off fat in great strips. These strips you cut into cubes and the cubes you melt in your cauldrons. When the oil has cooled, you pour it into barrels. When all the barrels have been filled, you sit and wait for your captain to return. When he finally comes, if you are lucky he takes you back to Sydney, if not he has another load of empty barrels that need filling. When your ship reaches Sydney, a fraction of the oil is sold and the greater part packaged for transportation. Campbell is paid, the firm he works for prospers, everyone is happy except for you. But at least you are a man and not a seal. Heaven forbid you should ever find yourself at the sharp end of a lance.'

He returns to his cot.

The wind shrieks and the thunder crashes and all through the night I thrash restlessly, Faure's words whirling in my head. There is an icicle in my breast that no fire can melt. I am at the bottom of a deep well, the world above no more than a pinprick of light.

And I shall sink still deeper.

◆

COME MORNING it is the Frenchmen who rise and I who would linger abed. 'The storm is gone, George,' Faure says. 'We mean to make use of the day before it turns against us. Will you join us for breakfast?'

Outside, the sky is grey but it has stopped raining. In the brightness of the clouds, there is even rumour of the sun. The swell is not large and the sea elephants loll without perceiving that this morning may be their last.

It is too early for many of the sealers to be awake and so the French resign themselves to a breakfast of salt pork and ship's biscuit. 'Not many weevils in this batch,' Faure says. I am no longer accustomed to the taste of dry hardtack. 'The pork is excellent, no?' Faure says. 'It was procured in Otaheite by your navigator, Bass. You know of him?'

'I know he's an explorer and that the strait bears his name.'

'An explorer certainly, although he might more properly be regarded as a businessman. He is said to have invested an enormous sum of his personal fortune on the *Venus*. Governor King induced Bass to sail to the Pacific, as pork was said to be plentiful in Otaheite. Bass spent a fortnight stripping iron from a wreck in New Zealand and fashioning it into axes for trade, and thence the pork cost him nothing beyond the labour of his men. I am told he means to make a fishery of New Zealand. My only regret is that we were denied the pleasure of dining with him.'

'Maybe you will when you return to Sydney.'

Faure looks away. 'I fear we shall not soon be returning to this hemisphere. Nor am I likely to set eyes on you again, George, unless you should have occasion to find yourself in France.' He pats me gently on the back. 'There is the necessity of making some observations, however. Please tell me, what is the highest point on your island?'

'There's a hill yonder that cops the worst of the weather.'

'Then if you will be so kind as to lead the way.'

Faure has me lug his case of surveyor's tools up the hill while his companions prepare their longboat for departure. There are nearly always high winds up here. I watch the weather while Faure sets up his instruments. The theodolite is made of brass and the tripod of mahogany. I have never laid eyes on such wondrous things.

'Made by master craftsmen W&S Jones of London,' Faure says. 'The Republic spares no expense. *Mon dieu*, those reefs look beastly.'

Faure does not need his telescope to perceive that New Year Island is beset on every side by rocks and whitewater and that the west coast is by far the harshest. And the gale –

'The whole west coast of King Island is the same?' Faure says.

'You won't find a kinder landfall than this one.'

I follow Faure's gaze as he appraises the scene. The only sandy beaches are on the east of New Year Island where we make our camp and directly across the bay on the parent isle. 'New Year is breaksea for King,' he surmises. 'There are no such breakseas further south?'

'None that I know of. You'll want to stick close to shore.'

'That is sage advice, George.'

I stand by as Faure adjusts the theodolite's telescope and peers at its compass. He opens his notebook and makes his markings. He is at this business some time. Finally, he packs up his instruments and we trudge down the hill.

'Did I tell you that eight stowaways were discovered aboard once we had left Port Jackson? The Commodore had them put ashore, each man with ten pounds of bread.'

'Might Lieutenant Robbins not return them to Port Jackson to face justice? Every one of them is a convict, I believe.'

'Nearly all of us are convicts, Pierre.'

'I must confess I find you English difficult to fathom. There seems no reliable means of predicting when you will be harsh and when lenient.'

'Only way to tell is to see whether they're reaching for the cat.' The scars on my shoulders and the backs of my legs can attest.

On our return to the huts, the sealers are at their meat and the other Frenchmen have taken the opportunity of a second breakfast. As we take our places by the fire, Faure notices a quantity of skins neatly stashed in the longboat.

'It is a gift?' Faure says to Grant, the latter grunting in assent. 'Then you have my deepest gratitude, Monsieur Grant. I only wish we had something of value to offer in return.'

'Just tell Robbins we want off this fuckin' island,' Grant says.

'I will convey the essence of your request, although perhaps not in those precise words,' Faure says. 'Surveyor Grimes means to make a study of King Island to further the claims of your government, and thus I expect *Cumberland* will soon call upon you here. Perhaps Lieutenant Robbins will take you away from this place?'

'Only a twenty-tonner, int it?' Grant says. 'No room aboard for the likes o' us. When I set my eyes on Campbell I'll snap 'is bleedin' neck. Sailed to fuckin' Peru.'

'I can make representation to Commodore Baudin on your behalf, although it is my belief that *La Géographe* sails for Kangaroo Island next.'

'We ain't starvin' and we ain't in need of rescuin',' Grant says. 'We want payin' and that's just for starters.'

'I shall relay your message to the Commodore.'

When we have finished eating, I walk the Frenchmen to their longboat, which is heavily laden and no doubt will be a chore to row. I help them push it down past the incurious elephants to the surf. There is a question on my lips on the subject of stowaways but I am too afraid to ask it.

'Cheer up, George,' Faure says. The others mean to be off but the surveyor lingers. 'I will recommend you to Lieutenant Robbins if I possibly can, and if I cannot then you must make representation of your own. It is a strange fate to which you have been assigned but I do not believe it fatal. Perhaps we four will drown and you will be called upon to bury us, for the world has a way of upending our senses. For who can say what tomorrow will bring?'

◆

DAYS OF leaden skies and teeming rain, Grant and the others restless in the knowledge that *Harrington* is far away. No trypots to stir nor casks to fill, the sealers sink in their malaise. When they see fit to rise, it is in an attitude of malevolence and only then do the sea elephants feel the point of their knives.

Days beyond recollection I have spent at my lookout imagining the moment of greatest import to be close at hand. A thousand times I have perceived a sail only for it to dissolve into foam before my eyes. Times beyond counting my heart has leaped only for it to fall dashed. My whole life lived like this.

One morning my vigil is partway rewarded. I have become so fixated on the northern cape that I often fall into a trance. Hours slide away in such reveries and I am steeped in my daze when the critical moment arrives. If my eyes are to be believed, then it is another longboat beached at the southern end of Seals Bay. It is possible the Frenchmen have doubled back but I think it more likely to be a boat belonging to the *Cumberland*, the British ship of which Faure spoke. It is not nearly as cold today and I content myself with walking back to camp. At any rate my intelligence is negligible for the sealers have seen the sail.

First one visitor and then another. It seems our exile is ended.

In the afternoon, a schooner I take to be *Cumberland* appears in the bay and anchors in our island's lee. She is a stout-looking vessel of modest dimension, and we watch as her longboat is lowered into the water. The weather is happily benign. The longboat runs up the beach and lands in the same place the French landed a week earlier.

'Robbins, is it?' Grant says to the lanky fellow we take as the boat's leader. 'Them frogs-legs said you'd be comin'.'

'I am Charles Robbins.' Dressed as a ship's captain though he may be, Robbins is a skinny youth without a hope of filling out his coat this season or for several seasons hence. 'And you must be Percival Grant?'

'I am.'

'The French passed this way? Sailing from the north?'

'In a boat no bigger'n yours.'

'How long ago?'

Addled by drink, such computation is beyond Grant.

'Seven days ago, sir,' I say. 'It was Surveyor Faure and his contingent.'

'And your name is?'

I tell him.

'A surveyor, you say? Did this man speak of the intentions of the French Republic?'

'No sir, he just said he'd been sent to make a map of King Island.'

Robbins frowns. 'First it is a map and later comes the settlement. Governor King was right to send a party in furtherance of our claim. At this very moment, Mr Grimes is busy compiling an inventory of the objects that have fallen to our share.'

'Faure said *Harrington's* sailed to Peru,' Grant says. 'Is that true or was he pissin' in our ear?'

'*Harrington* out of Sydney Town? Yes, I believe it has.'

'I'll 'ave that bastard Campbell,' Grant says. 'Marooned us 'ere, he has.'

Robbins is shown the extent of our operations here and his attention lingers longest on the cache of barrels under the lean-to. 'How many do you have?' he says.

'At last count near on two hundred barrels,' Grant says. 'We've ceased labourin' for want of more. Sixpence a gallon we were told.'

'And each barrel holds how many gallons? Forty?'

'Nearer fifty.'

'And you say you could have taken more? It seems there's no shortage of sea elephants.'

'Could've taken twice that.'

'I can assure you the Governor will hear of this upon my return, but that may not be for some weeks. Our instructions are to make a survey of Port Phillip once our business here is concluded, and Mr Grimes is very thorough in his endeavours.'

'Meanwhile we're to sit on our hands, are we?'

'If Captain Campbell is indisposed to attending to his investment, then surely another company representative will be found. If none such exist in the colony, then I shall sail to your relief in a vessel suitable to the task. I have no doubt that the Governor will be gratified to purchase this oil for the King's Stores. Sixpence a gallon, I believe you said? I may even be in a position to act as intermediary.'

Grant evidently draws encouragement from this, for a gap-toothed grin has broken out on his pockmarked face. At sixpence a gallon, a barrel will net him nearly a pound and hence the lot is worth perhaps £150. He is too dull-witted to perceive that this is a mere fraction of the oil's true worth.

Robbins and his men consume a hearty meal by the fire in the big hut, washed down with tots of brandy. I take my place just inside the door, but of meat and drink I am given neither. They knock back mug after mug, toasting French brandy but never the French.

'By Jove, I put a fright into them,' Robbins says. 'The look on Péron's face when he saw the Union Jack flying over his tent! He asked what it was and I told him that servants of His Majesty are obliged to fly our nation's colours over every corner of the Empire. The French naturalists were dumbstruck while I stood reaffirming the Declaration.' Here Robbins parodies the French accent: '"Ours is a scientific mission. You must not interfere with our samples." They think us fools but the truth is we are wise to their schemes. Months they have spent in Van Diemen's Land, and doing what? Collecting butterflies and observing the natives, if you can believe that.'

'Run them off, did ye?' Grant says, holding out his mug for a refill.

'Not hardly. Baudin won't leave without his precious surveyor. I'll have to ask Grimes if he knows the man. But we must be getting back over to King Island before nightfall. I thought you might like to accompany us, Percival. I need a good man for whipping the shore party into shape, and it seems you're presently sitting idle.'

'Need a man for whippin', do ye?' Grant's eyes gleam at the thought of such a task.

Robbins and his men get to their feet. The day has turned blustery and I wonder whether I might steal an hour at the fireside. As they go out I try to get in but one of the other sealers shakes his head no. I am left to follow Robbins and his entourage down to the beach. They are tipsy, not least Grant who is even fouler drunk than sober. They get into the boat and I get waist-deep in icy water helping see them off.

'Lieutenant Robbins, what does it mean to fly the flag upside down?' I ask.

'You'll have to speak up, boy. I can't hear you over this infernal wind.'

'Flying the Union Jack upside down.'

'What's that? Upside down?'

'It must be an easy enough mistake to make, the broad white stripe in the top left corner the wrong way around.'

'Faure told you the flag was flown upside down?'

'He told me Commodore Baudin thought it was a flag used for straining water. Those Frenchmen weren't dumbstruck while you were reading the Declaration, Lieutenant. They were wondering what you meant by flying the colours upside down like that.'

'Balderdash! What did I tell you about never trusting the word of a Frenchman?'

Robbins' voice is level but his face has gone bright red.

◆

TWO DAYS later I observe another ship. This unknown schooner I first mistake for *Cumberland* and for a while I am puzzled by its madcap pattern of coming and going. Finally, I see both ships in the bay together and the mystery is resolved. It is too small to be one of the French corvettes but perhaps it is the boat Faure described, *Casuarina.* If so it has either completed its survey of northwest Van Diemen's Land or else been blown off course. But from observing the behaviour of the two vessels, I think they are both British and sent by Governor King to press his claim in these waters.

Now that Grant has gone with Robbins, the remaining sealers are even more indolent. Day and night they swill their rum and brandy and none are inclined to go after the black seals. The sum of their knowledge is that one day Captain Campbell will return for his investment and if not him then someone else. Now the sealers kill for fun if they kill at all and for the most part the sea elephants lie peaceful in their slumber.

After another night of incessant rain, *Cumberland* returns to anchor and the longboat comes ashore again. Neither Grant nor Robbins are among those landed and the gentleman in the fine jacket I take to be Surveyor Grimes. He has a case of instruments much like Faure's but unlike the Frenchman he has a man whose job it is to carry it. Grimes' jacket is studded with gold buttons and his mop of curly hair is no less red than my own.

'Where's the boy who Faure took a shine to?' Grimes says. 'It's you, is it? With Mr Fleming and I, then.'

The sky is overcast and the ground wet as we make our way up the hillside. When we get to the top, Grimes sets up his theodolite in almost the exact spot Faure chose. It is even made by the same company, W&S Jones, but perhaps a newer model.

'Baggs, is it?' Grimes says.

'Yes sir.'

'Tell me about Faure.'

I describe my interactions with the French surveyor. Already his visit seems to me in the manner of a dream. Grimes only gives my narrative half his attention while he fiddles with his instruments.

'Did he say where they were sailing next?'

'He mentioned Kangaroo Island. I have not heard of it.'

'The isle is at a distance of some five hundred miles. The French have no intention of returning to Van Diemen's Land?'

'Not if I understood him correctly. He described another boat, *Casuarina*, surveying the Hunter Isles. I thought I saw it in the bay.'

'That was the *George* you saw. Captain Rook has set down a party at the lagoon yonder.' Grimes indicates to the south end of Seals Bay. 'Have you seen this lagoon?'

I tell him no.

'Then perhaps it will please Mr Fleming to describe it.'

Fleming is closer to my age than to Grimes and he is dressed far more humbly than the surveyor. 'She's a rough country all right. A week it's taken us getting round and it can't have been more than twenty miles. The timber's poor, the ground's swampy and everything's covered in black vegetable mould. And it rains all the bleedin' time.'

'Except when it's hailing,' I say.

'Except when it's hailing. That lagoon is salt although it does turn fresh two miles upstream. Everything's sodden and the mosquitoes never stop biting. Four days of that and we were properly miserable. There's a marquee up but it may not withstand this blasted wind.'

Fleming and I walk over to the cliff edge. 'Barely a week we've been at this damned survey and I am footsore,' he says, his gaze upturned to a sky turning black. 'Every mile of this accursed country filled with swamps. We'll be another week getting back around.'

'And then Mr Grimes is to continue his survey at Port Phillip?'

'Clever little bugger, aren't you? Who told you that?'

'Lieutenant Robbins may have mentioned it.'

Fleming shakes his head. 'He's out of his depth is Charles Robbins. Never should have flown the flag over the French tents like that, and nor should he go about divulging our movements to all and sundry. Indeed, we go to Port Phillip next.'

'And where is that?'

'A lot bloody closer than Kangaroo Island. Across the strait on the coast of New Holland.'

'First comes the map and later the settlement,' I say. 'That's another thing Robbins said, although I think he was referring to the French.'

'There will be a settlement at Port Phillip, although whether sooner or later will depend on Mr Grimes' survey.'

'And King Island?'

'A miserable place from what I've seen. No, any southern settlement will be in Van Diemen's Land proper. Faure spoke not of the French intentions in this regard?'

'He said he just makes maps and someone else decides what to do with them.'

'And some men make balls for firing from a musket. Ought they to be condemned for where they land?'

'I couldn't say, Mr Fleming.'

◆

I MUST escape this hellhole, Campbell be damned. Masters such as he instruct you to do as they command or else face their wrath, but then they leave and who can say if they will ever return? *Sailed to fuckin' Peru.* Percival Grant is no different, first whiff of a better offer and he's off. I can only hope the bastard drowns. I am told that William Rook, a man I know from *Harrington*, is master of the *George*. He was Chief Officer and I just a boy under sentence but perhaps this connection will count for something. Faure would not take me away from this place and I cannot bring myself to ask the same of Fleming for I know his answer. One ill-conceived barb about the upside-down flag was enough to sully my good name if I ever had one. In truth I am thought of not at all.

The night after Grimes and Fleming leave, a fierce tempest whips up in the west. The timbers of my rickety hut whine and quiver and I am afeared the gale will cleave it in two. If I were a black seal I would dive into such depths that the storm could not follow. I would find a dark cave to secure myself from harm. I'd need nothing of land for that is the region of lament.

By morning the sea is a thing to be despised. Waves boom on the misty beach and the elephants have abandoned their wallows and evacuated to the deep. One of the schooners toils out there in the cauldron, though whether *Cumberland* or *George* I cannot say. The seas are too rough to work in, the schooner rising and falling on foaming grey-green hills betwixt New Year and King. It is a piteous spectacle and one that has drawn the attention of the sealers for there is the prospect of the craft being driven ashore. If she could get around to the north she could ride into Bass Strait, but if she must come ashore better that she does so here and not on the sealing rocks.

And she rides, my word she does, through towering spray and a sea raving mad. No cable can withstand such battery and so it proves for the schooner is being swept closer with every pummelling wave. Only a miracle of navigation will see her clear of the rocks and we watch as she is driven to precisely the place that would do her the greatest ill. Too late to go, no chance to stay, and thus her fate is sealed. She is running toward the reefs as though at her master's behest.

I am running too, not up the hill but to the spume-flecked rocks beneath it. No place for sailors, nor sea elephants, nor me. I glance over my shoulder and see the sealers trudging in a line but I am more fleet of foot. Here the beach gives out and I proceed to the sealing rocks offering scant protection from the inrushing waves. The black seals are disinclined toward flight and so I dart between the shallow rock pools in their midst. It seems these creatures fear nothing of the weather and nor are they alarmed by my presence. The schooner has vanished behind the southern cape.

Suddenly I am out of the wind and it is an eerie feeling for I find myself alone at the foot of a crumbling cliff. What waves there are plash gently and there is no other sound but for the cawing of seabirds and the snorting seals. I hear a cry not from a bird's throat but from a man's, and then I espy a knot of timbers run up against the rocky shore. The schooner must have been torn apart for the water is filled with debris. As I pick my way along, I come upon a ragged chunk of the stern upon which my own name, *George,* is written. It is a desolate scene: broken casks, sodden clothing, a tangled mess of rigging and cable. Pork hocks and seal steaks picked at by squabbling birds. Plates, mugs, a sealer's knife. Skins freshly taken and not yet flensed, lumps of gore and fat. Two men lay washed up in a cove, battered and bloody and half drowned. Their clothes are cut to ribbons and they are covered head to toe in lacerations. One of the men nurses a badly-broken arm and he cries out in agony, his eyes rolling back in his head. The other lies shivering and uncommunicative and it is all I can do to offer some vague condolence before carrying on.

Voices.

A party of survivors fish whatever seems most valuable out of the drink, which is a foolish scheme for the weather is turning fouler. The waves are double what they were a moment ago and who is to say they will not double again? In an hour there might be nowhere for them to stand. I tell the men this but they are too engrossed in their salvage to listen to a bedraggled youth.

With a moan of timbers, their attention and mine is drawn to what remains of the *George*. The greater part of the ship has wrecked not thirty yards offshore and it lays stricken in no more than two fathoms of water. The schooner's bow has snagged on the reef but it won't be long before the force of the tide serves to bash it to smithereens. Amid the swirling white-water I see a man coming up from belowdecks and it is William Rook followed by a second man heaving a wooden chest. To my amazement, I see it is Percival Grant. The shore party is trying to launch a longboat but it is taking on too much water from the slopping waves. Rook sees this and I see him wondering how in damnation he's going to get himself and his precious chest ashore. If they are quick they might abandon their plunder and swim, but what seemed possible a moment ago now seems suicidal. The timbers creak and groan and whatever is to be done must be done. Rook has the chest open on the tilting deck and he is bent over stuffing papers into his pockets and Grant the same.

Rook looks to see if a rescue is in the offing, but those on the shore are reduced to the status of onlookers with a sinking boat. There's nothing for it but to leave the chest and try to swim ashore, but for some fool reason the two men are making their way toward the bow. The tilting of the deck is such that they must clamber up and hold fast to the rigging and I cannot for the life of me see the sense in their stratagem. The bow is rising out of the water and suddenly I see what they intend. If the deck tilts any higher it will soon become possible to scuttle along the spar of the bowsprit and jump onto the ledge of the nearby cliff. This madcap plan is one borne of the purest desperation for if the pair slip they will plunge onto the foaming rocks. Rook goes first and as Grant tries to crawl after him he is waved back, for it seems the former is afeared that the bowsprit might crack under their combined weight. The ledge in question is no more than a rookery for birds and only marginally less precarious. Rook has made it halfway along the bowsprit but there is a vault of air between him and safety. I clamber up the cliffside for a better look. Rook is like a man atop a flagpole or a gallows and Grant cannot wait a moment longer before beginning his ascent. As the wind rears, their jackets billow like sails, the papers whipping free of their pockets and cavorting like seabirds.

Rook can climb no higher and he is confronted by the depth of his folly for it would take a leap beyond the means of any man to bridge that gap. It is perhaps five yards but it might as well be fifty and it is a killing drop. I have climbed nearly level with him. Grant is approaching the end of the bowsprit but there is nowhere to go and the sea has all but submerged the *George*'s deck. Rook calls out to me but his words are lost on the wind. Grant is trying to get alongside him and thence to leap but Rook is having none of it and kicks at the other's hands.

There is a sharp crack and what remains of the schooner begins to right itself and I lose sight of the dangling men. I scramble to the slippery ledge and look down and see the severed spar of the bowsprit on the rocks below. Somehow Rook is still clinging to it. *George* is sinking and will soon be out of sight.

I pick my way down to Rook and I am the only one to do so for his men are cut off by the rising waters. The man has cheated death by dint of an undeserved miracle for the severed bowsprit has jammed between the rocks in a manner that could hardly be more fortuitous. He has only to let go of the spar and step down onto the rocks, which he does with my helping hand. He seems dazed but otherwise uninjured.

'Thought it was George Baggs,' he says. 'When I saw you I thought you were bringing a cable, but you didn't have any cable, did you? Now where's that daft bugger got to?'

More debris begins to wash up around us. I scoop up a bit of sodden paper and offer it to Rook.

'Finders keepers, George,' he says. 'Percival won't be needing it any more.'

I look to where Rook is pointing and see Percival Grant facedown about ten yards out. He is not moving except on the tide and the water around him is stained dark red.

'What is it?' I say, trying to make out the writing on the wet paper.

'Promissory note worth a pound,' Rook says. 'You'd best hang onto it until you see port again. Quickly now, let's see if we can't find another.'

IN THE FURNEAUX

1809

THE SKY LOOMS heavy with cloud and the sun will not show us its face. The schooner *Governor Hunter* stands at anchor in the lee of Badger Island in the Furneaux Isles, but the gale has turned easterly and waves pound the shore. As we watch from the deck, sandy shoals shift beneath our keel.

'What d'ye reckon, George?' Jimmy Brown says. The wind tousles his dark hair and his eyes are like two bright shining coals.

'I reckon we should've quit the islands when we had the chance.'

He scowls at the maelstrom washing over rock and shoal. 'Aye, but Rook were greedy, weren't he? Now who's the April fool?'

More than four months we have sealed the Furneaux Isles at the eastern end of Bass Strait, taking more than eight thousand sealskins. Given that our gang is being paid a hundredth lay, that's eighty skins for me, eighty for Brown, and same again for Bush, Johnson and Stepney.

'Might be we're the bigger fools, Jimmy,' I say. 'Eighty skins isn't enough to pay my debt to Nichols and it wouldn't buy me a farm on the Hawkesbury even without the debt. Seventeen pounds seems like a lot of money but it isn't that much.'

Brown pulls his cap low over his face. 'I wouldn't count on yer eighty skins just yet, George. She's a wind to blow the horns off a bull.'

The sea is in turmoil and we are bucking in a roil of waves and spray. One of the longboats lashed to the deck has come partway loose and is threatening to crash into the bow, and only the anchor cables are between us and shipwreck. The rain comes at us sideways in frozen droplets, sleet stinging my face and hands. The crew scurry about on the slippery deck as we sealing men try to ride it out, our breath turning to vapour.

A crack of thunder splits the sordid heavens. The deck is awash, waves lapping at our feet, and then the hail strikes us from on high. I am stung a dozen, a hundred times, and then a hand drags me into the longboat. It is Brown. We cower listening to the flurry of hailstones on the oilskin cover, and after a moment young Tom Stepney tumbles in.

'How's it lookin', Tom?' Brown says. 'Any sign she's blowing over?'

'I d-d-don't think so,' Stepney says, his teeth chattering. I take the boy's hand, frigid like a corpse's, and guide him to where we lay in the bilge. We huddle together for warmth and listen to the groaning timbers. There is a great crash and splintering of wood.

We hear the hue and cry: 'Fore cable's snapped!'

'Mary mother of Jesus, we've lost an anchor,' Brown says. 'Out we go!'

We throw off the oilskin cover and emerge into the horrid day, the boat rolling badly in the fierce riptide sweeping between the islands. The captain and first mate are peering over the starboard at the rocks looming before us. There is an uneasy sound of timbers turning on nails.

'We'll 'ave to cut the aft cable, else we're for that reef!'

the first mate says, and I cannot but think of the day long ago when I saw the *George* torn to splinters in such a fashion.

'We'll run her up on that yonder beach,' the captain says.

That yonder beach is a boil of foam where waves boom and crash. The remaining anchor drags horribly and there is a great rending as the hull is thrust against jagged rocks. Then as the first mate cuts the cable we are unsnarled and careening for that spiteful shore. We are flung about and falling in a disarray of tangled rigging and flailing limbs, and in a frozen instant I catch a glimpse of low-lying Badger Island, the rocky beach and the forest beyond. Then we are swept up in the roll of waves.

'There go yer eighty skins, George!' I hear Brown cry, but before I can retort I am flung upon the deck. I scramble to my knees and try to brace for impact as the stricken schooner runs up the beach in a manner no vessel should dare to try. By some miracle we shoot straight up and come to a kind of troubled rest, but the rain is teeming and the waters surging and there are injured men groaning and pleading for help.

I try to get up but fall into darkness.

◆

I AM sitting on a boulder on the beach amid the gentle sucking of water on the rocks. It is the following day and we have spent the intervening hours in a manner too wretched for recollection. The schooner is not quite a wreck but it will not sail without repairs and we have no carpenter among us. We aren't going home to Port Jackson, at least not in *Governor Hunter.* Badger Island is a sight bigger than New Year, but I'll be damned if I'm spending another year of my life in such a place. I am warm enough in my sealskin jerkin and kangaroo fur moccasins, however. Before me are the windswept islands of the Furneaux. To the east are the largest islands, Flinders and Cape Barren, and a host of smaller ones. To the north lies mountainous Chappell Island with its slithering snakes and oft-visited seal rookeries. To the south but hidden by the bulk of Cape Barren lies Preservation, where the *Sydney Cove* foundered, and Clarke, named after the purser of that ill-fated ship.

'There ye are, George,' Brown says, dressed in a heavy woollen short coat and a crudely made sealskin hat. He hauls himself up beside me.

'Has Rook admitted defeat yet?' I ask.

'No, but he's cuttin' a forlorn figure.'

'Not half as forlorn as he'll be when he tells Nichols what he's done to the man's ship.'

'There is a curse on Isaac Nichols, I'll wager. I reckon we ought to've stayed with Lord & Co after all.'

Our employer is indeed a man acquainted with misfortune. They say he got his start hiring out his horse and cart for ten shillings a day, and that's when the trouble began. First a fire nearly burned his house to the ground. Then Mrs Nichols was found floating facedown near Goat Island, the *Sydney Gazette* reporting that she'd been out carousing. The inquest returned a verdict of *Accidental Death, by Insanity*. Now Nichols is married a second time and thinking to try his hand at the sealing game. Not long ago a convict was crushed to death under an immense log they were rolling onto a raised sawpit in his shipyard, the man's head so badly crushed they reckoned you could have used it as a frying pan.

'What about the curse on us?' I say. 'We've been at this endeavour all summer and for what? It's not the first time it turned out I was working for the joy of giving.'

'Ye've still got yer own skin, George.'

That I have. When I finished my indenture with William Campbell, I started working for Henry Kable, but Kable's terms were just as harsh and before I knew it he was in league with James Underwood. Next season the pair of them joined up with Simeon Lord. Now it was Lord & Co and the terms were worse still. Brown and I went over to Nichols out of desperation, and in doing so I ended up working under Captain Rook.

'The Furneaux's played out, George,' Brown says.

'They'll have us sailing further afield, Kangaroo Island or else New Zealand.'

'Plenty of islands for puttin' down the likes o' us. And then ye're waitin' months if not years. Provisions long gone, living on seabirds and eggs.'

'If we can't get those skins in we'll have fallen even further behind. Seventeen pounds already.'

Brown claps a paw on my shoulder. 'A man can't get ahead on a hundredth lay, not for all the seals in the sea. I'm sayin' we don't go back, George. Not now, not ever. Down here we won't be needin' no master.'

A brazen fellow, Brown. Hardly a deep thinker but a good man and a better sailor. Might we be mates forever, Messrs Baggs and Brown?

◆

THE NIGHT is brisk but we are content by the fireside, our bellies filled with Cape Barren geese. Captain Rook is taciturn in nature and not given to hectoring nor outbursts of wild frivolity. His brow is dark and furrowed and we can almost see him forming the words he intends to deliver. *Governor Hunter* cannot be re-floated without repairs and those repairs cannot be attempted without a carpenter. Such a carpenter must be sourced in Sydney and, even if there were a passing ship, no relief would likely be forthcoming until spring. Rook is therefore faced with a grim choice. Winter here and wait, or risk taking the longboats over to Cape Barren, thereby abandoning *Governor Hunter* and its eight thousand skins. There is a chance Captain Bader of the *Active* may yet be at Kents Bay on Cape Barren and there rests Rook's hopes.

'The storm is passed,' he finally says in a low voice. 'And so we must salvage what we can and pray the Lord guides us safely to Kents Bay and to Bader.'

The men murmur. 'And if Bader ain't there?' Brown says.

'He was there a fortnight ago and I pray he remains there still.'

'He might've gone the other way round Cape Barren,' Brown says.

'Pot Boil's through there,' the first mate says, a stocky fellow with a ruddy face. 'No man who's sailed these waters would risk it.'

The Pot Boil is a region many an unsuspecting mariner has ventured into once but seldom twice. Located at the eastern end of the sound between Flinders and Cape Barren, it is a maelstrom of black swirling water imperilling all who dare to enter, a watery hell of illogical winds and furious riptides where waves explode. To the north is Babel Island, forever shrouded in sleet and rain and squall, thus named for the muttonbirds who descend upon it each September.

The conversation splinters into separate mutterings and whispered asides, and Rook strains to raise his voice over the hubbub. 'If we arrive at Kents Bay to find Bader gone, then we shall overwinter there.'

'Mr Rook,' Brown says, 'surely we're safer here on Badger? Plenty of geese around.'

'Cape Barren is not far enough away to offer undue impediment.'

'But what about the skins? Eight thousand we took, that's eighty to a man.'

'The skins are secure in the hold.'

'And what if they aren't there when we come back? Our gang will have slaved all summer for nowt.'

'In that event, I'm sure Mr Nichols will offer compensation.'

'No, he bleedin' won't. Ye know the Articles as well as I. No skins, no pay.'

'Then what is your suggestion?'

'Ye take yer men over to Cape Barren if it pleases ye and meanwhile the gang'll stay here'n guard the skins.'

Rook chuckles. 'I'm to leave you here with eight thousand skins?'

'Take both boats then. We'll be marooned.'

Rook glares at Brown and then the others, none daring to speak. 'You're all to come with me,' he says. 'You are in the employ of Isaac Nichols and he has seen fit to make me your master. You sealers shall each have your eighty skins as payment for your labour and I shall be answerable for the remainder. Now let us retire and with any luck we shall be on our way tomorrow.'

The stars are not my fellows but at times they offer better comfort than a fellow ever did. In quiet moments beneath such a sky I find myself aching for a home I barely had, for a land that thought nothing of grinding me into the mud. Where a boy might bleed or breathe his last in the gutter or ditch without a soul to mourn his passing. A cruel land, England, one filled with cruel people. In my darkest dreams I roam those streets but cannot find even a single soul to remember me. Better that I try to carry it within me, this home inside.

Sydney is not my home and I have my doubts it ever will be, but perhaps I will find my place in Van Diemen's Land. The brotherhood of men is not without its comforts, but what a man truly needs is a wife. The doxies of Port Jackson will do for an hour, but those dissolute waifs with their poxes and their grog will not serve for long. The colony is awash with men, many of whom are characters of the worst depravity, and yet Britain thinks nothing of flooding these shores with more. What surprise is it if, in the absence of the fairer sex, these poor wretches commit unnatural acts upon each other? The only women I have lain with are those for whom I paid, and those times were few and the prices extortionate. A sealer home in port with his season's wages is a lamb soon fleeced. My word he will sail again. He is deprived of everything a man would want to have, the only outlet for his fury the seals he sets upon. He will slay a hundred and then a hundred more and the slaughter will not cease until he has earned his lay, if he ever does. It is a cruelty done to him and one he means to repay in blood. Cruelty upon cruelty, poxes raining down from the sky.

◆

TOMORROW COMES. A rolling sea batters the beach, forestalling any thought of our departure. It is a bitter wind, last night's fire no more than a sodden patch of blackened ashes. Sullen men shelter in flimsy lean-tos that rattle and threaten to take flight, gnawing on weevilly ship's biscuit and cursing the sky.

Badger Island isn't a place you'd want to be stuck long. Flat and low and at the western edge of the Furneaux, the prevailing winds whip through the tussock and the stunted scrub and they chill a man to the core, making him long for a warm bed far from here. And unlike nearby Chappell, there are no seal rookeries on Badger. What the island does have is she-oak, paperbark and tea-tree. Good for a fire but not for boatbuilding. The only island further west is desolate Goose and beyond that is the vast expanse of Bass Strait. Two hundred miles of turbulent water lie between us and King Island, where last year Captain Rook was paid £120 for bringing in three hundred tons of elephant oil. Now they say the sea elephants of King are finished.

When the rain finally slackens, Rook consents to letting our gang go exploring. The five of us traipse through a wet dripping forest and soon arrive at a craggy shoreline. Petrels and oystercatchers nest in their hundreds and our ears are filled with the sound of their squawking. No cove down there, no sheltered beach, just a grey-green sea heaving itself onto a punishing shore. Breakers crash on a smattering of tiny islands flung across the bay.

Badger's western end offers even less shelter, exposed as it is to the force of the prevailing winds. We stand on a point looking across the channel to nearby Goose Island, where salt spray drifts over the fields of billowing tussock. We make our way down to a rocky beach. Two distinctive rocks rise from the outcropping like a pair of stone shark fins and they seem to watch us as we collect driftwood.

At our fire, we sit chewing stringy salt pork and discussing our paltry stratagems.

'He's a wily one is Rook,' I say. 'I'm surprised he let us out of his sight.'

'Least he's giving us the skins we're owed,' Tom Stepney says.

Brown pokes at the spluttering fire. 'What use are skins this far from port? We've nowhere to trade 'em.'

'Port Dalrymple maybe,' Bush says. 'I heard a gang made it over there from Cape Barren.'

'That was to beg supplies because they were starvin',' Brown says. 'Besides, the port's not open for trade.'

'Then where do we sell 'em?' Johnson says.

'Nowhere, that's the point,' Brown says. 'Rook knows the best way of makin' sure we don't scarper is by giving us our skins now. He thinks it's a cinch we'll carry 'em back to Port

Jackson. But I took a lot more'n eighty skins this summer. I ain't been wadin' up to my neck in blood'n blubber just to pay a debt to Isaac Nichols.'

'Rook means for us to go with him and I'll wager he'll have his way,' Bush says. The man has a weaselling voice to grate the nerves.

'Aye,' Johnson says. A duller fellow you will not find, he forms each word with tremendous effort. 'If Bader's still there, me and my eighty skins are off to market.'

'Problem with men such as yerselves is ye're always thinkin' in terms most meagre and piddlin',' Brown says. 'Blast the pair of ye.'

'I'm listening to you, Jimmy,' I say. 'How can I get away from Nichols and get something for the skins?'

'I mean to tell ye, George, but privately. This pair'll go bleatin' to Rook if they think it'll win 'em an eighty-first skin, damn their eyes.'

'Brown's as full of piss and wind as ever,' Bush says. 'I'm off back.'

'Coming, boy?' Johnson says.

Stepney's eyes dart but he keeps his backside firmly planted on the sand.

Brown waits for Bush and Johnson to clear off before continuing.

'Now Tom,' he says, 'George and I have sealed together many a season. We're like brothers, see?'

The boy swallows and nods. 'Aye.'

'Whereas ye're the new chum, aren't ye? First season out.'

'Did the job of a man, din't I?'

'That ye did, lad, but what I'm sayin' is there's more to bein' a sealer than just sealin'. It's like an oath ye take. If ye want to go back with Rook that's what ye'll do. Ye've earned yer eighty skins.'

'But what if I go with you?'

'I was hopin' Rook would leave us on Badger long enough so as we could get them skins off and make a stash,' Brown says. 'Even if he din't trust us with a boat, maybe we could fashion a new 'un from the wreck.'

'We'd probably drown in that channel, Jimmy,' I say. 'How many times were you figurin' we'd need to go back and forth for eight thousand skins?'

'We wouldn't be needin' every last one of 'em, George. But p'raps it was a foolish plan.'

'But you've a better one now?'

Brown pokes the fire. 'It's a fair way round to Kents in an eighteen-footer, int it? Ye might run up on a shoal or wash up in the wrong bay.'

'You're thinking of scarpering?' I say. 'Bush and Johnson won't be party to it.'

'Then we'll heave 'em overboard and good bleedin' riddance.'

'You'd drown two men?' I say. 'For skins you've still to share with Tom and I? Or will you drown us too when the time is right?'

'No, I'd never. There's the boiling-down works at Kents so we'll be snug till spring. Then we find ourselves an island off Van Diemen's Land, somewhere we won't run into no redcoats.'

'What about native clansmen?' I say. 'They might not take kindly to us.'

'Then we'll steer right clear o' them too.'

High above our heads, I spot muttonbirds heading south. First one, two, six, twenty, a hundred, the sky filled with their black wings and the din of their discordant shrieking. One thousand, two thousand, too many to count, a vast exodus signalling that their season and ours is at an end. None can say where the muttonbirds overwinter, but they will be back in

September, nothing surer. As we watch for what seems like hours, the advance guard disappears into the vanishing distance while the stragglers continue to pass overhead, a swarm of gigantic black moths blocking out the light of the sun.

To Brown and I it is an omen that we have outstayed our welcome here.

'Right ye are,' Brown says. 'Are ye wi' us, Tom?'

'I reckon.'

◆

NEXT DAY the skies are no less ominous but we are underway nonetheless. Rook has thought it prudent to split our gang between the two boats and thus I toil at the oars under the watchful eye of the master. Bush and the ship's cook complete the quartet, leaving Brown and Stepney to contend with Johnson and the remainder of the crew in the other boat. He's a wily one is Rook.

By launching our frail craft into this cauldron we have handed ourselves over to fate. Despite our best efforts, we make little progress but for the capricious tides swirling around us, the waters inky and sinister. We surge forward into the lee of mountainous Chappell Island rising from the dark water like some antique leviathan. Those fur seals that have hitherto escaped our wrath bask in the warmth of a timorous sun. They snort and disport, bearing their yellow tusks at one another while their true enemy passes by unnoticed. High above, the whole face of the mountain is alive with the wriggling white specks of cavorting seabirds. For a few blessed moments the tide draws us onward to our goal.

The eastern sky glows darkly in promise of further mischief, the whitening sea frothing and foaming. Amid the gathering gloom I perceive an outline of the white towering peaks on Flinders Island and I take this as my cue to pull harder. Rook murmurs in encouragement. For a moment we are master and servant no longer, each owing our lives to the perseverance of the other. It is but a moment but in it I perceive a stubborn truth: in different circumstances, Rook and I could have been fellows too. But there is a gulf between us that no understanding can ever brook because I have been a convict and he has not.

Now is the moment of urgent necessity, the gale freshening and not to our advantage. To imagine we steer the boat through this maze is a deceit and a flattery. As if to taunt us, the skies above Flinders are clearing, the white mountain flanks bathed in sunlight, a faint pinkish tinge haloing the summit. The wind has swung around to the nor'west and it drives us away from the passage between Flinders and Cape Barren. We row for all our worth to avoid running up on the shore of Cape Barren with its great sheets of mountainous rock rising from the water.

For the moment we are in a pocket of sunshine and I have a premonition that I won't be feeling the sun on my neck for many a month. The sea cannot sink us but land assuredly can, and I cannot escape the thought we could have been snug and secure back on Badger. We are for a safe beach, indeed any beach. There is one on Long Island, nestled up against the nor'west corner of Cape Barren, and though it is far short of Kents I know Rook will have it in mind. Though he is not by nature a gambler, his desire to reach *Active* has given him over to acts of wild desperation. A man sunk so low in his thinking believes he has nothing further to lose and thus imperils the lives of his crew. It is bust or it is Bader.

This southern coast of Cape Barren is dotted with bays unsuitable for vessels the size of *Active*, the channel between Cape Barren and Clarke full of tricky shoals. At the western entrance to this channel lies Preservation Island. To the south lies Clarke Island, more substantial and more akin to Cape Barren. Rugged and thickly wooded with tea-tree, the ground there is mostly sterile and punctuated by granite outcroppings. There is a good harbour in the northeast and the island teems with geese and kangaroo.

There comes a series of flashes and a sharp peal of thunder from the gunmetal sky. There is precious little strength in my arms and all is a tumult of swirling darkness. To my recollection there is a beach around the headland of Cape Barren's sou'west corner, and though it is some way short of Kents it forms part of the same coastline.

Passing on our starboard side, the other boat appears to be having a better time of it. With five men aboard, their boat is doubtless heavier but one of those men is Brown and he is a bear among men. As we slide past the perilous cape, the gale has become a hurricane. We will soon be swamped but we dare not allow a man to bale lest we overshoot the bay and wreck on the rocks beyond. Somehow we dodge the rocks and shoot along the coast. When we round the next point Kents will hove into view, and either a hundred-ton brigantine will stand at anchor or it will not.

Rook inhales sharply. 'Quick, the spyglass!'

I hand him the telescope. I'll allow there is a smudge of white.

'It is Bader!' Rook declares. 'Thank goodness, men, it is the *Active*!'

As we run closer, *Active*'s features become apparent. She is a square-rigged two-master of perhaps seventy feet, a fine vessel for the open water but too cumbersome for navigating these channels. Anchored in the bay long favoured by sealers, *Active*'s dilemma is much the same as ours: to stay or go. From the looks of the men hauling casks on the shore, it is the latter.

We haul up amid this scene of frenetic activity and Rook addresses us. 'I've never set eyes upon a more bedraggled band but you've done me proud even so. When I see Mr Nichols I won't fail to remember you to him.' Without another word, he turns on his heel. The first mate commences a slow trudge across the sand while the remainder linger to await an eventual judgement upon their fate.

Brown and I take the opportunity to slink away from the crowd. 'I've a mind to get back in and start paddlin',' Brown says as we sit on the dunes above the beach. Below us, the others are attempting to sort through the skins.

We soon see Stepney's head bobbing up the hillside.

'What ho, Tom,' Brown says.

'Bader's offerin' passage,' Stepney says. 'He means to be off this forenoon.'

'That so?' Brown says. 'Look at my hands, Tom. Just look at me fuckin' hands.'

Brown's hands are rubbed raw, his palms a labyrinth of bleeding cracks. 'I carried ye onto this 'ere beach and now some pig's arse of a captain is *offerin' passage*? What say ye, George?'

'I say Rook and Bader can go fuck themselves or each other, whichever is better to their liking.'

'Aye,' Brown says. 'Now ye've a choice to make, Tom, and Rook won't help ye make it. Right now he's rugged up nice and cosy with a glass of brandy in his hand, and he's dreamin' up all the lies he'll be tellin' Nichols. Ye can go acceptin' passage, and if ye do ye'll work yer way back just like ye always did. With a bit o' luck ye'll see Sydney in a month or two and ye'll get yer pay, minus all the deductions for the provisions ye've gone and eaten. But if ye're lucky ye'll come out ahead and ye'll spend a happy fortnight fritterin' it away. Ye might find yerself a sweet little floozy at the back of the tavern or down by the wharf, and if ye're luckier she might not give ye a dose of the clap.

'But soon enough ye'll have run through yer packet and ye'll be needin' work. Spring'll be in the air and notices'll start popping up in the *Gazette*, and ye'll sign on with Nichols or Lord & Co. Ye'll be on a hundredth lay or maybe an eightieth and they'll put yer gang down on an island more to the liking of seals than men. Maybe they'll even come back for ye. The graveyard's full of men who couldn't be done without, Tom, and yer little lady won't be waitin' long. I know it's a fearsome picture and it's not that the other's an oil painting, but if ye stay with George and I ye'll be yer very own man.'

'But what about the skins?' Stepney says.

'Forget the skins, Tom. I know it's hard but put 'em out of yer mind.'

'Do you have family in Sydney?' I say.

The boy shakes his head. 'Naw, I's an orphan.'

'Then there's nothing stopping ye,' Brown says. 'We've two perfectly good boats and there ain't enough room on the *Active*'s deck for even one. They've no choice but to leave 'em.'

'But we'll be labelled absconders, won't we?' Stepney says.

'That's only fair given as we're abscondin',' Brown says.

'We aren't forcing you, Tom,' I say.

'I don't much care for that bastard Rook,' Stepney says. 'He's taken a strop to me more'n once. I'll come.'

Brown clambers to his feet. 'I give my word ye won't be seeing William Rook again in this life and prob'ly not the next. Now let's get ourselves good and hid.'

◆

WE ARE at the place called Bishops Creek and everywhere are signs of the work done here over the season past. A handful of scraggly huts sit back from the beach, most of them dilapidated and likely to tumble down come winter. The walls are poorly fashioned from sheoak and the roofs thatched with rotten tussock. We scavenge what we can: dirty spoons, filthy rags, old cooking pots congealed with grease. Everywhere bones and ashes, a great many seal skeletons and decomposing carcasses. Here are the remnants of kangaroos and geese, an assortment of bones and fur and entrails. The boiling-down works are at the sandbar at the mouth of the creek, and here we find splintered casks, rusted sealing knives and a miscellany of useless things.

That afternoon we build a bonfire on the beach. We have a supply of black powder and broken-up casks to use as fuel. We drag the timbers from a fallen hut and roast a pair of geese. 'I reckon we're in for it soon enough,' Brown says, his bearded chin wet with goose grease.

'You aren't worried about Bader?' I say.

'It isn't Bader that concerns me, George. Look around and tell me what ye see on that there hillside.'

It is approaching dusk but not too dark to see the low-lying scrub, rocky outcroppings and granite peaks. 'I don't see anything much.'

'Not much tucker, is there?'

'There's kangaroo.'

'Aye, but what did ye think to catch one with? Yer bare hands? It int like creepin' up on a dozy seal, ye daft bugger. We'll be needin' guns or huntin' dogs and prob'ly both.'

'Why didn't you say anything about this before?' Stepney says.

'Because I figured ye'd be jumpin' ship on me.'

'Then we'll find some dozy seals,' I say. 'I know the rocks sou'east of Clarke.'

'Ye're dafter than I thought if ye want to try them waters,' Brown says. 'Once the weather sets in we'll be needin' to stick close to land.'

'We could make spears such as the clansmen use,' I say.

'Seen one being fashioned, have ye?'

I admit I have not.

'I've seen plenty o' clansmen in Van Diemen's Land and more than my fair share of their spears,' Brown says. 'I was part of a gang left at Oyster Bay. Much better country than here and the clansmen keep the scrub down with their fires. We built a hut and took two thousand skins, and then we ran over to Maria Island thinking to take a good deal more. When we got back we found the clansmen had burned down the hut and all our skins.'

'Why'd they do that?'

'They din't like us takin' their seals is why. To our way of thinkin' they've nowt connectin' 'em to the land, but 'tisn't so. We had some muskets but takin' a kangaroo with one int so easy. They're mighty skittish.'

'Then what did you eat?'

'We had some biscuit and salt pork but it din't last long. Some thought to walk to Hobart Town but it's near enough a hundred miles and there's clansmen up and down that coast. Luckily we were saved by a Kable sloop, *Nancy*. We spent the remainder of that season workin' Prime Seal Island, but *Nancy* wrecked up at Jervis Bay. We would've starved if not for the kindness shown by the clansmen thereabouts. And I learned a valuable lesson.'

'What's that, Jimmy?'

'The clansmen'll be yer friends if ye'll just let 'em, but they consider all the kangaroos and seals to be theirs. That's why the Oyster Bay mob burned down that hut. I don't reckon they're particularly interested in skins but they'll trade for carcasses. If we could get some dogs they'd trade for them too.'

'We're back to sealing, or stealing,' I say. 'In either case we'll be needing the boats.'

'Don't ye worry George, we'll be using 'em soon enough. Now I've a riddle for the pair o' ye. How does a man on an island hunt with nary a musket or even a bleedin' spear?'

'That's what we're wanting to know, Jimmy.'

'Answer is he doesn't hunt, he fishes.'

'What with?' Stepney says. 'We ain't got no fishing pole.'

'We won't be needin' no pole, Tom.'

'For Christ's sake, what do we need then?' I say.

'Fish traps,' Brown says, 'and before ye ask I know how to make one, don't I? I've seen them used by those Eora clansmen. They have a way of pilin' up the rocks just so, and when the tide goes out the fish get caught. Ye can near enough grab 'em with yer hands. Them traps are right intricate.'

'And you're figuring on making one at the mouth of this creek?' I say.

'Hungry man'll try near about anythin'. Just ye see if I'm wrong.'

◆

OVER THE following days we spend a good deal of time trying to construct Brown's damned fish trap, which necessitates a great many boulders being hauled into the water to form a weir. When this is done, Brown has us build a second weir twenty yards further upstream. All the while, good eating fish dart around us and between our legs. At low tide, so the theory goes, fish will be stranded in the mudflats on account of the weirs, but either the creek is not adequate for this purpose or, more likely, Brown's comprehension of the scheme is lacking. After the better part of a week, we have impounded precisely one fish. We are thus reduced to prising the black shells of muttonfish from the rocks for our supper. Even if this wasn't perilous already, attempting to lever off the stubborn muttonfish with a freshly sharpened sealing knife assuredly is. Small and lithe, Tom soon proves adept at hunting crabs. At day's end we cook it all up in a pot and we find it a poor fare unworthy of our toil. The flesh of the muttonfish is chewy and the unsalted crabmeat no more appetising. This wretched dinner is barely enough to stop our bellies growling and then in the morning we find it has given us a terrible flux.

We are trapped in our hut on account of incessant rain. It is the eighth day of our freedom. I know this because we have started keeping a tally on the trunk of a nearby tree.

'I'm cold, Jimmy,' I say. 'What I wouldn't give for some salt pork.'

'Ye don't hear young Tom complainin', do ye?'

'S'cold,' the boy says from his corner.

'Aye and it'll be colder still,' Brown says, 'but I've an enlivenin' tale for ye of the time I nearly stole the *Estramina*.'

'How many more tales of your foolishness must we endure?' I ask.

'Nowt foolish about this. When we first landed on the Derwent, Robert Sturt was the fellow most of us *Calcutta* lags looked up to, and he was hell bent on gettin' away. He had a plan to steal *Estramina* and for this he had a couple of men make off with a boat owned by the Reverend Knopwood. Davy Collins caught wind o' it and they were rounded up and given a floggin'. Sturt convinced the pilot at the Derwent to loan him the cutter and meanwhile I robbed the store. We meant to commandeer *Estramina* and be on our way.'

'And I suppose Davy Collins caught wind of this as well?'

'I reckon so. *Estramina*'s master rounded us up and took us back to Hobart Town in chains. Sturt and I were sent up to Sydney to be tried. We thought we would hang but then Governor Bligh arrived all a-bluster announcin' an amnesty to all those awaitin' trial. That's how I ended up workin' on the sealing gangs. If I hadn't taken up with Sturt when I had, I'd still be on the Derwent shooting fowl for the Reverend's plate. And that's just me point, see?'

'How long was your sentence, Jimmy?'

'Seven years transportation for thievin' silk handkerchiefs. Got me a greatcoat and trousers and plenty more besides. Got sprung soon as I fenced it, o' course.'

'And what year was that?'

'1801. Spent the best part of two years on a hulk in the Thames.'

'Then your sentence would have expired by now, Jimmy.'

'Ye don't know much about Hobart Town, do ye? There int half the difference between lags and ticket-of-leavers as ye might think. The soldiery is still squattin' in wattle'n daub huts not much better'n this. Launceston's worse than that from what I've heard.'

'Maybe we'd be better off working out of Sydney,' I say. 'Least there we could get a pint of porter with our dinner.'

'The game's rigged against us, George. Between the New South Wales Corp and the likes of Lord & Co they've got the whole game fixed. There int no place in Port Jackson for an honest man, just ask Governor Bligh.'

It rains steadily for one day and then two, and soon we cannot recall a time it wasn't raining. Sometimes it lets up just long enough to dash our hopes by coming back even stronger. One morning the storm swells to a hurricane no less severe than the one that did for *Governor Hunter*, threatening to blow down our frail tenement. Our fire has long since died. We have dragged the boats high up into the scrub and even there they are endangered by the rising waters. Bishops Creek is a creek no longer but instead a thunderous river and our pitiful fish-trap weirs are destroyed. Peering at the foaming sea, we forget both the cold and our hunger. As we watch, the roof of one of the other huts is sucked down into the vortex.

I get to my feet, my legs so numb they are little better than two stiff planks. Brown and Stepney are in their corners. I reckon I couldn't get much wetter and so I push the board aside and step into a world made of wind and water. The sky is so foul it could be night and the rain comes at me from every side, sucking at my ankles to drag me down into a watery pit. I scramble over a debris of tree branches, my only thought to make it to higher ground. I hear a cry and it is the others scrabbling up the hillside. Higher up, we cling to the thickest boughs and observe the tumult below.

It is all we can do to hang onto that which we hold dearest and that is our very lives.

◆

WHEN I wake, I am jammed awkwardly into the crook of a tree and cannot tell whether it is the same afternoon or early the following morn. My head is pounding and I find I am too dizzy to stand. I put my hand to my throbbing temple and it comes away wet with blood. My mouth is dry and my thirst immense and I am very cold, but what has woken me is none of these. It is instead a vast shrieking cacophony of seabirds, not the sooty muttonbirds but apparently every other bird in creation. The sky is thick with them, a plague of birds engaged in some endeavour my foggy head cannot comprehend. I hear another noise and it is Brown coming to like a grizzly bear from its winter hibernation. He is caked with black mud and his jacket torn to shreds.

'Ye've banged yer head and it looks like ye fell in a bucket of yesterday's shite,' he says.

'I'd ask you to look in the mirror, Jimmy, only we haven't one.'

Brown helps me to my feet and we pick our way down to the beach. Bishops Creek is still thundering into the bay and the sandbar is gone. Of the seven huts that stood here yesterday, only the two set furthest back from the rivermouth remain. Even our tally-tree has been uprooted.

'Bugger me, even the boiling-down works were carried off,' Brown says. 'Those trypots must've weighed a ton. Now where's that boy got to? There he is, the blighter!'

We go down to what remains of the beach and only then do I understand why the birds are swarming so. The storm has thrown up an immense quantity of fish and now the birds are feasting. Stepney cradles an armful of fish and my stomach starts growling the moment I set eyes on his catch.

'Good fishin', was it?' Brown says.

'If only I had something to carry them in,' Stepney says, dumping the pile at our feet. Most of the fish are still flopping.

'Tell me you've still got that black powder, Jimmy,' I say.

'Aye, it were in that satchel, but did I think to grab it from the hut or din't I? It might be I set it on a tree branch, or p'raps I thought of usin' it for my pillow.'

Stepney goes over to the scrub and retrieves the satchel from where he's had it stashed.

After days of wretched eating, our hunger is such that we can think of nothing beyond cooking up every last fish we can lay our hands on. This proves troublesome as the satchel has gotten drenched along with everything else. Brown and I choose the driest spot and the one best protected from the wind, and there we pile up branches and bits of driftwood. Meanwhile Stepney is employed gathering fish and it is soon enough to feed not three but thirty men. We dump the contents of the satchel onto a flat rock and consider the nature of our plight. What was an orderly collection of paper cartridges, each one filled with black powder and a musket ball, is now a soggy mess of wet paper, loose balls and damp powder. It is the best we can do to try to separate the three, and in the meantime the boy goes hunting for something to hold the powder in. He returns with a mug and spoon he has salvaged from God knows where and we spoon black powder into the mug.

'If this don't work we'll be eatin' 'em raw,' Brown says, working on getting a spark. Before long we have a little fire. We crouch over it and build it up and roast the fish, gorging ourselves and not caring if the flames should lick at us.

'Did I not tell ye things would be turnin' for the better?' Brown says.

''twas a fluke and nothing more,' I say. 'We've got to get out of here before we're flooded out. I hope our boats aren't damaged.'

'The pair of ye have a gander and I'll keep watch over the fire.'

Stepney and I go searching. Now that I've eaten I'm no longer as dizzy and the head wound does not trouble me unduly. We find one of the boats a good way inland, having come to rest upside down in a thicket. By some miracle the hull is undamaged, but when we get it right side up we find one of the oars broken in two and another missing. Of the second boat we can find not a trace.

We find Brown asleep upon our return.

'Wake up, Jimmy,' I say.

He groans and opens one eye. 'What is it now, by Christ?'

'One boat gone and the other barely usable. This creek's a hazard to our lives, Jimmy. We need to get over to Clarke Island. We've no food beyond this fish and nothing with which to salt what we can't eat today. We've no more black powder. No guns, no warm clothes.'

'And what makes ye think our condition'll be greatly alleviated by crossin' that channel?'

'We need meat and furs,' I say. 'I know it isn't the right season but I'll wager Bader won't have sealed that reef this season.'

'That's a dangerous reef even in the right season, George.'

'You said yourself a better thing was around the corner. We'll cook up every last fish and scavenge anything we can find, then at first light tomorrow we'll get going.'

'Ye've taken leave of yer senses. Best sit tight, I reckon.'

'You're for staying and I'm for going, so we'll let Tom cast the deciding vote. It's his life the same as ours.'

'What'll it be, Tom?' Brown says.

No more than a boy is Tom Stepney and I can see that the decision weighs heavily.

'It int safe here,' he finally says. 'I reckon we'd better go.'

◆

IT IS bitter come first light but we see no portent of rain. The current between Cape Barren and Clarke runs swiftly from the west and we know of sailors drowned in those tidal rips. As we get underway, the sea is ominous in its calm as though foxing to lure us in. Brown and I row for all our worth and before long we are in the lee of Clarke's eastern shore. The sky has a wild look about it.

'Spell me awhile, Tom,' I say.

Clarke is the most southerly island in the Furneaux and beyond it lies the northeast coast of Van Diemen's Land. Stepney and I switch places and I commence scanning the coastline. I recall a seal colony at South Head but one long since fished out. Latterly the seals have taken refuge on the offshore reefs that are hardest for a boat to land a gang on. The scrub abounds with geese and kangaroos but we are lacking both musket and powder. Strewn along the coast are outcroppings of granite boulders and thickets but no signs of habitation.

In the afternoon we haul up on a strip of white sand beach. We drag the boat up onto the dunes, upturning and using it for our windbreak. We eat cold fish, wishing we had a fire. Out there in the chaotic dark we hear the wash of rushing leaves and a splintering of branches. The wind whips up plumes of sand and we listen to the spray against our eggshell hull. There is a dry rasp in my throat and I lay long hours trying to stifle a cough. Finally I hear Brown's snores.

My mind races with a thousand half-formed thoughts that tumble against one another, and in my delirium I imagine myself rescued and en route to Port Jackson. I will have a wife and home and all the things a man would want to have. I will have a child, one and then another. *Sire nothing on a woman unless you know how the littluns are expected to eat,* my old mam says. I turn to tell her about the fish and find she isn't there. I am held tight in a black bubble rising from the deep and when I reach the surface my world shall pop. Somewhere behind the veil I can hear mam's voice, but what words she has can't be reckoned for I have gone to a place beyond the sea. *First it is a map –*

Morning finds our condition not much improved. In the dimness I perceive that Brown still slumbers but the boy is absent, and when I slide out from beneath the boat I find it half-buried in sand. I take a draught of rainwater from an old cooking pot and there is an evil taste in my mouth. I spit up a little blood.

Stepney comes out of the dunes and shows me the clutch of bird eggs he has collected. 'Now all we're needing is a fire,' I say.

He goes back to the boat to see what can be done in the way of breakfast and I stand looking across the water. I can see the white flecks where the waves are breaking over the distant reef. There are some nearer rocks but I do not think we will find good sealing there. Two men will row while the third gets up onto the reef and I have decided that the third will be me. Brown is the strongest and needed in the boat and Stepney is too frail to wrestle seals, and they would both be back at Kents were it not for my insistence.

The others are supping on raw eggs and sandy fish. It turns my guts to see this fare let alone try to get it down, and it only serves to redouble my resolve that we will have seal meat tonight. A man can just about live on seals alone as they afford him not only sustenance but also warmth in the form of furs to wear and oil to burn. If I were a seal I'd never come ashore for that is the realm of men.

'Ye've got that look in yer eye, George,' Brown says. 'I don't fancy clamberin' up on them rocks.'

'You won't be doing any clambering, Jimmy. I'll be the one going up.'

'Plenty of eggs to be had on the shore and I wouldn't be the least bit surprised if our Tom came back with a nice fat goose.'

'I'm freezing in these rags. Just row me out and I'll do the rest.'

'Ye're a daft bugger, George. What if there int no seals?'

'There's going to be a fucking seal.'

◆

WE MAKE first for the pair of rocky islets about a mile offshore. Little more than granite slabs wet with spray, an unlikely patch of moss offers a hint of greenery. There is nothing like a cove where Brown and Stepney might rest their arms, and nor a seal. When I was a lad, the seals would have lain two deep on such a rock.

The reef is further into the strait in a direction you wouldn't want to go, for if a westerly whips up you might find yourself blown out beyond any prospect of land. In an eighteen-foot boat with only two oars, we would be dead men. New Zealand is yonder ways but I could not say how far. The sea has an oily look about it and through the spray I perceive a blob of white that can only be the sealing rocks. I can feel the swirling eddies sucking at the boat, and before long the reef rises out of the water. A misting haze begins to fall and I strain my eyes looking for movement.

'I see 'em,' Stepney says. 'Up on that ledge.'

'Right you are,' I say, gathering my club and knife. Two reddish-brown clapmatches of a decent size loll on a bed of black weeds at water's edge, any pups they may have had already weaned. No sign of a bull. I spot a third and fourth clapmatch, nearly indistinguishable from the smooth boulders around them, and as the boat draws closer I catch a whiff of their stench.

'I'll get ye alongside, George, but ye'll have to jump!' Brown shouts over the surf.

'Close as you can!' I shout back, and I get up onto the thwart in a crouch. Brown manoeuvres and I fling my tools up onto the ledge. I get up onto the gunwale and then it is a matter of timing and luck. I must leap across and find purchase between the slippery rocks or else slide down into the slop. I am up before I know it and I see Brown and Stepney trying to get the boat around. I must work quickly. Walking in my wet moccasins is like skating on a cake of soap and I find better purchase barefoot. The jagged reef cuts into my bare feet but pain is for later.

There is a seal on a rock not five yards distant, and she barely stirs as I creep up and lift the club to still her. The club comes crashing upon her snout once and then twice and the fight is already over, but that is the easier part. I must wrestle the deadweight into a secure position lest it slide into the water, the carcass probably weighing the same as me. We are in death's dance, the water streaming with my blood and hers, but now I must take my turn with another. The second has more fight, baring her teeth and spitting blood after the first thwack, but I do for her nonetheless. The remainder have some inkling of the killer among them but they are slow to get moving and hence I club a third.

There is a bile rising within me and such is the power of the swell that I can no longer tell if it is raining. Those remaining seals are taking flight and I too must think of quitting. The boat toils away and I wave madly to it, standing on a promontory above the thrashing sea. Brown is trying to get the boat around but it won't be long before a breaker crashes over them or a rock stoves them in. He works it through sheer persistence and I see the narrow gap he is making for. It is barely wide enough but it will have to do, and so I commence dragging my companions down by their meaty flippers.

The rock bites into my flesh but I am outside myself. I decide it will be no bad thing to slip beneath the waves. Up here all is turmoil and discomfort but down there I might find rest. Just then I am called back by Brown's cries. He has the boat wedged up against the rock and I must haul the heavy carcasses. The boat is fast filling with water and Stepney is busy baling. I do my work slipping and jolting, but the seals are too heavy to lift alone and the boy comes to my assistance while Brown tries to hold the boat.

On the slime-green ledge we heave the first seal up and over, but the second is heavier and we struggle to lift it, inch by miserable inch. I am trembling and the boy is not much better and the weight of the third is agony itself. Somehow we do it and then I go back to the promontory a final time for my club and knife. I reach into the crevice and in that moment hear an almighty boom, and when I look back white foam is cascading where the boy stood a moment before. I wait for the water to subside but the boy is no longer on the ledge and nor is he in the boat. I search the waters which roar and slide but he is gone. Brown is calling to me and I tumble into the boat and take an oar. I look back in the hope I might see the boy but he is gone. We are clear of the rocks and turning into the wind and I will not release my grip until we next touch land.

My heart is sore and I think only of Tom. A king wave must have come over just as he tried to get back to the boat, and I see from Brown's face that he is haunted by such a vision. I look back again and there is nothing, just a blob of white signifying the reef and a stormy sky already blowing over. Shivering youth sent tumbling to its doom, the whites of his eyes flecked with blood. In my mind a stillborn memory of a time, not more than a fortnight ago, when he asked if we'd see Sydney again and I promised that we would. Said I'd swear it on the Bible if only we had one. The truth was I didn't believe a word of what I said. I could have confided my heart's own truth although it would be of comfort to none.

We are orphans, Tom. Whatever homes we had don't want us back. Now we are banished, whatever plans we have just stories to fill the emptiness. We go where we go and nowhere else. That wave took you and not me and what of it? You were the issue of a colony which didn't want you, your mother a pauper and a prostitute, your father likely a convict and a drunkard. A cruel town, Sydney, one filled with cruel people. It was never your home. The only home is the one you carry inside.

The boat rides lower than it ought but the wind is at our backs and the shore not half as far away as it was. We are saved, Brown and I, but it brings me no joy. Mine is not a drowning fate but a fate to see those drowned. It is a darkness enveloping me and swallowing me entire.

◆

IN MY dream I am a boy on a raft in rising waters that plash and gurgle and I have no oar with which to steer. I feel the current sucking me beyond the estuary and I go where the water decides. Looking back at the evening land, I find it does not tug at me unduly. I look down at my hands and find I can see right through them. I look for my reflection upon the water and there is none. One thought holds me back and it is that I should like to call on my mam, just to set eyes upon her and to hear her speak. Nothing like peace in this letting go, only the bitterness of a life unfinished and of tasks undone.

Get up, George, she'd say. *Get up and don't you go falling down.*

'George, George.'

I open my eyes and a black bearded face looms above me, tree-trunk fingers pressed against my skull. 'Fever's broken, looks like. See if ye can get this soup down.'

I am propped up within the hull of the upturned boat and cloaked in something warm and reeking, a sealskin not yet dried. Mug in hand, Brown crouches next to me and lifts the spoon to my lips. He is wearing a jerkin, wet with dark blood. The soup is warm and meaty and there are chunks of bobbing fat. Three spoons is all I can manage.

'Let's have a look at them feet.'

I shimmy forward and the sealskin slides off me. My torso is slicked with half-congealed seal's blood, but the blood encrusting my feet is my own.

'Won't be walking for a while,' Brown says. 'Thought I'd be buryin' ye.'

I whisper: 'How long has it been?'

'Best part o' three days. Way ye were carryin' on that first night I thought ye wouldn't see the dawn, but I'll grant ye're a tough bugger. Second night I thought maybe ye'd pull through. I'll cut that third skin into a jacket later on. They ain't proper dry but needs must, eh? Skins, meat'n blubber, just like ye said.'

'I thought I was dead, Jimmy.'

'Ye weren't far wrong. Now rest up before ye go catchin' cold. I mean to boil down some o' that blubber and then we'll have oil for a lantern. Wasn't time to flense the skins proper so p'raps I'll have another turn at that.'

'Did you see what happened to Tom?'

Brown turns away. 'Aye and it were a terrible thing. He weren't more'n two paces away when that wave came over. When I looked up I caught sight o' him before he were swept under. He was a good boy and I would remember him to his kin but he called himself an orphan, din't he?'

'He did. I was always hard on the boy and now I feel like I've killed him.'

'It was me who convinced him into runnin', George. Said I'd get him eighty skins, din't I? All we have is three but broodin' won't bring him back. If ye hadn't gone for yer tools ye would've been washed away as well. No way I'd have got the boat back.'

Brown goes back to his tasks and I am left holding the mug of soup. I don't trust my trembling hands and so I sit clasping the mug with both hands lest I drop it. I hold it to my nose, inhaling the pungent odour, but my eyelids are heavy and the mug falls to the sand. A warm trickle runs down my leg and pools at my feet. I huddle into the clammy sealskin.

Stepney returns and although he speaks in a voice too faint to hear I know he reproaches me for the manner of his drowning. We never should've gone out to that damn reef. I am locked in a battle against the cold and the boy stares at me from across a frigid sea. As I watch, the water freezes over, entombing the boy, and yet his eyes dart back and forth.

I would remember him to his kin.

His lips are almost black and when he opens them his tongue is frozen solid. From the look in his eye, I think it best that the dead cannot speak. I can sense his anger.

But he called himself an orphan.

When I wake, I hear the crackling of a fire and I crawl over to the opening. Brown sits on the sandbank feeding the flames and stirring a pot of blubber. He has a sealskin pegged out next to a huge mass of slimy meat. Further up the sandbank, the squabbling birdlife fight over guts and offal.

'Give us that skin and I'll flense it,' he says. 'Other'n should be about ready.'

As I unpeel myself from the wet filthy skin I find bits of gore sticking to my flesh. Brown has fashioned head and arm holes in the dry skin and when I put it on I am much warmer. He cooks up the first of the greasy steaks and although my appetite has not returned I know I must try to eat. The meat is chewy but I get most of it down.

'Thought I'd walk to South Head tomorrow, can't be more'n a mile or two,' Brown says between mouthfuls.

I look to the south through the gathering gloom. 'Weren't many seals last I saw, back in '05, and I reckon none now. Four years is an awful long time in the Furneaux.'

'It must be the end of April or early May, don't ye reckon? We'll be needin' a better place than under the boat or we'll be catchin' our death. We'll be needin' traps and snares for huntin'. We'll be needin' a hut or else a good cave.'

◆

BY MORNING, something has been at the seal carcasses and what remains is crawling with ants, but nothing will stop Brown from setting out on his trek. I watch as he disappears into the distance. I try to eat part of another steak but it is even less appetising and the condition of my innards is precarious. When the rain lets up, I sit for a long time looking out at the islets and thinking about what I might have done differently. It was my inability to lift the carcasses that brought Stepney to my side. With Brown's strength, he and I could have had them in the boat in a trice but then who would have held the boat?

I can see myself and Stepney on that slippery ledge, straining every sinew to lift that stinking weight. Second by second and inch by inch we lift, but still I must clamber up that rock one final time to retrieve my tools. An almighty boom, a rain of spray, and it is done.

Such it has been my whole life. Where the wave hits or the musket ball lands, I am not. I might have hung at Execution Dock but I received my pardon instead. I might have drowned off Badger or in that storm on New Year, and I was clear of that ledge when I had to be.

'I've news for ye both good and bad,' Brown says when he returns.

'Let's have the good news first.'

'The good news is there's huts standin' at South Head.'

'And the bad?'

'I saw a seal, two in fact. Good size clapmatches. We needn't have gone out to that fuckin' reef after all.'

◆

EACH TIME we depart a place we leave a trail of bones and the charred remains of fires. Anything that might come in handy goes into the boat, the rest left to be picked over by birds or scattered to the wind. The sky is filled with the promise of rain but the shallows on Clarke's protected side are tolerably safe. I am weak and the slosh of waves aids me none. I find myself glancing back as though I might catch a glimpse of the boy.

South Head is a rocky and windswept place unfit for habitation but we are six months out of port and have forgotten what it is like to sleep in a bed. The huts are where the beach curves outward before ending abruptly in a tumble of rock. I recall another cove closer to the old sealing ground but it is southerly facing and subject to the full force of winter. Van Diemen's Land is clearly visible from that place whereas here it is hidden behind a wall of rock upon which thousands of birds nest.

'Ye've turned three shades greener, George,' Brown says as we drag the boat through a tangle of seaweed.

'I reckon I'll live,' I say, but my throat is sore and my forehead clammy.

'Get out of the wind, and if ye feel better later ye can help with the fire.'

The hut is old and evil-smelling and the wind whistles through it. Built of timber planks beneath the rocky cliffside, it has seen its share of sealers. Nothing salvageable inside, not a stitch of clothing or a single utensil, and yet the faint smell of woodsmoke and seal blubber lingers. The floor is more rock than sand but it is tolerably dry.

As I start to drift off, it occurs to me that scurvy might be my affliction. We had boiled lime juice every day aboard *Governor Hunter* and not so much as a sprig of wild parsley has passed our lips since then. I've known men to eat something they called sea celery, and I've heard of men who tried the wrong berry and bloated up dead.

I mention this to Brown when I get up. He has a fire going.

'Scurvy, George? Could be'n all. To be honest with ye I've been feelin' poorly meself, though I thought it were a pox I'd caught.'

'We need greens. I reckon that lime juice did something for us after all.'

'Plenty o' bird eggs to be had up there,' Brown says, pointing to the grey cliffside. 'But as for greens, I can't rightly say.'

'Did you know those Eora clansmen to eat vegetables?'

'Nothing like a turnip or a potato, although I recall some roots they favoured.'

'What about at Oyster Bay?'

'I reckon they eat a mountain of muttonfish, George. Huge piles o' shells along the beach. There'll be muttonfish here but I don't fancy muckin' about under that cliff.'

'What about seaweed?' I point to the great mounds washed up not twenty yards from where we sit.

'It don't look right to me.'

'You can see where it grows on the tide. All we have to do is look for some that's washed up fresh.'

'Now that ye mention it, I did see that Eora mob eatin' seaweed though maybe it weren't the same kind. Cleaned it in the stream and cooked it over a fire.'

'Did you try it?'

'No, but it din't seem to do them no harm.'

There is seaweed washed up along this coast but it mainly accumulates in the corner where the rocky head juts out. I pick up the freshest-looking bunch by the whip end and drag it toward the hut, a mass of strands trailing behind me like a twenty-foot tail. 'Which part makes for the best eating?' I say. 'These long strands?'

'Don't know, George.'

I detach a strand from the bunch and cut a six-inch section from the fleshiest part. Brown shakes his head but hands me a pot of rainwater and I wash off the worst of the sand. Then I spear it and hold it over the flames. After a couple of minutes the seaweed is starting to brown. 'I'm imagining it to be a fresh cucumber,' I say, biting into the warm rubbery flesh.

'Well?'

'Salty. Chewy.'

'Can ye get it down?'

I swallow.

Brown looks at me and then at the tangled mound. 'I think I'll wait a day or two 'fore tryin' it meself.'

◆

I AM not dead the next day or the day after that and finally Brown concedes that eating seaweed won't kill us. I am feeling better and Brown worse and it serves to fuel my suspicion that it is scurvy. Finally he consents to trying some. He spends his days huddled in the corner and I try to care for him as he did me. When he is sleeping I go foraging. I spot a single clapmatch out there beyond the breakers but she will not come ashore. The boy still visits my dreams but not with the same intensity of that first dread apparition. We know not the day, week or month but there can be no mistaking the season for anything but winter. Oftentimes we can do little more than sit in our hut with no more light than in the bowels of a hulk.

'Best part o' a year spent in chains on the *Fortune*,' Brown says. 'Weren't called *Good Fortune*. Ye'd have thought I'd learn me lesson, but it din't stop me from taking up with Sturt first chance I had. Even cheatin' the hangman din't stop me. I'd nick anythin' wasn't nailed down. I was charged with thievin' a pig, property of Thomas Arndell, Esquire. Acquitted on insufficiency of evidence. Ye'll never guess the name of the man who turned tattle. Go on, have a guess.'

'Henry Trotter?'

'No, William Hog! He had plenty o' evidence, some were in his belly. It's true I fired at the porker but I missed, din't I? Course then I battered its brains out. Me'n Hog butchered'n salted it and we buried half in a cask. Only reason Arndell found out was I had the other half hangin' in me hut.'

Brown has proven himself a master of getting a fire started and keeping it alive but even he has had to concede it is a lost cause now. We have to travel further along the beach for driftwood and the scraggly tea-tree won't burn after all this rain. Even the caves are starting to flood.

'Never thought I'd be livin' on raw eggs and seaweed, George. When ye turn side on ye near enough disappear. Soon I'll be lookin' right through ye.'

His words remind me of my dream of seeing through my own flesh. Never a real life but only the ghost of one. I look at my hands and they seem real enough.

'Another month and we'll be too weak to travel even if the weather does turn good,' I say. 'Maybe I'll walk down to the south beach and see if something's washed up.'

'Won't be a grain o' sand left after the batterin' we've had.'

Our little bay is well protected from winds blowing from the south or west, but only a man who values his life cheaply would try to climb directly to what I call the south beach. Instead I walk north and east through the rising scrubland dotted with shallow pools. The easier route to the south beach lies that way. I'm nowhere near the clifftop before I start to feel the power of the southerly wind. As I ascend, cold air pushes me back. Standing away from the edge, I peer down at the grey waves thundering in. If there is a beach down there it is one unsafe even for birds.

◆

ONE MORNING I wake to see light streaming in through the gaps between the planks. All is silent but for the sound of Brown's snores. I get up and open the door.

It is a miracle: *the sun.*

For long moments I stand squinting, basking with my face upturned. Not a single cloud in the brilliant sky. I am a blind man suddenly restored to sight. I have never seen so rich a shade of blue.

'Jimmy, come quick!'

Emerging from the gloom, Brown is a pale spectre with sunken cheeks and red bleary eyes. He stands at the threshold before taking his first faltering step. We look over the glassy water and our thoughts can only be the same. Today is the day for getting off.

'Might be weeks before we have another day like this,' I say.

'Aye.'

Clumps of seaweed lay in varying states of putrefaction, some we have been eating and others thrown up by the most recent storm. There may be bird eggs on the higher cliff ledges but lately we have been too feeble to climb. We have passed to a place beyond hunger, our grey twilit thoughts a mirror to our surrounds.

'How far is it to Swan Island, Jimmy?'

''tisn't a long haul except as we're weak as kittens.'

'But from there we can get over to Van Diemen's Land.'

'Nearer don't mean near, George. Wish that it did.'

Brown shuffles back inside. I drink deeply from a place where the rainwater collects and eat a few strands of seaweed. I go into the cave where we store the boat, finding that the storm has pushed it into the far corner. Brown is asleep when I get back and I have to cajole him awake. On his feet, his arms hang loose as though they are no business of his.

'You want to die here?' I say. 'I need your help with the boat.'

He mutters woozily and in my anger I slap his face. In normal circumstances he might raise his hands to throttle me but now he allows himself to be led. I make him drink but he will not eat. The sunlight seems to have brought him to his senses for he helps me drag the boat clear and I sense something of the old Brown returning. I sit him down on a rock while I go about gathering all we hold dear and it isn't much beyond some strands of seaweed, pots filled with rainwater and our sealing clubs and knives. It is a good thing the sea is benign for Brown is in no fit state. We can die miserably in a dank and smelly hut or we can try the sea again. If I must perish I would rather it be out there on the open water. I do not know the correct date but it must be past the eighteenth of June and thus I have attained twenty-two years. I have outlived many men and I've an inkling I will outlive more still.

Brown helps me drag the boat. I ask him to row and he rows. The swell is nothing much and yet it takes all our strength to get out against it. Already my arms are protesting this labour. I have one last look at the little cove we have called our home and then we are around the head. Banks Strait is becalmed and we toil under a sun too strong for our liking. Swan Island is to the sou'west and our progress is negligible. I look at Brown who is slumped forward, chin resting on his oar.

We are becalmed.

I drape some rags over him to try to keep the sun off his face. Swan is still a long way off in the shimmering distance and my eyes will not stay open.

When I open my eyes, the sun has gone behind a cloud. Hours must have passed because I can feel the sting of sunburn. The current has brought us closer to our goal, however, for I find we are not far from Swan Island.

'Jimmy! Wake up!' I try to shake him awake but he is moribund. His skin has taken on a grey, chalky quality and his breathing is shallow.

Brown warned me that Swan Island was no paradise and he didn't lie, the island little more than a narrow strip of sandhills. Running horizontal to the mainland, the only vegetation aside from tussock appears to be patches of brushwood and stunted shrubs.

I have a decision to make. There is a suitable cove on the northside of the island and I might direct us there on the tide. If not, we will make landfall on the eastern side of what I take to be Cape Portland. The country looks more promising but I know nothing of its clansmen. I am undecided and thus Swan slides by.

We are for Van Diemen's Land.

◆

THEY ARE watching, three clansmen naked but for the kangaroo skins draped across their shoulders. They stand motionless, their thin spears taller than a man. We have made landfall on a wide expanse of beach adjacent to the mouth of a river. It is late in the afternoon and the sun has disappeared behind a bank of cloud. The country is well-treed and the grassy plain is dotted with yellow flowers.

'We made it, Jimmy,' I say. 'But we've got company.'

Brown does not answer.

There is a little water swishing in one of the pots, so I raise it to his lips. When I look up, the three men have come closer. They are around my height and probably a similar age. Their bodies are covered in intricate patterns of welts or tattoos and their hair is long and twisted into wrinkles that have dried with a kind of red glue. The men speak to each other and point at the sleeping man, but they do not raise their spears.

'He's sick,' I say. 'He needs food.'

It is clear these words are not understood.

'Food.' I open my mouth and pretend to put something in, repeating the word several times. 'He needs to eat. All we've got is seaweed.' I point to the dry clumps. The men mimic my action and we can agree there is a thing called eating. One of them reaches into a pouch on his hip and withdraws a piece of cooked kangaroo tail. He hands it to me.

'My God, yes,' I say, biting into the flesh. I look for something suitable to give in exchange but the men start walking away. It seems the food is intended as a gift. 'Thank you a hundred times,' I say to their backs.

Better than salt pork, better than rabbit stew, this kangaroo tail is life itself. Every ounce of me cries out for it and yet I must think of Brown lest I gobble it all.

'Wake up Jimmy,' I say, holding the meat under his nose. I break off a small piece and pop it into his mouth, but it sits there on his tongue where he is liable to choke on it. 'You've got to chew.'

Brown is too weak even for this and there is the stench of death about him. The meat falls off his tongue.

'If you won't chew, then I'll do as birds do.' I chew the meat into a paste and feed it from my mouth to his. Chew by chew, mouthful by mouthful, I get the meat down into his gullet. We are both covered in fat and slimy pap but if he can eat then maybe he will live. I've lost one member of my gang and I shall be damned if I'm losing the other. After a while, he lays with his head back but the food has done him good. The clansmen are watching.

What we cannot do is sit here in the boat or else we will be washed out on the tide. We must find shelter in the trees and Brown is in no condition for that. Nor can I drag the boat with him sat in it.

'Are they still there?' he whispers.

'Yes.'

'In a while they'll go ask their chief what to do. They'll have their camp nearby.'

'What can I give them? I don't reckon they'll want these old pots and suchlike?'

'Dogs, hatchets.'

'We've neither, Jimmy.'

'Seals.'

'Seals we can get tomorrow if you think you can row.'

'S'late.'

The wind has picked up, ruffling the water, and the first drops of rain begin to fall.

'I need you out of the boat, Jimmy. I'll drag us up near them trees.'

'Wait till they go.'

It is a queer standoff, the clansmen waiting for us to leave and us waiting for them to leave so that we might stay. They watch me and I watch them and the waves lap at the keel of the boat. If they come with hostile intent I have my club and knife but they are three to my one and they will slay me where I sit.

Eventually they go. It is past dusk and getting difficult to see when I help Brown down onto the sand. He is wracked with fever but there is a stubbornness in him and he holds onto the bow while I push from the stern. Thank God the beach is free of seaweed for otherwise I would not have the strength. We take refuge beneath a stand of trees, the ground sodden and the shelter slight. After a while I decide we are better off under the boat. It has stopped raining but the wind is stronger and we will not sleep a wink like this. I get the boat tipped over with Brown underneath and we try to get warm. There is a foul odour and I fear Brown has shat himself but we must hunker nonetheless. When I put my hand to his forehead it comes away wet and clammy.

We have come a great distance and yet find ourselves no closer to safety and it is bitter to imagine we ought to have gone to Sydney with Bader. Tom Stepney would be alive and Brown tucked up warm in bed and we would have our hundredth lay. A hundredth of something is better than the nothing we have. Brown said we'd have our freedom and this is it, two starving men crouching in the darkness at the mercy of the elements and the clansmen both. This is the freedom we have won.

◆

MORNING COMES and Brown is not dead, but his breath is laboured and the smell worse than ever. Though he cannot form proper words I know he is asking for water and so I turn the boat over and let in the day. The sun is high and the morning advanced and Brown is like a tortoise flipped over, its underbelly exposed. I tell him I am off in search of water.

Pot in hand, I am headed in the direction of the river when I spot the clansmen. Today they are five in number, armed not only with spears but with waddies too. I put the pot down and hold out my hands to show I am unarmed. One is older than the others and perhaps their chief for his long hair and beard are dressed in the red glue and it is spread all across his torso. He comes up and looks me in the eye and a string of words issues forth. He is pointing to the boat with Brown propped up against it and I have an inkling he is telling me to get in the boat and be gone.

'He's too sick to row,' I say. 'I can't manage the boat on my own.'

The chief walks past me to observe the sick man. The others hold their spears at their sides. The headman speaks to me again and points in the direction of the dunes. I take this as sign of progress for the expression on his face seems not of anger.

'He needs water,' I say, pointing to the river and then my mouth. 'Water.'

The chief looks at the sky and then all five of them are talking among themselves. The chief points to Brown and then at each of his men and finally the dunes where he indicated before.

'They're going to carry him?'

The men put down their spears, leaving only the chief with weapon in hand. They do not seem to consider me a threat. They stand over Brown, touching his clammy skin, lifting his hand and letting it drop again. The warriors screw up their noses and grimace at the stench but they have been given their instructions.

'They're going to lift you, Jimmy,' I say, but he appears not to have heard. Nor does he object as the four men commence hauling him off. I am to follow with the chief.

Just beyond the rise of dunes is a grassy plain not more than a two-minute walk from where Brown and I spent the night. It is here that the clansmen have made their camp and a thin plume of smoke rises from their cooking fires. They could have easily slain us and have chosen not to. There are a number of domed bark huts and for the first time I see the clanswomen. They sit or stand in their nakedness except for the kangaroo skins they drape across their shoulders. Unlike the men, their hair is cropped short. Several of the women suckle infants at their breasts while older children play by the fire. The women wear shell necklaces and their bodies are decorated with patterns of scars like the men. Everyone turns to look at me and I feel I am a ghost and not a man, such are their expressions. Some of the people are old and wizened but none of the greybearded men seems to hold sway. It seems I was correct in my assumption that the red glue is a sign of privilege or rank, and thus the man I identified as the chief is in fact so.

The four warriors carry Brown to one of the openmouthed huts and I am given to understand that he will be in the care of the older women. I am invited to sit on a log by the fire. It is good to warm my bones and I am given a meal of cooked muttonfish, crawfish and some kind of tuber. It is as good a meal as I have eaten in months and I am at pains to express my gratitude. Everyone seems pleased and I am the object of much fascination. The shock of my presence is starting to wear off and now I am even worth a cautious smile. They want to touch my white skin and ginger beard and they are interested in my sealskin jerkin. *I'm as alive as you or I,* I want to explain, but it is myself I must convince first of all.

When the meal is over, I walk back to the boat with the chief where his huntsmen commence gathering up our meagre possessions. They are particularly interested in the knives and I try to explain that they are for hunting seals. I point in the direction of the Furneaux Isles where the outline of the great mountains is visible. 'Plenty of seals off Clarke,' I say. 'When Brown's better we can get you as many as you like.'

The chief looks at me and there is a strange glint in his eye as though I have confirmed some idea of his. He grasps me by the hand as if to confirm I am a man and not some unwanted vision and there follows a long string of words, the meaning of which I haven't a hope of comprehending. He points to himself and says something which might be his name or the name of his clan, and so I tap my chest and say 'George Baggs.' He does not try to repeat the words but I believe he understands that I have told him my name. I point to the islands and try to explain by way of gesture that we have sailed across from them and this pleases him greatly for he claps me on the back in the manner of an old friend. I have conferred some vital information and I know not what it is.

The men are already starting back across the dunes but it seems the chief is intent on giving me a tour of his domain. He points at the sky and says some words, and then the sea, and finally the Furneaux Isles. It is clear the islands hold some special significance for he points at them repeatedly. It is my turn to speak and so I tell him that the small island across from us is called Swan and that the larger islands go by the names of Clarke, Cape Barren and Flinders. I try to explain that I came from a bigger boat which foundered on an island called Badger. The chief is attentive as I try to show him how *Governor Hunter* ran up onto the beach. I want to tell him about Tom Stepney and the reef and the winter stuck at South Head but I fear it is beyond the limits of what might be achieved through pantomime. When I am done I have no idea whether I have made myself understood in the slightest.

The chief indicates that I am to walk with him and we make our way along the beach to the rivermouth, where I am startled to spot several women in the deep water. At first I think their purpose to be bathing but I see them duck their heads beneath the surface and stay submerged for longer than I would have thought possible. The chief seems quite unperturbed as the women come up with hauls of crawfish which they heap in piles on the banks. The women are lithe and lovely and although I have laid with women I have never before seen them in such a state of the frankest nudity, not one let alone six at a time. The women swim back and forth and it must be part of their ordinary labour for they give no sign of acknowledgement.

Further along, I am surprised to see black smoke rising from the forest inland of the rivermouth. As we approach, I see flames licking at the boughs of trees and a group of huntsmen nearby. These men wield burning torches and they are setting fire to the underbrush all around. Again this must be a routine matter for the chief shows no surprise. He is explaining the purpose of the fires to me, although the meaning is lost.

In the afternoon the chief instructs me to stay near the camp and he and his men go off somewhere. When I go to visit Brown I find him fast asleep. The women usher me out of the hut and I go back to the fire where an old man tries to engage me in conversation. I respond as best I can but we make little progress beyond me telling him my name. After a while he nods and moves away. By now the fisherwomen have returned and it is clear there will be a feast. The women point at me and whisper but they do not attempt to engage me in conversation and it is just as well that they do not. The blood surges within me and I must quell it for fear of causing offence, so I lie down beside a log and close my eyes.

The fire crackles, birds sing, wind rustles in the trees. I let the words of the people wash over me and I listen to the happy cries of their children at play. Between the sun and the warmth of the fire, I am comfortable and yet probably in mortal danger. If Brown recovers we can be on our way but only if the chief allows it, for we haven't a hope of sneaking out without attracting attention. If Brown dies, it must be all of a hundred miles to Launceston and I would not know the way. If I can persuade these people that I mean to be their friend and ally, then perhaps I can be of use to them and them to me.

The sound of the men returning from their hunt awakens me. They have slain two kangaroos and they place these near the fire to be skinned. The sky is clear, the sun touching the trees. I must have slept for hours and it might be the best thing I could have done because no one is staring at me anymore. They can see I am a man and one who eats and sleeps the same as they, and this is pleasing to them. I want to check on Brown but I fear this will be frowned upon and so I sit back and watch the preparations. The chief sits next to me and explains how the women undress the kangaroo. They do not have knives and instead use rocks with razor-sharp edges to cut through the thick fur. They work swiftly and with the dexterity of master butchers as they peel back the hides. The butchers' hands are slick with blood as they cut through the kangaroo bellies and release forth a torrent of innards onto the sand, and they reach into the cavities and pull forth long strings of intestines. Before long, the rich smell of roasting flesh begins to rise from the hot coals. I rub my belly to indicate hunger and several people laugh in appreciation. I am not a ghost and everyone is happy to find it so.

The first stars begin to appear in the evening sky and the chief points them out to me. I watch and listen and I signal my agreement. Some of the younger women have gone off somewhere and they now return carrying dripping baskets. One of the women brings a basket to the chief and I think I recognise her from the river. The basket is made of dried seaweed and is used for holding water which the chief demonstrates is for drinking. He passes the basket to me and I drink deeply from it. The chief is happy and seems to be referring not to the basket but to the woman herself. She is slender and beautiful and no more than half his age so perhaps she is his daughter. I smile and thank her and she goes off to attend to the others. She is a vision of loveliness and I cannot but stare.

The meal is ready and there is not only roasted kangaroo but an assortment of other delicacies. I particularly favour the crawfish but there is more than I could possibly hope to eat at one sitting. It is a banquet of kangaroo, seaweed and a vegetable which reminds me of sweet potato. I recognise the seaweed as the same kind that Brown and I subsisted on for so long, although it is far more palatable toasted like this. There is singing and clapping and soon the people are on their feet and dancing by the firelight. The men and women dance not together but separately and I first watch the men, soon realising that their dances are a storytelling or stage play. The men mimic the bounding of the kangaroo and then a hunter unleashing his spear. They sing about the fire and the stars and perhaps even about me for they look over and point in fear, and then their fear turns to laughter. Then it is the turn of the women and I think their song is about fishing for they make out that they are diving down and then bursting from the water. They jump up and crouch down, both predator and prey, and it is all a whirl of flashing limbs and shapes against a backdrop of flames. The young fisherwoman whom I take to be the chief's daughter looks at me and I look at her. As she dances, all else vanishes.

◆

THE DAWN comes and I find I have slept near the fire. The people lay everywhere sprawled and it takes me a moment to realise they are sleeping and not slain. It is a spell I dare not break. A kangaroo skull looks at me from where it has been placed atop the smouldering coals and by its very silence it seems to pose a question but I know not what it is. Creeping away from the fireside to empty my bladder, my thoughts turn to Brown. I must know whether he still lives and if I might seek his advice.

The hut where he lays is unguarded, a flap of skin covering the opening. I gain entrance. He is laid out on a bed of kangaroo skins but in the dim light I cannot tell whether his pallor has improved.

'You're still alive, Jimmy,' I whisper. He opens his eyes. I help prop him up so that he might see me better.

'Them women make fine nursemaids,' he says in a low growl.

'They've washed you.'

'Aye and it brought the fever down. I'm feeling a sight better.'

'What'll we do now?'

'We'll have to get away, George, soon as we can. Prob'ly the only reason they didn't spear us was because I was so poorly. They might let us go if we ask 'em.'

'They might not like that. The chief's taken a shine to me.'

'Ye'll have to ask his permission then. They'll be out there listenin'.'

I peek past the flap of skin. At the campfire, several people are on their feet and looking this way. I duck back inside. 'You're right.'

'Then go talk to them.'

'Aren't we better off waiting?'

'I reckon they'll try to run us off, George.'

I walk over to the campfire. The chief intercepts me but at least he is not brandishing a weapon. He speaks in a commanding tone and points at the hut and I know I am being admonished. He is asking a question or demanding a response and it is all I can do to hold out my hands in what I hope will be taken as a gesture of goodwill.

'Brown's feeling better,' I say. 'We'll be heading back to the Furneaux.' I point across the water. He turns to face the sea and I stand alongside him, pointing first at the boat in the dunes and then at the islands. 'We will bring you lots of seals.' I point to my jerkin and then to my lips. 'Good eating.'

The chief's stern expression cracks into the broadest smile and it is like night becoming day. He is talking and pointing and I am in complete agreement with whatever it is he is saying. I signal to Brown and tell him to come out and everyone watches as the flap is pushed open. He creeps forward slowly and I can see it takes all his strength to do as much as this. 'Tell yer women thank ye,' he huffs at the chief. 'They've saved me life.'

The chief nods and all is well in the world.

The whole camp is awake and bustling with activity. The women are preparing provisions which I hope may be for our journey and at least a dozen people follow us down to the beach. I can feel their gaze upon me and I know I must grow larger to fulfil whatever role it is they imagine. I can see that Brown is tiring and this seems a foolish scheme for if he cannot walk he certainly cannot row. The conditions for sailing could not be better and yet I can't help but feeling we are making a mistake. Were it not for Brown I might have thought to throw in my lot with these people, but maybe he is right in thinking they tolerate us only as visitors. I do not think they have seen white men or perhaps only fleetingly, and they do not seem to understand that the British are already settled in Van Diemen's Land where they mean to stay.

'We'll be needing our knives,' I tell the chief as we drag the boat down to water's edge. I mimic a cutting motion and the chief sends several men back to the camp. By the time we are nearly ready, I count more than forty souls gathered on the beach to see us off. Men and women, the old and the young. The chief is pointing things out to me again and perhaps he is showing me the best place for seal hunting. Swan Island is no good for this purpose if I understand him correctly, and I try to explain that we will head for Swan first on account of its proximity and go from there. The chief points to the east and makes a motion with his hands that might be to suggest the way a seal swims, and I thank him and say we will try those rocks when we can. The hunters return, bringing not only our sealing implements but every last thing we possess down to the rustiest pct. The women give us kangaroo and crawfish from last night's meal and two seaweed water carriers.

We are about to leave when the chief comes over again. Brown is sitting on the thwart with oar in hand and anyone can see he is in no fit condition for sailing. The chief looks at me and puts his hand on my shoulder and indicates to two of the fisherwomen standing there, one of whom is the daughter who so entranced me with her dancing. He is telling me something and it is a matter of the greatest importance for he repeats the same phrase many times. I think the two women mean to try to lift Brown out of the boat but surely he is too heavy, and then I realise they are getting into the boat. The chief means to send them a'sealing, for when I look back he is smiling and pointing in the direction of the islands.

◆

THE CHIEF'S daughter does not speak my tongue and nor I hers and yet there is a thing like language between us. The sight of her quickens my blood and she smiles in such a way to say she knows it to be so. There is a heaviness in the air like a gathering cloudburst. At night-time, she lays down abed and I am awake half the night waiting for a sign that will not come.

Brown is as unfit for sailing as I feared and so we go no further than Swan Island that first day. The women have plainly never held an oar let alone tried to row, but it doesn't take long before they are pulling like a pair of old hands. The bay I judge safest is on the north shore facing Clarke and we land there without incident. Swan Island is not much good, all tussock and sandflies and the godawful wind. What miserable stream there is will soon run dry and the water here makes me thirst for rum. There is a kind of kangaroo rat but it frightens upon my approach. Vanishing into its burrow, I am left clutching empty air. The women laugh and point and beckon me down to the shore, Brown watching from the fireside. The women wish to demonstrate their hunting prowess and I tell them I am happy to have it demonstrated. I think they understand the sentiment if not the words and they stride out waist-deep and dive into the foam. The day is not warm and the sun not shining but I do not think it bothers them unduly. There they are, two bobbing heads and a flurry of arms.

After a while, the chief's daughter returns to the beach while the other goes in search of muttonfish. The chief's daughter wants to show me her skills and I tell her she is a fine huntress. Now she points to the water and tries to take my hand and I tell her no. I hold her hand in mine and tell her the water is too cold for my liking and besides I never learned how to swim. She cajoles me and perhaps promises of a reward if only I will come. I take off my moccasins and let her pull me ankle-deep into the shallows, the bottoms of my trousers wet. I know what is coming and so I remove my jerkin and fling it up onto the sand, and then I think to hell with it and step out of my trousers too. She is seeing me the way I see her all the time and the thought does not displease me. *Warmer in than out,* she seems to be saying, ducking into the water and splashing me. In my foolishness I cannot but follow.

Shock, the bracing rush, and I must thrash about or perish swiftly from the cold. I am stumbling and falling, my arms windmilling without effect, but there she is to guide me with her hands and her voice. She moves through the water without disturbing it and my efforts at imitation are inadequate, but I am a willing disciple. The water is a little deeper here and when I duck down I can almost forget the cold. In my time I have bathed in many a river but rarely the sea and it is a different sensation entirely.

She would have me swim out further and I tell her no, and so for a time I am content to watch her to-ing and fro-ing. No poorer a swimmer than a seal is she but one immeasurably lovelier, and this is our courtship dance. She surges toward me in a swirl of limbs and I would possess her in my arms but she is too nimble. Back and forth this goes in splashing laughter and finally she consents to being held. She whispers in my ear and I think it is along the lines of *I shall be the one to decide* but she is giving herself to me all the same. Now we are one but all too fleetingly.

We are warm, the sea our bath, and with two fingers pointing at my eyes she gestures that she would show me the world beneath. She demonstrates inhaling sharply and her chest heaves, and then she disappears. I pinch my nose and duck below the surface, but all I see is a murk of sand and seaweed. I come up coughing and hacking. Long moments pass, long enough for me to begin wondering whether I might have imagined her out of nothing. She surfaces before swimming back toward me, grinning with a wriggling crawfish in each hand. It is only when I am on the beach that I feel the bite of the wind. I hold my garments in a sodden bundle and race over to the fire, and meanwhile the chief's daughter rejoins her companion.

A little colour has returned to Brown's face. 'No one could say ye weren't game, yer daft bugger.'

That night I wait for her to come and she does not. I lay restless but intent on making patience my virtue and the dim dark wanders on regardless. In my dream, I am a man known to all and assailed on every side. I cannot take a step without brushing past the outstretched hands of supplicants, and I avert my gaze so as not to see their pleading. I shall leave this place in the manner I have left all others, without a backwards glance. No home but the one I carry inside. I shall find a place alone and turn away even from that.

It is early and the world is still. The fire burns low but I am warmly ensconced and there is light enough to see a whole world poised to shrug off its cloak. The light leads me down to the water and I look out over the islands rising from the mist. Those unearthly blue hills tug at me, places of this earth where no one dwells. I walk along the beach awhile toward the lightening sky and come to the place where the chief's daughter stands. She glances at me but does not speak and the faintest breeze comes rippling off the water.

'I spent all winter over there on Clarke Island,' I say. 'You see that low island in front of Cape Barren?'

'Longtartennerner?' she says.

'Place where no one'll bother us. We could travel there. What do you think?'

'Longtartennerner,' she says, and I take this for a yes.

MᵒE

1812

Y WIFE MOE, the chief's daughter, says I am a dead man walking this land. Arriving in her country aboard a strange vessel, with a near-corpse as company, has lent me a certain notoriety. Moe says that when we perish we shall be reunited in England, the place of shadows, and there is nothing I can say to persuade her otherwise. I put her hand to my chest saying *Can you not feel my heart beating? Can you not feel me, blood to blood?* but she is unmoved. I am a man, this she will admit, but I do not truly live. Visitants are abroad in her homeland but this has always been a place where spirits roam.

Jimmy Brown and I are seal hunters and this is something the clansmen understand, but trying to explain our purpose for the skins is more vexing. Now that we have dried, salted and bundled a boatload of skins, we must sail to a faraway place called Launceston in order to sell them. If we spot other ships along the way we must make ourselves hidden, lest we find ourselves captured and sent back as prisoners to a place called Sydney. Sydney is filled with Englishmen but they are no friends of ours. Warring clans, bitter feuds – Moe's people know all about that. What she thinks about during the long hours under sail I cannot say, but her eyes are forever scanning the coast for sign of the hostile clans that would do us ill.

These January days are endless and dusk is a long time coming, but our destination draws near at last. We are not far from Low Head at the mouth of the River Tamar and we dare not have a fire for fear of soldiers. Two men fell in with us along the coast, and although they are adequate oarsmen I would not want to vouch for either. One is called Staples and I know little of the man beyond the fact he has spent time on a whaler. He will not say if he has been a convict and if so whether he has served out his sentence. The other, Hendrick, is rather more forthright, often expansively so when at his drink. Hendrick will attest to having served time on the chain gang for stabbing a fellow and I can well believe that he has.

That makes five of us, or six if you go counting the bairn.

I had wanted to name my daughter Mary after my dear old mam but Moe will not allow it, saying a child so young has no need of a name. She says the child will let its name be known when the time is right. I can never say my wife's name to her satisfaction and so I call her Moe instead. In return she calls me *GeorgeBaggs* as though it were all one word.

That night I am roused by an unpleasant dream of fleeing from a foe who will not show me his face. Oftentimes my nights are plagued by just such an adversary and my rest is meagre as a consequence.

Brown is on watch. 'Can't sleep, George?'

'Bad dreams is all. How goes the night?'

'Damn sandfleas have been pesterin' me.'

'They always did prefer the taste of you, Jimmy.'

'They're creatures of some discernment.' He grunts and scratches himself. 'Wish I could say the same for the lassies I've been acquainted with, by and by.'

'That's the real reason you want to go to the settlement, isn't it? To visit the brothel.'

'Easy for some to look down their noses. I never went after Sal when she ran off, did I? Trouble is I'm too much of a gentleman. Men I've known would've had her in chains.'

'But then you are a gentleman.'

'That I am, and so off to town we go.'

'I can't risk taking Moe and the bairn up there, Jimmy. Only three things those fucking redcoats are good for.'

'Drinkin' and shootin' and I believe ye mentioned the third already. Moe's a fine lass and ye're a richer man for havin' her share yer bed, even if it is crawlin' wi' sandfleas. I hear York Town's abandoned but there must be a hut still standin'. Moe and the littlun'll be safe while the rest of us go up to Launceston.'

'And what if the Major has us thrown in gaol?'

'Now why would that fool Gordon want to go doin' a thing like that? Nobody gives a tinker's cuss who we are or where we've been, George. Won't find a man from the Governor down who ain't absconded from somethin'.'

'I won't leave Moe alone, Jimmy. She'll run off and I wouldn't blame her if she did.'

'If I had such a woman I prob'ly wouldn't let her out of me sight neither. Just means one less set of arms for rowin' but then I always did the work of two, din't I?'

Jimmy settles down and I take his place at the watch.

◆

THE BOARD nailed to a tree reads 'GEORGE TOWN' and though I am no man of letters I do not fail to recognise my own name. This place must be intended as a site of future settlement but for now there is nothing here, just a stand of trees near a muddy cove. When I explain the name to Moe, she asks whether it is my kin who will be coming and I tell her no, there is another George and he is the King of England. I cannot imagine where she places this in the scheme of her understanding but she is deep in thought nonetheless. Of kings and wars she is familiar and I think our peoples are not so different as is often said.

This is not my first time on the River Tamar and I do not think it shall be my last. I was aboard *Governor Hunter* when it came here in '06. Then the main settlement was still at York Town, although there was already talk of relocating the port forty miles upriver to the place where three rivers meet.

It is not nearly as far as that to York Town. Not wanting the boat to become mired in the mudflats, I have Brown land us a short distance up the Western Arm. From there it will be about three miles on foot to the old settlement.

'We'll return for ye in a fortnight,' Brown says.

Hendricks and Staples say not a word between them.

'Just turn your attention to getting a good price for those skins,' I say. 'And don't go spending all our money on women of infamy.'

'Ye know me better'n I know meself, George.'

'A fortnight, you said? I shall be counting the days.'

'Now ye're quite sure ye can count that high?'

'Don't go abandoning us if I'm not stood here the moment you get back.'

'I won't go leavin' ye, George. Ye never left me yet.'

'No, I didn't. Godspeed to you.'

On the river path, Moe carries the bairn in her shoulder sling and I shoulder the musket and those few provisions we have. I do not think it is possible for a man to go hungry with Moe at his side, for to her way of thinking the country is a banquet waiting to be had. She thinks nothing of diving for crawfish or turning up edible roots in places I would not think to look. Where I see naught but prickly bushes and dry scrubland she sees food and plenty of it. The fact that her people do not practice animal husbandry is seen as a sign of their backwardness but they have ways and means besides.

Three miles is no great distance but the day is hot and there is a hint of smoke in the air. The baby is fretting from the attention of the flies and so we stop and rest in the shade awhile.

'Kartummeter pleengenner? Kartummeter parkutetennar?' Moe says, pointing to the path ahead.

'I bloody hope there's no soldiers, it's supposed to be abandoned. Do you smell fire?'

'Pannerkarner marebrunner tangehaller.' Clansmen burning the bush, she reckons. They have burned much of the country this season and it must be lingering smoke I can smell. Moe is right to be leery of soldiers, parkutetennar. We have just the one musket and I am loathe to use it for anything other than deterrence. There is no more vulnerable musketman than he who has just fired his piece. Already the clansmen have learned to stand off from the first barrage before commencing their assault.

'I'll go into town by myself,' I say. 'You stay in the bush and look after the bairn.'

'Luewottenner nartick. She's hot.'

'Then rest in the shade, I won't be more than an hour or two.'

'Meena wongherne in the bush.'

'Stay in the bush and for God's sake keep the littlun quiet.'

'Wollighererperarner, GeorgeBaggs.'

'Goodbye, Moe.'

I get a glimpse of York Town as I round the last bend in the river. Viewed from across the mudflats, the old settlement appears much as it did in '06, but as I get a little closer I see that many of the rooves have fallen, particularly among the convict huts on the lower ground. Ramshackle structures of warped timber, adorned with bark and shingle, lay scattered along the forest's edge. The storehouse by the wharf is intact and the government garden is filled with apple trees and figs and peaches. A thin column of smoke rises from the chimney of one of the larger cottages.

I slake my thirst at the rivulet, refilling my pouch and thinking about how best to proceed. I dare not approach the storehouse directly for fear of being spotted by soldiers. A lone man dressed in kangaroo skins will be taken for a bushranger and shot. Another man might think to storm the cottage and take its occupants prisoner, but instead I hide the musket in the reeds, go up to the front door and knock.

A man's voice: 'Who's there?'

'Just a hungry fellow is all.'

'I've given you rascals all that I'm giving.'

'You've never laid eyes on this rascal, I'll promise you that.'

The door opens a fraction. 'Just the one is it?'

'Just the one.'

The man comes out and closes the door behind him. He is unarmed and does not look like a soldier. 'Ran off from those bastards in Launceston, did you?'

'No, I've been three years in the bush.'

'Long time for a man to be living alone.'

'Didn't say I was living alone, did I? I've been a'sealing in the Furneaux Isles.'

'Then you've come an awful long way just to knock on the door of Henry Barrett. I didn't catch your name.'

'George Baggs.'

'Never heard of you, George, and I don't recognise your face. Come inside and let's see what the missus is cooking.'

Henry introduces me to his heavily pregnant wife, Mary. 'Stew's not ready but there's plenty of cold cuts,' she says. 'And fruit preserves if you'll take those with bread.'

'Thank you kindly.'

I cannot recall when I last sat at a kitchen table eating jam and bread. Woven baskets occupy corners and nooks, housing the essentials of daily life – dried herbs, spoons, and scraps of cloths. The air is tinged with the scent of timber and a whisper of smoke from the hearth. Henry pours us rum and I begin to grow drowsy until I remember Moe and the bairn out there in the hot sun.

'I've taken a wife from the clansmen, Henry,' I say. 'She's down by the river with our littlun.'

'Then why didn't you say? I don't give a tinker's cuss what colour a man or woman's skin might be, it's their intentions I'm more particular about.'

'We're afeared of soldiers is all, Henry.'

'You'll find none hereabouts, just the storehouse guard. Did you hear that, Mary? The man's wife and child are out there in this terrible heat.'

'I've two working ears, don't I? I'll wrap up something to see them through to dinner.'

'I'll show you a good place to bed down,' Henry says. 'And I'll have a quiet word to Douglas, the guard. Reckon he's nursing a sore head anyway.'

Mary gives me a bundle of food wrapped in cloth. 'Bring her up for supper later, she's more than welcome.'

'Thank you again, Mary.'

Henry and I leave Mary to her cooking and he points out a cottage near the rivulet. 'This was built by McDonald but he's long since taken off to Hobart Town.'

The cottage is similar to the Barretts', with the same two rooms and earthen floor. 'You're sure no one'll mind?'

'Nobody here to mind. Different story a fortnight ago, you would've seen Governor Macquarie and his entourage. Quite the flurry of activity we had. Place was fairly swarming with soldiers but you needn't worry as they've all buggered off. Good riddance to the lot of those long-winded bastards.'

'Why are you still here if everyone's gone?'

'I'm still the gardener, aren't I? All this was laid out by Colonel Paterson before he left. Loved nothing more than gardening, God rest his soul. He was forever taking observations and boxing up flowers to send back to England. They say he never even lasted a month at sea before breathing his last.'

'You've been here from the beginning? I was last here in '06 and I don't recall a gardener. I sailed aboard *Governor Hunter*.'

'*Governor Hunter*, that's the schooner refloated in Bass Strait a while back?'

'Refloated? Where'd you hear that?'

'Read it in the *Sydney Gazette*. Refloated after more than a year, they said. Isaac Nichols. I guess you'd long since nicked off by that point, not that I blame you.'

'Are you still under sentence, Henry?'

'Fourteen years I copped and I'm barely through five, but I imagine there's worse fates than tending the Colonel's garden. Mary's sentence expires this year and so we've asked for permission to marry.'

'Then you have my congratulations. I doubt Moe and I will ever be married in a church but she is as good a wife as a man could hope for. Speaking of which, it's time I was off.'

'We'll see you at supper?'

'If I can convince Moe to come.'

'Good man.'

By the time I get back to the river, Moe is nowhere to be seen and a dead heat smothers the land. She wouldn't travel far with the bairn in this weather and I expect she's found a cool place to kip. I am looking for her when she comes up out of the shadows. 'Partrollarne?' she says.

'Damn, I left it back in the reeds.'

'Nartick, nartick,' she says, showing me the place where she's left the baby sleeping under a tree.

'I know it's hot. I met the gardener and his wife and they're good people. There's a cottage we can stay in.'

'Wongherne legana.' Moe scoops up the bairn and sits with her back to me.

'We can't stay here, there might be parkutetennar for all I know. You hear me, Moe?'

'Luewottenner nartick.'

'I'll go and fetch the musket and when I get back you'll be ready to travel, you hear?'

'Wollighererperarner.'

◆

IT IS dusk by the time I get Moe and the bairn inside McDonald's cottage, for my wife fears the dark and would rather camp beneath the stars. She sniffs the musty air and claims it to be a bad place. I tell her we are lucky to be given the use of the cottage without payment but this means nothing to her. I do not think she will ever understand that my life and the life of every Englishman is governed by scraps of paper and the ink symbols marked upon them. Many times I have tried to explain the debt of seventeen pounds I owe to Isaac Nichols and that he will throw me in the debtor's prison if he can. But what is this seventeen pounds? Is it a tool, meat or an item of clothing? I tell her no, it is a mark on a tally or words on paper. She asks if I have stolen one of his daughters and I assure her it is nothing like that. It is purely a matter of business, but what is business? Men cutting one another's throats by other means is how I describe it, but then she is thinking of spirits and evil eyes and that isn't right either.

Moe will not come to dinner despite me telling her we must take up the Barretts on their offer of hospitality. I can only hope she remains in the cottage until I return.

Henry is dressed in overalls the same as before but Mary has changed into a blue dress. She serves up a stew of kangaroo and vegetables. 'Your wife couldn't come?' she says.

'The baby's poorly,' I say. 'Too much sun, I think.'

'Poor thing. I hope they both feel better in the morn.'

'Won't be long before you're a mother yourself, Mary. That was my mam's name.'

'We'll not be seeing our mothers again now we've been sent to t'other side,' Henry says, pouring the rum. 'Mine nearly cried her heart out when I was stood in the dock.'

'I never saw mine again after I ran off to London,' I say.

We eat our stew and drink our rum and share our memories of the old country. I tell them of how I came out on *Harrington* and a little about my life a'sealing since then. Mary is interested in my kangaroo-skin jerkin and she asks if native women wear them too. I tell her they prefer not to dress in this fashion but they like the warmth such garments provide. Henry regales me with recollections of the Governor's visit, which he says caused quite a stir:

'A fine military gentleman, never thought I'd see the likes of him. A proper Scotsman, not like that sourpuss Bligh. Named half the island after himself and the other half after Mrs Macquarie. They say he took one look at Hobart Town and started laying out a chart of how he wants the streets set out. Lord knows what he makes of mucky Launceston. He put everyone in their places and not before time.'

'They weren't in their proper places already?'

'I know you're pulling my leg, George. Christ Almighty, it's been a free-for-all since day dot round here. Colonel Paterson was a good man but he was oftentimes poorly and all he wanted was to faff about in his garden. Meanwhile the so-called gentlemen went about grabbing the best land and making off with all the government stores. They're making a killing selling pork and grain to His Majesty and Macquarie's hopping mad at having to foot the bill. Major Gordon's gone soft and won't put a stop to it. Bunch of brigands the lot of them.'

'For all you know, Henry, Mr Baggs might number those men among his friends,' Mary says.

'Mr Baggs ain't got no friends, least none that matter,' Henry says, tipping his mug with one hand and lifting the bottle with the other. 'Isn't that right, George?'

'I don't know a soul in Launceston and that's God's honest truth.'

'Hear that, Mary? He don't know Messrs Garrett and Piper. He ain't heard of Captain Brabyn nor Peter Mills.'

'I don't see what you're driving at,' I say.

'A likely story,' Henry says.

We eat in silence but I can see it is only an intermission. I think of taking my leave but the look on Henry's face gives me pause. Mary busies herself with clearing the plates while I sip my rum and wait for him to speak his mind.

'One day a man appears dressed in skins,' he says. 'He admits to being an absconder but says he's been living with sealers. Fair enough, he wouldn't be the first. Fellow says he has a native wife and a babe-in-arms and yet somehow he's made it halfway across Van Diemen's Land without a boat or crew. He knocks on the door of Henry Barrett just days after the last of the soldiers have scarpered and there's no sign whatsoever of him being armed. What does he want, this man? Apparently nothing except for a place for his family to bed down. Now that's curious.'

'You think I'm a bushranger come to rob the store, is that it?'

'Wouldn't you think that if you were sat in my chair?'

'What about the guard? Isn't it his job to protect it?'

'The guard's gone on a jag or didn't you know that either? Pure coincidence.'

I turn to face Mary and the wrong end of a musket. 'You sit quiet or I'll blow your head clean off,' she says. 'A hundred places we could bury you and no one would ever know.'

'Where's your friends?' Henry says. 'That'll do for starters.'

'You needn't point that thing at me,' I say. 'My friends have taken our boat to Launceston to trade sealskins. I didn't want to take the missus because I was worried about what might happen to her there. I ought've worried about here'n all.'

'And where is she, this phantom missus?' Henry says. 'We've seen neither hide nor hair of her. What say we take a stroll over to McDonald's and see how the lassie's travelling? Perhaps if you really do have such a wife we'll be more inclined to believe the remainder of your story.'

'It's getting dark out there, Henry,' Mary says. 'Could be there's an ambush.'

'You've let your imaginations run away from you, stuck out here on your own,' I say. 'There's no ambush and if there was what good would one musket be against it?'

'Won't make no difference to you with half your face shot off,' Henry says. 'Give it here, Mary, and go fetch a lantern.'

Henry gets to his feet and Mary hands him the musket. I am worried about what will happen if McDonald's cottage is empty. I knock back the rest of my rum.

'Don't think about getting up until after you've been asked,' Henry says. 'I wouldn't want to go putting a hole somewhere I never quite intended it put.'

Mary puts a lantern on the table. 'I'll not set foot outside,' she says. 'Reckon you'll have to ask George to carry it.'

'On your feet,' Henry says. 'And if you think about making a run for it, I'll fire with a clear conscience, God help you if I do.'

'Look at me, Henry Barrett,' I say. 'If you cut me down it will be on your conscience for you'll have slain an innocent man.'

'I'll happily pour you another drink if it turns out you're in the right.'

I take the lantern. The night is hot and moonless and the crickets and frogs are in their element. 'I can't tell where I'm going in the dark, Henry.'

'Just keeping walking and don't stop until I tell you.'

I want to call out to Moe for even if she is not inside the cottage I expect she won't have gone far, but the barrel of the musket poking into my back gives me pause.

'I'm about ready for that drink, aren't you?' I say.

'My word I am. McDonald's is there on the left, but it seems awful quiet.'

'She might've heard us coming and scarpered.'

'I'd pray she hasn't if I were you.'

'I'm praying, don't you worry.' I push the door. 'Moe? Nobody's going to harm you.'

I shine the lantern and it illuminates the whites of my wife's eyes.

◆

WHEN HENRY is satisfied there is no skulduggery afoot, thought of another drink is forsaken for I must stay with Moe and offer what consolation I can. Henry tells me to hang onto the lantern on account of how he could find his own cottage in a blindfold. I bid him goodnight and the bairn commences a plaintive wailing. Moe is petrified and won't sit still, a torrent of language bubbling forth from her throat. Much of it I cannot understand but I pick up the words parkutetennar and partrollarne rightly enough. I try to explain that Henry Barrett is no more a soldier than I but she is having none of it. The sight of a white man with a musket in the night invokes a singular terror in her. She speaks of karpennooyouhener, bad men appearing on clan shores and in their midst. It is an ill wind on which these demons ride and a foul tide washing them ashore. A darkling land this England, or so it seems to Moe.

The night is endless and I find myself banished to the far side of the hut. There I lay in the dirt looking at the play of shadows in the lamplight. The tireder I become the more morose my thoughts and yet sleep will not find me. At such times Tom Stepney comes to me with the same accusations he has always had. Men like Monsieur Faure had kind words for me when I was a lad but I had few for young Tom. If I could go back and trade places with him I'd do it in a heartbeat for then I would be spared this torment. There is a stone in my breast and it has sympathy for none. This stone seeks dominion and I am no less a tyrant than the worst men I have known. Tom Stepney will not rise again and it is on my conscience that he will not.

By morning it is a little cooler, and since I am waking I can only surmise that I have slept. Moe and the bairn are fast asleep but I fear the slightest movement will wake them. The expression on my wife's face is of a serenity seldom seen by day. I lay a long time looking at her. She is far better than I deserve. I knew it the moment I first set eyes on her.

In time, the bairn stirs and so does Moe and the misery of the night is forgotten. We go outside and find the Colonel's garden a wonder bursting with summer fruit. We pick figs and nectarines and strawberries and they all speak well of the labours of Henry Barrett. There is freshwater bubbling along the rivulet and we are much revived after washing away the sweat and dust. Moe takes my hand and her smile is my reward. I cradle her and she the bairn and for a time everything is as it should be. The child is fascinated by the gurgling water and the shafts of morning light amid the trees and Moe instructs her on the names of everything. The sunlight Moe names *teewoorer* and the water *legana* and there is plenty more besides. I too am under instruction and I repeat the words until she is halfway satisfied. We are there a long time before Henry comes down to meet us. He is carrying a pitchfork and not a musket but I can feel Moe stiffen nonetheless.

'Morning, Henry.'

'Morning, George. I'm glad to see someone eating that fruit before it spoils. Those nectarines are the best we've had. I'd have Mary making jam but for the want of jars.'

The look on Henry's face reminds of how startling it is to look upon a woman's naked breasts, especially with her husband sat next to her. Moe's solitary concession to modesty is a hand placed loosely before her sex, and it is plain Henry has never seen a woman in such a state of undress outside his marital bed. I walk with him to spare his blushes and because I will never see his wife the way he has seen mine.

Much of the present disorder stems from this, I believe, for the English have been years without women and in many cases they have not had them at all. Suddenly these native lovelies appear before their eyes and they can think of nothing else. In their pursuit they are untroubled by slaying any who would stand before them and to our shame they do not call it murder. Brown and I have supped with men who kept women in circumstances unfit for cattle, but if government knows of such practices it remains silent. No surprise that the clans would take up the spear against us.

'I feel terrible for disbelieving you last night and I wish to make amends,' Henry says. We have been walking along the rivulet to where York Town gives out in favour of the hillside rising from the bush.

'Don't vex yourself, it was late and you had your wife to consider.'

'Three times we've been robbed this past year and one of those was at gunpoint. I don't know what I'd do if anything happened to my Mary.'

'I feel the same about Moe.'

'Then we understand one another. Will you dine with us again tonight? Mary would like it very much. If I know that woman, she'll spend all day working up a feast.'

'Tell her she needn't bother on our account, but we'd be much obliged if you'll allow us to stay in McDonald's cottage until our friends return. It'll be a fortnight, I expect.'

'I'll sleep better with a second man around. If I had another firing piece I'd gladly give it to you.'

I am about to say I have my own but something stays my hand. Both of us have our wives in mind and we make a swift return. Moe has not moved and I can only presume that Mary is safe in her kitchen.

'I'll leave you and go to my chores presently,' Henry says.

'Warrander in bush,' Moe says when he is gone.

'We aren't running off into the bush, Moe. Look, the baby's falling asleep.'

'Luewottenner parhamoeniyack.'

'I know she's tired. It's getting hot.'

Moe squints up at the sky. 'Nartick.' Then she points to the hill beyond the settlement. 'Kartummeter pannerkarner.'

'Lots of clansmen? We're safe here, aren't we?'

She shrugs. 'Kartummeter partroller.'

'If they're setting fires in those hills then we'd best stay near the river.'

'Wongherne legana.'

It seems we are agreed but then I am never entirely sure. Conversations with Moe are like reaching through a tangled thicket and coming up with nothing, and she is forever slipping away just when I think I have her pinned down. It is not in my wife's nature to sit tight and nor in mine and yet we must.

◆

DAYS PASS and the heat will not release its grip, the air oftentimes thick with smoke. It is the sea we crave and not this pestilent mudflat. The sea gives endlessly of itself and I am ill-at-ease when beyond its reach. My wife misses it the same if not more. We rarely venture far from the rivulet and it often falls to me to keep an eye on the bairn while Moe is out hunting. One afternoon I am at the rivulet with the bairn when I spot two white men coming along the bank. Neither appears armed, and from the way they stagger they seem much debilitated from the heat. One drinks from a flask while the other mops his brow, and their faces are wet with sweat. They shuffle past not ten yards from the patch of shade where the bairn and I are sat. Just then the littlun offers a disgruntled remark and this draws their attention. One of the men reaches into his jacket and withdraws a flintlock pistol but before he can think to employ it I am beseeching him not to fire on an unarmed man let alone one with a babe-in-arms.

'Who the devil's there?' the man says, waving his pistol. 'I'm inclined to fire on ye, babe or no.'

I tell him my name.

'Leave off, Jeremiah Douglas,' the other man says. He is younger, about my age and from his accent an Irishman. 'You'll not shoot a man just for sittin', will you?'

Douglas scowls and mops his brow. 'There's no telling just what I'll do.'

'So you're the fellow meant to guard the storehouse,' I say. 'A fine job of it you've been doing of it lately.'

'Put that away for pity's sake,' the Irishman says. 'Baggs, you said? Met a friend of yours t'other day, I'll wager.'

'That would be Jimmy Brown. He made it to Launceston?'

'Prob'ly by now he has, although we met at the Whirlpool Reach. The name's Peter Mills. I'm the harbourmaster so Henry maybe mentioned me. This'd be your wean then? Pretty as a picture. Reckon I saw its mother swimmin' a ways back and she weren't hard to look at neither.'

'That's my wife you saw, Peter. I hope you didn't frighten her off.'

'That native wench mucking about in the mudhole?' Douglas says. 'Lucky for her she din't come close enough to frighten.'

'Now the lassie's the man's wife and a fine one at that,' Mills says. 'What say we call on Henry Barrett like we planned? I'm a mite parched.'

'Won't catch me carousin' wi' blacks,' Douglas says. 'Wouldn't want to end up wi' nothin' I hadn't had.'

'Jeremiah's been pinin' after one of Garrett's porkers,' Mills says. 'He's had his beady eye on a big fat sow 'cept he's been pourin' all his wages int' drink and the good doctor won't extend him a line of credit, will he?'

'Shut your bleedin' mouth lest I should find cause to fire on you instead.'

'Put it away, now there's a fellow. I recollect you sayin' you were thirsty? I wouldn't say no to a drop.'

I wait for the men to disappear inside the Barretts' cottage before going in search of Moe. I cry myself hoarse shouting for her. Finally she appears from a hiding place in the reeds. She's throttled a pair of black swans and has gathered up a clutch of their eggs.

'There you are, Moe. You had me worried sick.'

'Ya, GeorgeBaggs. I see boat legana.'

'A boat?'

'Boat.' She points toward the bend in the river.

'No doubt belonging to the men I just saw. You saw two pleengenner come this way? Two white men?'

'Pleengenner, pleengenner.' She's seen them all right. 'Larngerner boat.'

'We can't make off with their boat, Moe.'

'Larngerner boat, pernickerter!'

'You can show it to me but we're not thieving it.'

The flies are many and the mosquitoes pestersome and in this heat each step costs twice what it ought. Moe puts the baby in her shoulder sling and soon enough we come across a boat tucked away in the reeds.

'It's a jollyboat,' I say. 'Just a littlun.'

'Jollyboat,' she says, pointing to the oars. 'Two beege.'

'Two oars.'

She points at herself and then at me. 'Two.'

'Two oars, two oarsmen. Where would we go?'

'Legana.'

'Yes, but whereabouts on the river? We're trying to stay away from Launceston. Kartummeter pleengenner there, hundreds of them.'

'Tebrakunna.'

'You have my word I'll take you home but not right now. We need to stop here, wongherne, and wait for Brown.'

A flash of anger. 'Nummerwar wongherne!' Then more I cannot follow.

'I know you don't like waiting but we've no choice. Parkutetennar will shoot us, understand? Kartummeter parkutetennar. I said I'd keep you safe and by God I intend to try.'

'Kartummeter parkutetennar, kartummeter pannerk-arner, kartummeter karpennooyouhener.'

'You're right about that, a bunch of bad'uns the lot of them.'

'GeorgeBaggs karpennooyouhener.'

'Now you're being unfair. If you'll just come along I'll see if Mary will cook up one of those swans for our dinner.'

If I knew the right words I'd explain to Moe why we cannot act the way she proposed and must do as I say instead. She inhabits one world and myself another and it is these worlds which have been thrown together as much as we ourselves.

Such is Moe's anger that I have a devil of a time keeping up with her, the way she strides. 'Wongherne!' She throws a hand across me and I halt midstep.

'What is it?'

'Plentenner.' She points at the black snake on the path. Another step and I would have trodden on it. I have heard of sealers meeting hideous ends after being bitten by snakes and it is only Moe standing between myself and such a fate. The snake is unmoved, but once I am out of the way she strikes it dead with her waddy and drapes it around her neck.

That evening I dine with Peter Mills and the Barretts. The guard will not show his face and better that he does not for I am not above stoving in the teeth of such a villain. There is scarcely room enough for the four of us at the Barretts' table. As we tuck into roast swan, the air is close and stifling. The rum flows freely and our tongues are sure to follow.

'Those sealskins your man Brown is lookin' to offload, does he not realise such trade is prohibited?' Mills says.

'Who says it's prohibited?' I say.

'I'm the bleedin' harbourmaster and I'm the one saying it. By order of Major Gordon.'

'Pull the other one, Peter,' Henry says. 'If I had a shilling for every little thing that happened round here which was *expressly prohibited* – '

Mills grins. 'Just statin' the facts is all. The harbourmaster might choose to overlook certain irregularities as he sees fit. We're all in need of makin' a livin'.'

'What he means is he's prepared to turn a blind eye just so long as he gets his share,' Henry says.

'I've two blind eyes for the turnin',' Mills says, and we drink to that. 'Now Baggs, I'm headin' back to Launceston tomorrow and I'm short an oarsman. I thought there'd be men here but it seems they've all taken off.'

'My wife and I are laying low,' I say. 'I figured we'd best stay clear of the settlement. I don't know how they treat the natives.'

'Not always kindly, I'm afraid. But if you come with me you'll find yourselves under the protection of the harbourmaster and the acting deputy surveyor.'

'Next you'll hear of how he came to be thusly appointed by the right and honourable Governor Bligh,' Henry says.

'I was just gettin' to that and now you've gone and spoiled it! As I was sayin', no harm'll come to you or your lovely missus. We've business to transact and we cannot complete such business anywhere but at the settlement. I wouldn't be surprised to find your man Brown's fallen afoul of the powers-that-be, smuggling prohibited goods as he is.'

'You've a cheek,' Henry says. 'Some might call you a sheep-stealer and a brigand.'

'Then let them say it to my front and not my back. What say you, George?'

'What if Brown's already found a buyer for the skins?'

'Then I'll have no choice but to have such sale annulled for violating the terms of trade.'

'You see George, that's the way things are done round here,' Henry says. 'Only difference between a magistrate and a lag is one holds the whip while the other is obliged to bare his back.'

'Mr Baggs isn't interested in your tiresome bleating, Henry.'

'You'd be the one knows best about bleating, Peter, but then I'm just the gardener.'

'Yes, you are the gardener and a man under sentence besides. Now I'll have your answer, George. Are you with me or do I have to go roundin' up your smuggler friends?'

'We'll come with you, Peter,' I say. 'Now I'll go check on my wife before that fucking guard decides he wants something he hasn't had after all.'

◆

THIS LAND is home to many rivers but the Tamar is the grandest of those I've known. It is to the north what the Derwent is to the south and the means by which the English penetrate the interior. Men have explored these rivers to determine their origin but found nothing except further turns and subsequent bends. If such origins exist they are high in the mountains and invisible to those who toil in the ebb and flow. We set our sails and turn our oars a thousand times and are never certain where it is we are heading. There is a road beginning across the sea at Portsmouth and I know not where it ends.

I ask Moe the name for the river and she tells me it is Kunermurlukeker. To her people's way of thinking Kunermurlukeker is less road than clan boundary. Moe says it is not uncommon for the clans to wage war upon one another and to raid their neighbours for women. If we are caught unawares then Moe will be taken as a trophy and the bairn and I shall be slain. I tell her not to worry but her expression remains doubtful. *What do you know of the next bend in the river, GeorgeBaggs?*

I try to think on what mam would have said. *Just put one foot in front t'other*, no doubt. Poor woman never had the chance to wonder what it was all for. A man eats better here than he ever did in England, but at least there he knew in his bones that he was in his homeland. If I have made a wrong turn, I am years down the wrong track by now and without the means of turning. Mam would have said *that's why God gave us eyes in the front of our heads and not the back.* I never ought to have run away but it has been the pattern of my days.

Mills seems to know where he's headed, however, and he has plenty of energy for rowing and pontificating both. He has nothing but scorn for the Governor. 'Calls this the County of Cornwall, thinks he's the King of his very own England,' he says. 'Macquarie's the kind of fellow who thinks he knows best about everything under the sun, and there's nothing he likes better than finding fault with a man's honest labour. He's a stickler and a pedant.'

I ask if Governor Macquarie found fault with Mills during his recent visit.

'My word he did! I'm supposed to be the acting deputy surveyor, and what is that? A fellow obliged to sit on his hands while the gentlemen race about taking up all the best land. If there are clansmen the soldiers run them off and if a few get shot then they ought to have run that much faster. I'm supposed to give an account of who owns what and who said he could have it, but the whole thing's a muddle and that's the kindest word for it. There are those who've built farms on land not belonging to them and others who've taken government stock and called it their own. Macquarie reckons I myself have built on land not belonging to me. Now he's having me clear out but says I'll be duly compensated. *Two hundred acres so long as it does not interfere with the purposes of government*, it says in the letter. And what is the land for which government has no purpose? The very worst of course, requiring the greatest labour for the smallest reward.'

'So what will you do? Go to Hobart Town?'

'I'll not afford him the satisfaction. Connections are what a man needs here, connections and capital. Fifty pounds a year for a salary ain't near enough to get ahead, but there are ways and means besides.'

'And what are those?'

'Told you this place was a muddle, didn't I? Macquarie's gone and thrown it into an even greater state of confusion with all his edicts. A man might just about take what he reckons is his.'

'You mean if he has the right connections?'

'My countryman Garrett's the chief surgeon here and I reckon he owns a greater share of the north than any man. And Brabyn's my father-in-law and the Captain of the Guards, no less. At one time he was the commandant.'

'And yet you never cease complaining about the settlers and the soldiery.'

'Truth is it's a family affair and always has been.'

By the time the sun has reached its height we have covered a good distance, but Mills says we shall not see Launceston this day unless we propose to row the night through. Fresh water and a patch of shade are what we need and Mills assures me they can be had not far from here at the Supply River. As we push through the Tamar's narrowest section, I do not need Moe to tell me we are within the range of a well-thrown spear.

In the boil of the sun, I thrash at the water as I might a mortal foe, imagining it the enemy who has oft besieged my nights. No respite from the sun out here on the burning water.

In my fervour my vision dims and the horizon narrows and there is naught but this earthly labour. We are a devouring flame consuming all we touch. I know why the clans fire the land for there is an ecstasy in the flame.

Fresh water and a patch of shade.

I open my eyes to discover a haze over the river and a wall of smoke engulfing the southern sky. I espy no lick of flame but gain no reassurance from the fact. Mills' face is red and peeling and the back of his neck is a horror.

'Every summer's the same, George,' he says. 'By the time the clansmen are done waving their firesticks there'll be naught but burned bushes and black earth for miles around. Though I reckon they ought to start their fires closer to Launceston. That'd set the English scurryin' for their boats.'

'It's madness to sail into that blaze, Peter.'

'Madness is going without a single blessed penny for all those skins o' yours. How long were you collecting them?'

'Two months or more, but I didn't go risking my life only to throw it away now. A couple more days won't make any difference.'

'The Major's within his rights to impound your skins and your boat and then where would that leave you?'

'You ought to have followed Brown if you're so desperate for your share.'

'Don't I know it, but I promised to take Jeremiah back to York Town and that's just what I did.'

We have not travelled much further before the smoke is so thick we can barely see the mountains rising from the eastern shore. The bairn is the first to start coughing and soon we are all a'spluttering. Moe says partroller, partroller thinking us blind or insensible, and mine is the task of explaining that the karpennooyouhener are intent on rowing to the place where the smoke is thickest. I think I see a face rising in the swirling fug.

My head is pounding and my eyes weeping but finally we are in the clear. I am ill and gasping but slow progress is better than none. When I look back, I see we have come through a wall of smoke by the dint of sheer pigheadedness.

'Reckon we'll need to find a place to rest,' Mills whispers, his face deathly pale. We steer toward the west bank with an eye out for clansmen but the heat and smoke has stifled all movement. The harbourmaster expresses his desire to enter the mouth of what appears a nondescript brook and by the time we reach it his eyes have narrowed to slits. The brook narrows to a rocky waterfall not far upstream. It is a landscape abundant in stones, rocks and pebbles of every size and shape, the stream fast-flowing and turbulent. Moe takes the oar and helps me get the boat into the shade below the falls. Once we are secure, I step out onto the slippery rocks and fill our pouches. The water is the sweetest I ever drank.

The bairn is poorly from inhaling too much smoke and even Moe looks queasy as she attends to the littlun. But it is Mills who fares worst. Now that he has relinquished his oar, there is nothing to stop him from slumping against the gunwale. His eyes roll back in his head and it is all I can do to dribble a little water into his mouth.

When everyone is resting as comfortably as circumstances will allow, I ask Moe if she thinks we are safe here on the Tamar's western shore.

'Kartummeter pannerkarner. Kartummeter parkuteten-nar. Not safe.'

'What ought we to do then?'

'Boat legana. Safe.'

'You reckon we're safer out on the water even in this damned heat?'

'Kartummeter teewoorer.'

'My God it's sunny. Look at Mills; he'll not row again today.'

'Pleengenner sick.'

'It's the sun and smoke what's done him in. I reckon we rest awhile. I'll keep the musket close at hand.'

There is a hint of a breeze and it is pleasant enough here in the shade. I grow drowsier by the moment but just then the bairn starts fretting. She is bored and wants to crawl around in the bilge but the harbourmaster is blocking her path. Moe picks her up and sings in their language and I find myself drifting off to sleep. She prises the musket from my fingers but I no longer have a care. Let the world burn if I can get some rest by the time it's down to cinders.

It is hours later and Moe is shaking me awake. 'Pernickerter, boat legana.'

'All right, woman, give me a minute.'

'Pernickerter!' She sits on the thwart clutching the bairn. 'Pannerkarner larngerner boat,' she says, pointing along the brook.

I see them, a party of four or five clansmen observing us from the hillside at what I pray is a safe distance.

'Peter Mills!' I say. 'You'll rise this minute or else nevermore!'

There is no response so I give the Irishman a swift kick in the ribs. The men are starting to advance and I do not think there is time to get the boat clear. I jump into the shallows and try to drag the boat free but it is firmly wedged. 'Get up, God damn you!'

Mills is coming to but much too slowly. The warriors are closing in and any moment their spears will commence their deadly rain, but the sight of a clanswoman waving a musket is enough to give them pause. I commence hunting for a cartridge and Moe screams her head off all the while. Mills has sense enough to start bringing his weapon into a state of readiness and it seems this flurry of activity has caused the clansmen to reconsider. Mills is hard at work with the ramrod and even the bairn contributes a war cry of her own. The moment for assault is lost for we have two muskets that can be brought to bear and doubtless the clansmen have seen their ruinous work before. They retreat to a distance they suppose to be the limit of our range. Mills raises his musket to a firing position.

'Now let's not go and ruin it,' I say.

'A warning shot is all I intend.'

'Never fire unless you purely have to, Peter. They can see our intentions well enough. We'd best be getting off before there's blood spilled.'

I pass Moe my musket and climb down into the water, raising my hands in what I hope will be understood as a gesture of peaceful intent. This time I go to the stern and give the boat a shove. The boat has shifted no more than a few inches but it is enough to dislodge it. I look up and the clansmen are holding their spears at their sides and not in a throwing position.

It is a fragile peace and I'll be damned if I'm the one to shatter it.

◆

NEXT MORNING we reach the place where the Tamar joins the North Esk. Thank God the weather has turned grey for I could not withstand another moment under the sun's barrage. I still do not think it wise to bring Moe into town and so we continue a little further to the South Esk and the Cataract. There is a thought gnawing at me that I oughtn't to have trusted the harbourmaster. Probably we should have declined his offer and stayed in York Town. Perpetual movement provides an illusion of safety but an illusion is all it is. Truth is we were restless and took off first chance we had.

It cannot be much further than a mile from the Cataract to the settlement and yet there isn't a soul here nor anything like cattle pasture. Grey cliffs rear before us and I can well imagine a mighty torrent roaring through this canyon come winter. Even now at summer's height the flow is not inconsiderable. Mills points to a cleft in the rocks where the boat can be moored and we steer toward it. All is greyness – cliffs, sky, water – and I fail to perceive a grey seal lying on a grey rock until we are very nearly upon it. Moe sees it sure enough and were she not rowing she would probably leap up and crash her waddy down on its snout. The boat fits snugly in the place the harbourmaster said it would and, as we commence unloading, the seal finally slips down into the water. This is a good place for seals and men to rest but not together.

'A man could walk into town from here?' I ask Mills.

'I suppose, but I can't say why he'd want to if he had a perfectly good boat.'

'Then we're walking, you and I.' I am in thrall to a restless instinct urging me on. No matter how fervently I might propose to stay, I find I am always leaving.

'Begging your pardon? This here's my boat and I'm the bleedin' harbourmaster.'

'If we leave Moe here without the boat there's nothing stopping you from handing me over to your father-in-law, is there? Captain of the Guards, no less. Then you'll be free to divvy up our skins and God knows what'll happen to Moe after that.'

'Jesus, Mary and Joseph, the thought never crossed my mind. I said I'd take a share and a share is all I meant. Now what's gone and put such unkind notions in your head? You wouldn't be thinkin' of deprivin' me of my boat, would you?'

'I'll not deprive you of your boat, but I'll ask you to walk nonetheless. Moe'll be needing your musket meanwhile.'

'Give her yours if it will put your mind at ease.'

'And with you carrying the other? I'll kindly ask for a loan of yours instead.'

'You're depriving a man of his boat and his musket both. If that does not make you a bandit, I do not know what will.'

'Ask yourself who is the bandit here, Peter.'

I try to explain my scheme to Moe but the language barrier proves insurmountable. When we speak of a thing in the here and now, we can point to it and give it a name and thus we stand on what seems like stable ground, but as soon as one speaks of things which cannot be seen or events that might happen we are left floundering. Moe knows the value of the sealskins because she has seen them traded and she knows Brown to be our friend, but does she understand that he has gone to the settlement for the purpose of trade? How can I explain that Brown might be locked up in a place where only Mills can get him out? And that even if Brown is free, we will need Mills to negotiate the sale of the skins? I fall back on phrases like *you stay here with the boat, you hang onto the musket, kartummeter parkutetennar in town.*

Moe is not happy. She is frightened of karpennooyouhener and wants to go home. She points downriver indicating where we ought to row, and I tell her we will go home soon enough. She looks at me with an expression that nearly breaks my heart for I know she is losing whatever faith she had in me. She would throw me in but she finds herself tangled up in the devil's work.

Mills and I make hard work of picking our way along the rocks, him sullen and myself greatly hampered by the shouldering of the musket. Then the path gives out altogether and we are left with the choice of swimming or trying to scrabble up the hillside. Further along the drop looks even more precipitous.

'That water's deep and I'm not much for swimmin',' Mills says, sweat pouring down his face.

'You've led us astray, Peter.'

'It's yourself who's done the leading, astray or otherwise.'

'Then we've no choice but to climb to the top.'

'Climb up there? The sun's addled whatever brains you had.'

I insist we try. The climb is not quite as reckless as first imagined as long as one does not make the mistake of looking back. Only then does my heart begin a fearful hammering. There was a time when I performed such feats for pleasure on New Year Island, but now I take no comfort from such exertions. I always had it in my head to attain the highest peak so as to make a survey of all creation just like Faure and Grimes. A boyhood dream perhaps but one that has lingered into adulthood.

We attain the ridge at considerable length but in pitiful condition for having done so. Mills is worse than I, first thundering through the scrub without consideration of what abrasions he might incur and then collapsing to the ground. He lays cursing my mother and the manner of my siring and on both counts it is a long time before he is satisfied. Eventually we are as fit to travel as we are ever likely to be and I see the rooves of the settlement in the distance. We are high above the Cataract and Moe is somewhere on the river below.

◆

LAUNCESTON CONSISTS of a dusty track leading down from the gorge and a handful of crude shanties along the way. A herd of cows is busy cropping the grass near the barracks and the jetty is a little further past that. Here we find our boat tied up alongside a forty-foot ketch which Mills says belongs to the surgeon Jacob Garrett. Scraggly huts no sturdier than the worst ever thrown up by sealers lay everywhere scattered, their inhabitants as filthy as ourselves. It is a village not remarkably different from a thousand like it except that the others are in England. As we pass, a curt nod is the very most we can hope to receive by way of encouragement. A cottage no less humble than the rest is said to be the seat of government and it is here that Mills would have us direct our enquiries. The Union Jack hangs limp on a flagpole nearby.

Eventually a scrawny soldier notices our presence. 'You'll 'ave to come back tomorrer. Matter of fact, the day after that. He's not well is the Major, heat's got to 'im.'

'Then I shall call on Captain Brabyn,' Mills says. 'Is he at the barracks?'

'No, he's gone off on a shooting party. Best part of a week they've been at it.'

'Then who is in charge while the Major is indisposed?'

'It might as well be me,' the soldier says, his smiling revealing a mouthful of broken teeth. 'Private Taylor.'

'Pleased to meet you, Taylor. I'm Peter Mills, the harbour-master and the acting deputy surveyor.'

'Mills, is it? That other surveyin' feller mentioned you.'

'You must mean that imbecile Meehan.'

'Seemed right decent to me. Bought me a drink, he did.'

'If he's so decent then why does he go around tearing up my maps and replacing them with his own? And why haven't I seen you around these parts before?'

'That's on account of how I came up from Hobart Town with Governor Macquarie. Gave us half a pint of spirits each to toast the King's health. Blimey, I wish I had that half pint again now.'

'I'm sure you do, Taylor. Now we're looking for a fellow who brought in some sealskins, goes by the name of Brown.'

'I don't know nothing about no sealskins but we was obliged to lock up a feller on account of his disorderly conduct. Strong lookin' feller with a big black beard.'

'That's Brown,' I say. 'Can we speak with him?'

'Not likely. Yesterday the Major was ravin' and today you can't get 'im out of bed. Reckon you'll have to wait for Captain Brabyn.'

'But that might be days, mightn't it?' Mills says. 'I expect you could make use of a drink? I've credit with the storekeeper.'

Taylor ponders this. 'I suppose I could just nip out.'

Mills' credit at the store is nearly as good as he supposes and we spend an hour imbibing Bengal's best before we go tottering off toward the barracks. Those few soldiers not adventuring with Brabyn are fit only for lazing around and no one objects to us seeing the prisoner. Behind a gate in the back of the barracks, in the dingiest, dirtiest room, lays a man stripped to his underclothes. It is Brown and the stench from his bucket is enough to make anyone gag.

'How about lettin' me out?' he says. 'Days I've been here now.'

'I can't let you out without the captain's say-so and he ain't here to give it,' Taylor says. 'I told these men they could speak with you. Right then, I'm off to see if His Nibs has awoken.'

'What did they nab you for?' I ask Brown.

'What happened is that fuckin' bastard sold me down the river,' Brown says, pointing an accusing finger at Mills. 'Said I'd have no trouble at all, din't ye?'

Mills hems and haws and I cut in: 'He told me you were liable to being locked up as a smuggler, Jimmy.'

'Disorderly conduct I believe was the charge,' Mills says.

'My conduct was in perfect order until they tried arrestin' Hendrick an' me. We were after a drink and Staples offered to keep watch over the skins while we had it. Haven't seen the bugger since.'

'I reckon the cur's made off with our goods,' I say. 'And where's Hendrick?'

'Got off scot free! The guards are all his drinking buddies, aren't they?'

'This whole thing stinks worse than your shite, Jimmy,' I say. 'We've been had.'

'Those two were keen on fallin' in with us, weren't they? Played us for fools.'

'This one as well. The gardener in York Town called him a sheep-stealer and a brigand.'

'I haven't taken a single sheep that wasn't mine and nor am I a party to this malfeasance,' Mills says. 'Captain Brabyn will soon have it straightened out.'

'Surely the harbourmaster holds sway in this regard?' I say. 'It is after all a matter of shipping.'

'Not after what Macquarie and his lackeys have been saying about me. They'd have me run out altogether were it not for the captain. He won't allow it, especially not now his daughter's with child.'

'What about my child, and Moe? Someone's pinched our skins and I want to find out who.'

'My money's on your so-called friends,' Mills says. 'I don't believe there'll be much trouble getting Brown released, but as for retrieving the skins, it could be you're better off cutting your losses.'

'Why? We've done nothing wrong.'

'Have you not? A little birdie told me you ran away from a sealer a good while back, *Governor Hunter* I believe was its name. I wouldn't be at all surprised to learn that you owe your former employer a pretty penny. Sealing men usually do. You're liable to being thrown into the debtor's prison.'

'I'll ring yer fuckin' mick neck and they can hang me when I'm done!' Brown says.

'Now why would you want to do that when I'm the one trying to help you?' Mills says. 'A cut of the sale is all I'm after and I shall have it yet.'

'And how is it you propose to assist us?' I say.

'Told you a man needed connections around here. That's the trouble with you is you haven't got a single one. Whereas I – '

'Whereas you're the bleeding harbourmaster,' I say. 'But you're on the way out as you yourself have said.'

'I'm not without a trick up my sleeve. In the Captain's absence, I shall call in a favour with Dr Garrett. His farm's not far from here. Oh and Brown? Garrett's a feckin' mick as well. I'd be careful about callin' him that if I were you.'

◆

IT IS not much more than a mile to Garrett's but it is a mile further away from Moe and that will make two walking back. Plainly the doctor has done well for himself for he has his own jetty, good green pasture and a herd of cows. His farmhouse is the finest I've seen this side of Sydney and there are a number of outbuildings around the place. Convicts toil in the fields and gardens, easily recognisable by their leather caps and grey prison slops. It is a veritable village and one employing nearly as much government labour as Launceston itself. Upon our knocking on the front door, a boy shows us through to a sitting room where a ruddy-cheeked man in a black frock coat is sat.

'Afternoon, Jacob,' the harbourmaster says.

'If it isn't the reprobate Peter Mills,' Garrett says. 'And who's this he's brought with him?'

I tell him my name.

'To what do I owe the honour, George? Looking for employment, perhaps?'

'I've come to ask a favour, Jacob,' Mills says, 'one concernin' Mr Baggs.'

'You'll take brandy?' He addresses me and not Mills.

'I wouldn't say no, doctor.'

Garrett calls the boy over and has him pour. Mills gulps his brandy down and I am not far behind, while Garrett sips. 'And what do you think of my establishment?'

'I'm impressed. How many men do you have working for you?'

'A dozen, give or take, some here and the rest at Norfolk Plains. Have your travels taken you up the South Esk?'

'Only as far as the Cataract.'

'Norfolk Plains is a good deal further than that. The finest farming land I ever saw and the Governor thinks likewise. The day may come where I move there for good, although I daresay I'll still have business to attend to here. Isn't that so, Peter?'

'I imagine it is, Jacob.'

'I must say our harbourmaster has a certain sordid quality about him today. Perhaps all the mud that people have been flinging is starting to stick.'

'Now you're quite sure none of it landed on you, Jacob?'

Garrett holds up his hands as if to demonstrate their cleanliness.

'Two men I'm supposed to have at my disposal but there's a labour shortage, isn't there?' Mills says. 'Wouldn't know it around here.'

'Men of any description are difficult to procure these days and good men only that much harder, although perhaps I ought to credit you with finding Mr Baggs. Let us hear of your deeds fair and foul, George.'

'I've been sealing since 1801,' I say, proceeding with the barest outline of my doings.

'A decade in Van Diemen's Land? You would have seen great changes. There will be changes again, but will times turn in our favour or to our detriment?'

'Pardon my saying, but it seems you've done well enough, doctor.'

'Perhaps by the standards of this miserable colony I have. Men disinclined towards grabbing with both hands don't last long in these parts. I expect you've found likewise.'

'I've done my fair share of holding onto whatever I thought I had.'

'I'm quite sure you have. And you say you aren't in need of employment.'

'You see it's like this, Jacob,' Mills says.

'I want to hear it in his words and not those twisted by you.'

'All right,' I say. 'You might recall the schooner *Governor Hunter* that came to York Town back in '06?'

'I recall the name. Go on.'

'I worked as a sealer aboard that vessel. We made it safely back to Sydney but a couple of years later we ran aground in the Furneaux Isles. A fellow named Brown and I went across to Cape Portland and we never did make it back to Sydney. We've been a'sealing for ourselves ever since. Four hundred skins we took this season and we thought to bring them to market.'

'Four hundred skins? Black fur or brown?'

'Almost all of them brown, although not without value even so.'

'And your former employer knows nothing of this? Was it Henry Kable?'

'No, Isaac Nichols.'

'Nichols, a litigious character. I expect you still owe him money but doubtless he considers you to have perished. We conduct business in our own manner so I don't see a problem.'

'I haven't arrived at the problem yet, Dr Garrett.'

'Then let us have it.'

'I have a native wife and infant travelling with us. I had Brown leave us at York Town and continue upriver because I was afeared of what might happen to them here in town. Mills said we'd be safe with him and he needed a man for rowing. When we got here we found Brown a prisoner and the skins stolen.'

'A sad tale but hardly an uncommon one. Where is this wife of yours now?'

'I left her at the Cataract this morning.'

'You neglected to mention that you left her in my boat and waving my musket,' Mills says.

'You are as indifferent a harbourmaster as you are a surveyor, Peter,' Garrett says. 'Now what is your interest in this matter?'

'There ain't supposed to be any trade at all and if there is it'll be by my say so. Brabyn's out campaigning, the Major's lost whatever sense he had and the soldiers are free to lock up whoever they like. It needs someone to straighten it out.'

Garrett roars with laughter. 'And so you thought to turn to me? You know very well the Crown no longer sees fit to employ my services as magistrate.'

'There's money to be made here, Jacob. That's normally enough to pique your interest.'

'I'm unlikely to involve myself in so trifling a matter. Do you know how much the government has paid me to feed the people this past year alone? These skins are worth what, three shillings apiece?'

'The lot might be worth a hundred pounds to the right buyer,' Mills says.

'You're forgetting that they aren't even your skins, Peter. Even if they can be located they belong to Messrs Brown and Baggs. At most you might charge a modest impost.'

'I'll be much obliged if you'll consider helping us, doctor,' I say. 'A man can't have too many friends.'

'I beg to differ. I find that when a man attains a certain station he has more friends than he knows and every one of them with a compelling reason why he ought to be furnished with a loan.'

'No one's asking for a loan,' Mills says. 'You can have Brown released just as easy as clicking your fingers. I'll have the boy prepare your horse, shall I?'

'I want it known that any assistance I might render is done as a personal favour to Mr Baggs. I can have your man released if he hasn't killed anyone and possibly even if he has, but there's precious little I can do about the skins. All you'll get is good advice not to make a habit of trusting he who first appears just when you're off to market.'

'I never forget those who've done me a good turn,' I say. 'Come on Peter, we'd best start walking or else the doctor'll beat us back.'

By the time Garrett rides into town, Mills and I have been sat in the dust the best part of an hour. The doctor's horse is at least fifteen hands high and content to stand quietly at the tether while its master disappears inside the barracks. Not long after, Garrett returns with Brown in tow.

'All charges dismissed,' Garrett says. 'I've been assured your boat is cleared for departure and thus I'll leave you in the capable hands of our indomitable harbourmaster. I'd invite you to dine with me tonight but alas I have made a prior arrangement.' He mounts his horse and is gone.

As careworn as Mills and I must appear, Brown is that much shabbier. I tell him that Moe is at the Cataract and that we must hurry back. We make our way down to the government wharf. We have been duped and yet I am so fatigued that I can think of nothing more than a place to lay my head.

I am readying the boat when Brown calls out 'Look, George!' He is on the deck of Garrett's ketch holding something in his hands, but in the dim twilight I cannot say what.

'Our fuckin' skins, George! The doctor's gone and robbed us blind!'

'Skins are skins,' Mills says, standing on the wharf with his arms folded.

'I dried these skins and I say they're ours,' Brown says. 'I'm takin' 'em back every one.'

'You'll do no such thing,' Mills says.

'Are you certain they're ours, Jimmy?' I say.

'I'd stake my life on it.'

'Then bring one and hurry.'

'But what about the rest?'

'This cur will raise a hue and cry, won't you? Looks like you'll receive your share, or did Garrett cut you out?'

'I swear to God I knew nothing about it.'

'Then you are as indifferent a harbourmaster as the doctor said. Why don't you run off and tell him we've caught him red-handed? Come on Jimmy, poor Moe's been waiting long enough.'

We leave him standing on the wharf.

Night is coming and despite the presence of a bright moon I cannot find the place where we left Moe. I call and call for her. Finally from somewhere in the silvery darkness I hear her calling back. At first we hear nothing but the lapping of the waves but after a while I hear something scrabbling on the rocks. She comes down to us with the bairn on her back. She starts telling me something and I recognise the word yarnenner, swimming. She went swimming while the bairn was sleeping and now she's cold, tunnack. She saw no one all day.

'Wrap this around you if you're cold,' I say, handing her the sealskin.

◆

NEXT MORNING, when we round the final bend in the North Esk at Garrett's estate, we discover his ketch tied up at his jetty. 'What did I tell ye, George?' Brown says.

As we draw up alongside, a man comes up from belowdecks with an armful of skins. It is of course the harbourmaster.

'Morning, Peter,' I say. 'Is the good doctor in?' I show him the business end of his musket and it is to his credit that he hangs onto his bundle.

'If you'll be so kind as to hand that over.'

'I might say the same to you. Where are you taking those skins?'

'To the storehouse. After all they belong to Dr Garrett.'

'Like hell they do!' Brown says, toting his musket. 'I've a mind to blow a hole between yer thievin' eyes.'

'There's no thievin' here and these ain't your skins,' Mills says, but he puts down the bundle. He keeps glancing up at the house as if anticipating a rescue.

'Let's pay the doctor a visit,' I say. 'You too, Moe.'

'Kartummeter karpennooyouhener.'

'Yes, it's chock full of bad people.'

We go up to the house, Brown and I bearing muskets and Moe holding the bairn close to her. The houseboy opens the door and, perceiving our intent, calls for the doctor and gets himself hid.

'Can you not afford us a moment's peace, Peter? We are at breakfast,' Garrett says. 'Ah, it's Messrs Baggs, Brown and company.'

'We've come for payment,' I say. 'My apologies if we've interrupted your breakfast.'

Garrett is dressed the same as yesterday but he seems to have aged a decade in the interim. 'If you'll come straight through, I'll introduce you to Mrs Garrett.'

'Don't think I wouldn't fire on a man in front of his wife,' Brown says.

We move through to the dining room where a woman with red hair is sitting at the table next to a small native boy. The pair are being waited on by a scullery maid. The boy is about six and dressed in a tunic. Breakfast consists of sausages, bacon and fried bread with dripping.

'It's my pleasure to introduce you to my wife Bridget and young Cleveland here,' Garrett says. 'The lad has been with us the better part of six months. Isn't that right, my lad?'

The boy looks down at his plate and says nothing.

'The poor creature's parents were slain in an affray not far from here. My dear wife has taken to raising him as the Lord has not yet seen fit to bless us with a child of our own.'

'What's this about, Jacob?' Bridget says. She is in her middle thirties and robed in finery rarely seen in Van Diemen's Land. 'Are these men bushrangers or aren't they?'

'It is purely a business matter, I can assure you. I'll take these gentlemen through to my study.' Garrett turns to me. 'Perhaps your wife would care for some refreshment? You didn't mention her name.'

'I thank you kindly but I reckon she'd better stick close to us. Her name's Moe.'

'Moe, is it?' Bridget says. 'And what a beautiful child you have!'

Sensing the scrutiny the bairn is under, Moe clutches it that much more tightly.

There is barely room for all of us in Garrett's study. The desk and bookcase are oaken and a bible is laid open on the desk. Garrett sits down and reaches for his ledger. 'Let's see, those skins were purchased the day before yesterday for three shillings apiece, a fair price to both parties. The vendor gave his name as a Mr Samuel Dowling and the total paid was £58.'

'You spoke nothing of this,' I say. 'Nor you, Peter.'

'I didn't know of it yesterday,' Mills says.

'Perhaps you didn't, but the doctor certainly did,' I say. 'What did this Dowling look like?'

'The sale was conducted through a third party and thus I suggest you direct your enquiries at the commissariat.'

'How many skins were there exactly?'

Garrett peers at the ledger. 'Three hundred and eighty-seven.'

'And I told you we had four hundred stolen, didn't I? You knew they were the same skins. That's why you had Brown released, in the hope we'd clear out. Three shillings apiece? You'll sell them in Sydney Town for a sight more than that.'

Garrett clasps his hands. 'I can assure you those skins were purchased in good faith. I'll concede that I had suspicions after hearing of your misfortune, but as the purchase had already been transacted I felt my hands were tied. To act otherwise would be to expose myself to a significant loss.'

'Those bleedin' skins were all we had!' Brown says. Despite the cramped confines, he manages to level his musket at Garrett. The man doesn't even flinch.

'I advised Mr Baggs to choose his friends more carefully and I can only say the same to you, Mr Brown. You may have been robbed but not by me.'

'Let's not blow the man's head off quite yet, Jimmy,' I say. 'Now doctor, you'll concede we've been robbed and you admit of your suspicions, so you'll permit us our aggrievement. I'll accept you purchased the skins in good faith but nonetheless we require compensation.'

'Three shillings apiece is a fair price as I've said. Perhaps if I offered to on-sell them for the same value we could consider the matter finalised?'

'You'll accept £58 for giving our skins back, will you? But doctor, we don't even have fifty-eight pence.'

'Then I suggest you take it up with the commissary, or else Captain Brabyn. Perhaps the miscreant who stole your skins will be brought to justice.'

'This whole colony's crawling with miscreants,' I say. 'Henry Barrett was right. Fire away, Jimmy.'

'Now wait just a minute,' Garrett says, raising his hands at last. 'That will gain you nothing but the noose.'

'Then you'd best improve your offer, hadn't you?' I say.

'And we don't want no blasted promissory notes either,' Brown says. 'It's rum we're wantin' and plenty more besides.'

'I'm confident we can come to an agreement,' Garrett says. 'You would have accepted £58 in goods, correct? In recognition of the wrongdoing done to you, albeit through no fault of mine, I'm willing to extend that value in credit to you at the store. In addition, I'll offer you a cask of the finest French brandy as a gesture of goodwill.'

'That's more like it,' I say, 'although we were led to believe our haul would fetch closer to a hundred pounds.'

'I'm afraid the days of selling skins in Canton for a pound apiece are long gone. Six shillings per skin is the very best I could hope to realise, and you must understand that there are shipping and insurance costs to consider. No, I'm making a loss whichever way you look at it. £58 and not a penny more. Are we agreed?'

'What do you think, Jimmy?'

'Three shillings a skin, I reckon we could've done better.'

'And you could've done worse,' Mills says.

'Write us a note for the storekeeper and we'll be on our way,' I say. 'You mentioned a cask of brandy?'

'I'll have Peter bring it down to the wharf,' Garrett says, scribbling on a scrap of paper. He hands me the note and I pretend to read the words before pocketing it. 'One piece of advice before you go,' he adds. 'I think you'll find the money to be made from sealing has long since been made.'

'Where do you figure the money is now?' I say.

'Land,' he says. 'Land for stock and land for grain. Next time perhaps you'll call on me at Norfolk Plains and I'll outline the particulars.'

'Not for me,' I say. 'I'm never happy unless I can smell the sea air. I promised I'd take my wife home to her country, Tebrakunna, and that's just what I'll do.'

Hearing what is for her a magic word, Moe interjects: 'Tebrakunna? We go Tebrakunna?

'That's right, Moe. It's time I took you home.'

LONGTARTENNERNER

1814

WHAT DOES IT mean to be the first? To strike out in a new direction – unknown, unheralded – with little confidence that others will follow? We have strayed from the flock and now we hold both shepherd and wolf in contempt.

Clarke Island – Longtartennerner in Moe's language – is just such a place. Overlooked by its grander neighbours in Flinders and Cape Barren, overshadowed in historical import by nearby Preservation, the dark heart of Clarke is hiding in plain sight. As are we, Messrs Baggs, Brown and company. Absconders you might label us but banditti we are not. Free men and women of the islands is what we are, not English nor clan and yet both of those. Brown and I might have wintered here in '09 but we did not truly see the island.

I see the mountains across the channel clear enough, and how my soul craves to attend those eerie summits. The soul of the child trapped within the man. In my heart I am still a boy trudging up the hill alongside Pierre Faure. In the chest of every man beats a paradox and here is mine: on one hand it is my most fervent wish to flee, to shy, to deny, and yet on the other I would seek a perfect knowledge of all that transpires under God's watchful eye.

It is not far to Cape Barren, but where the channel is narrowest the waters run swiftest. It is an impressive peak on Cape Barren and I think the range on Flinders is even higher, but I am not ignorant enough to imagine I could spy the docks of Launceston from such a vantage, let alone Port Jackson.

Nothing true beyond the end of your nose is the way my mam would have put it. *Always somethin' needin' your attention in the here'n now.*

Under grey skies I get to my feet and brush off the worst of the sand. From the top of the rise a westerly wind washes over me and I bask awhile in the sea's salt tang. Below lies a white sand beach. As good a place to winter as any, tucked in a cove on Clarke's nor'west side. Not the Kangaroo Bay and the sealing point I knew in my *Governor Hunter* days, nor the old huts near South Head where Brown and I nearly starved. Long ago the westerlies taught us to seek shelter on the eastern shores but in truth there are safe havens all over the Furneaux. If we are bolters then these are our boltholes.

Down there in the swirling whiteness I spy a dark speck at water's edge. In days before I would have thought it a seal and readied my knives but there are no seals hereabouts in this or probably any season. The sand upon this beach is the finest I have seen and it squeaks underfoot to herald the passing of every step. I squeak down and the speck squeaks up and the latter grows into the shape of a person. It is my eldest child Daisy swaddled in skins, and despite such swaddling she comes at a fair old clip. Four years and more is she. She will be a beauty like her mother and already my thoughts turn to the matter of hiding her from evildoers.

'What is it, child?' I say.

She is breathless from her exertions and can only point back the way she has come. That way lies our caveside camp amid the yard-deep rifts of seaweed.

'Is it your mother?'

She shakes her head no.

'Then what?'

'There is a ship,' she says, and my thoughts go tumbling back to other such times and other such ships. A year and more awaiting *Harrington*, the ship which never came.

'A schooner?' I say. 'Big boat or small?'

'Uncle says it's a big'un.'

'Come on then, I'll race you.'

And we run, laughing and rollicking down to the cove the child knows as her island home. A sprite the girl may be but swift beyond her years. Though I am twice her size she beats me handily, although perhaps I abetted this victory. In the water there is no need of such deception for she swims no less ably than a fish.

Moe is at water's edge with the bairn in the sling and the other by her feet. I espy no sail but perhaps it has gone around the point.

'Was it a two-master?' I say.

'I reckon maybe three,' Moe says. 'Jimmy's gone up the hill a'lookin'.'

'It didn't try for the cove here?'

'She's away into the channel.'

'A big schooner, you reckon? Then she'll be for Kents.'

'Jimmy reckons maybe Kangaroo Bay.'

I pray it is not the latter for then Longtartennerner will be crawling with Englishmen tonight. We are in a quandary, Brown and I. On one hand we are still absconders and therefore subject to British law, but on the other we've heard tell of men who went back to Sydney and faced no inquiry whatsoever, let alone the noose on Gallows Hill. We're as poor as ever and in want of every provision, but the one thing we have in abundance is sealskins. A schooner gone to Kents in May is one heading home for winter, but maybe short of skins.

'Reckon we can catch up with your uncle before he's at the top, Dais?'

She flashes a smile and is away like the wind. That girl she was born running.

I pat my wife on her bare shoulder. 'I'll be back in a while, Moe.'

'Wollighererperarner, George.'

Daisy is out of sight but she knows the way as well as I. There are snakes afoot but it wouldn't surprise me to see one she's killed draped around her neck, just like her mother. This hill is no mountain but it is the highest point on the island and one affording the best view of the passage. If that schooner went to Kangaroo Bay we might see it.

Brown is at the summit with Daisy at his side and the wind has a certain bite to it. All that's needed is a surveyor's theodolite to complete the picture in my mind. Brown is not Pierre Faure but perhaps I look up to him as I did the Frenchman.

'Thought yer old man'd turned back, din't ye?' Brown says, ruffling Daisy's tangled mop of hair.

'Then you shall know me as the tortoise and not the hare,' I say.

'Never place a wager against George bleedin' Baggs, Dais. He's liable to come out ahead just when his goose seems cookedest.'

'Wouldn't say no to no cooked goose, Jimmy. Now where's this ship? Moe reckons it's a three-master.'

'Never came close enough for countin' masts, but there she is a yonder ways.' Brown points a finger and I am hard pressed deciding where he means, let alone spotting a sail amid the breakers. The keenest eye on New Year Island is what I had but that was years ago.

'I see it, uncle,' Daisy says.

'Right you are,' I say, but for me it is all a haze. 'How many masts, would you say?'

'S'too far away,' she says.

'Can you tell us anything about it?' I hoist her onto my shoulders and stand near the cliff's edge. Grey sky, grey sea, grey mountains. Maybe I do see a sail tacking into the wind.

'Two masts.'

'Good girl,' I say, putting her down.

'Migh·'ve come from England,' Brown says. 'Some of them try Bass Strait these days.'

'Only a madman would sail into that strait without foreknowledge.'

'Then p'raps a madman is just what he is.'

'A straitsman gone to Kents in search of seals is what he's liable to be, Jimmy.'

'Ain't no seals at Kents, George. Kangaroo Bay is where he's haulin' up.'

'Ain't no seals there, either. You'll go to Sydney if he'll have you, this madman?'

Brown pats me on the shoulder. 'Reckon I've just about had me fill of island life.'

The rest is unsuitable for Daisy's ears and thus we stow it in the cargo of unsaid things. This cargo might seem weightless but it has a heft which grows heavier by the year. Brown's first clan mistress ran away and her successor upped and vanished one summer's morn. I was inclined to make a jest of such species of misfortune but now I see the damage wrought in the lines on Jimmy's brow. That he needs a wife and littluns of his own could not be plainer.

In silence we begin our descent and we are halfway home before Brown breaks it. 'Reckon this aft we'll take the boat around. Load it wi' skins.'

'They're homeward bound, probably low on victuals.'

'Ship that size, they'll have somethin' we're after.'

'You won't run out on me, Jimmy?'

'Nay George, for all I know there's still a bounty on me head.'

I am doubtful as to the existence of such a bounty but disinclined from saying so. I have done little to merit the forbearance of such a friend, whose dark brow and steely scowl strikes fear into the hearts of men. My own countenance serves as inspiration for no such thing. Had he a wife and bairns it would serve to quell the urge that bubbles at his breast, but of wife and bairns the man has none. I fear only evil will issue forth from such a circumstance.

Moe and the littluns are at camp and she has a catch of parrotfish cooking in the coals. We sit and eat and even the youngest will take a scrap of fish although its mother's milk is still its preference. It is a fine cove and the breakwater is such that a sealer could berth here at a pinch. With the westerly howling it is a whiteknuckle ride to Kents or to disaster.

'What say ye, Moe?' Brown says when we have eaten. 'Will ye come wi' us to Kangaroo Bay?'

'What for, Kangaroo Bay?' she says. 'Good eatin' here.'

'For tradin' with those straitsmen,' Brown says. 'We've plenty o' skins and I know ye don't want to go all the way to Launceston again.'

'Never again that karpennooyouhener place,' Moe says. 'Don't want nothing of your rum. You kartummeter rowdy already.'

'It isn't just rum we're after,' I say. 'All manner of provisions.'

'What provision?'

'Salt, pork, bread,' Brown says. 'Warm clothes for the littluns. Ye won't need to hunt all winter long.'

Moe looks at her children, well-fed and content by the fire. 'They plenty nartick.' She sit and thinks about it awhile. 'You can't do without me?'

'My God, woman,' I say. 'You know the answer to that.'

◆

MANY TIMES the three of us have made this journey but now with the littluns we are six. The boat is packed with skins and rides lower than I'd like, and the day is clear and cold. No sign of mischief in the west. It is hard work in these conditions but a sight less dangerous, especially here at the passage's widest section. At the sealing point the passage narrows and the water is that much faster for it. Ain't no sealing to be had there either.

Moe and I work the portside oars, the peaks of Cape Barren rising on our left, while Brown muscles starboard alone. The bairns are snug in the bilge amid the skins but Daisy wants to take an oar just like her mam. I am about to tell her to get down lest she be swept overboard but Brown has her sit in his lap and thence they row together. Straightaway Moe and I sense a loss of power.

'Let your uncle do his work, child,' I say. 'He can't turn the oar with you holding onto it.'

'Give me my own then,' Daisy says.

There is in fact a fourth oar but it is the heaviest which is why we seldom use it. No sprite so fey could hope to shoulder such a burden.

'Go sit with your mam, pernickerter!' I say, and the girl reluctantly shuffles over. Moe sings to her in their language about the sea and we make our way.

Hostile shores, no bolthole here should the weather turn bad. Just to spite us, the sun has gone behind a cloud. We pick up speed as the channel narrows and after a while it is a matter of steering and not bullying the water. This is the time of greatest danger for should we misjudge we might wreck on that rocky shore, or overshoot and wind up at Kents on the wrong island entirely. There is a covelet, no more than a break in the rocks, but it is someway short of Kangaroo Bay and ill-fitted for our purpose.

'Which is it, Jimmy?' I say. 'That cove yonder or right the way round?'

'Call that a cove, do ye?'

'Right the way round it is.'

The sun is gone, winter almost here, but it will not rain today. If I say it a hundred times it will be so. I recall a day far fouler than this, in a similar boat and in the selfsame channel, with the captain from whom we intended to abscond at my side. Years have passed and yet here I am, toiling away in much the same place.

◆

IT IS a schooner not remarkably different from others I have sailed upon, and it rides at anchor at the entrance to Kangaroo Bay. In fine conditions this is as good a place as any but one considered unsafe in a nor'wester. Not much of a beach, the sand here coarser than elsewhere on the island, and you can wade out a hundred yards and still touch bottom. Moe taught me to swim here, or what I call swimming. The water is warmer here than elsewhere in the Furneaux, but it is not a place for a ship of thirty tons to linger.

We haul up at the western end of the bay near a bed of muttonfish. No sign of activity on the schooner's deck, no longboats. No fires burning on what beach there is, nor in the scrub. It is a picture of serenity, the lonely schooner creaking in the waves with the dark peaks of Cape Barren beyond.

'Big lillerclapperlar,' Daisy says, her eyes wide.

'Ye've seen bigger in Launceston, child, but p'raps ye don't remember,' Brown says. 'Where've they gone? A'sealin' I suppose.'

'They ought to have posted a watch,' I say.

'Aye, but they reckon the island uninhabited.'

We get the littluns up beyond the tideline while Moe goes to work on the muttonfish, knife in hand. She hasn't said a word since we landed and she doesn't need to for I know her views. Englishmen are to be avoided, present company grudgingly excepted, and sealers doubly so. Such men are notorious on these coasts for their rape and pillage. Moe won't put that knife down anytime soon.

'Reckon ye'll have to swim out and see who's belowdecks,' Brown says to me. 'What is it, all of three hundred yards? I've seen ye swim further'n that.'

'I'm not sure I could make it and I don't fancy a faceful of grapeshot. You go, Jimmy.'

'Ye'll do for me like ye did Stepney makin' me swim out there. Moe could do it, easy.'

I'm not sure whether my wife can hear us, but she has collected a day's feed in the time it has taken Brown and I to determine that neither of us will be swimming out to the schooner. Having stowed her haul, she comes up scowling and scoops up the littlest from where it has been crawling in the seaweed full of lice.

'Sell your skins, pernickerter!' she says.

'We're working on it,' I say.

'Is that what you call it? Standin' there yappin'.'

'Unless someone wants to swim we're going to have to wait. I'll get started on a fire.'

'Tradin' sealskins, are ye?' a voice calls out. A dishevelled gent wearing a tattered coat comes down from the dunes, flask in hand. 'Reckon I might be able to render assistance.'

Brown and I are defenceless, our muskets stowed, but Moe bares her knife and stands over the bairns, holding Daisy at her side.

'You're from that schooner?' I say. 'Stand back aways so we can get a proper look at you.'

'Joseph Halfpenny's the name,' the man says. He is barely twenty and has a gingery beard, though redder are his eyes. That he has been drinking is evident from his shambling gait.

'Pleased to meet ye, Halfpenny,' Brown says. 'How dry's that flask?'

Halfpenny tips it up. 'Second driest thing on this godforsaken island. Driest's my throat.'

We give the man our names and Brown explains that he would favour a tot of rum if one were readily available.

'Plenty more to be had aboard 'cept I'm a long way in arrears.'

'She's a sealer then?' I say. 'What's her name?'

'*Elizabeth and Mary* out of Port Jackson,' Halfpenny says. 'We've been months a'sealin' at Kangaroo Island. You know it?'

'Know of it but never been there,' I say. 'Good hunting, is it?'

Halfpenny throws himself onto the wet sand and sits up scratching his neck. 'Two thousand skins sounds a lot, don't it? Not when ye're on the lay it ain't.'

'It's a mug's game,' Brown says. 'What d'ye owe the jackals?'

'Two pound ten shillings at last count. She'll be a hungry winter.'

'Seventeen pounds flat is what I owe Isaac Nichols,' I say. 'Still breathing, is he?'

'Nichols? Aye. Run off from him, did ye?'

'That were years ago,' Brown says.

'Can't say I blame ye,' Halfpenny says. He lays back looking at the sky. 'I've a mind to scarper meself, although I'd be wantin' a mate or two.'

'We ain't yer mates if that's what ye're thinkin',' Brown says. 'All we're after is a man to help offload these skins. Where's everyone got to?'

'Sealin' at the point,' Halfpenny says. 'Captain's aboard though.'

'Doesn't your captain know there's nary a seal to be had?' I say. 'Hasn't been for years.'

'He did say words to that effect but the fellows were desperate. They're all of 'em behind on their accounts. It's a straight run to Sydney so this'd be their last chance.'

'There ain't no straight run to Sydney,' I say. 'First season out, is it?'

'Second,' Halfpenny says. 'I ain't so wet behind the ears.'

'Aren't ye?' Brown says. 'Rolling around drunk like that.'

Halfpenny sits up. 'Real thirsty fellow, ain't ye? Bet ye'd like a bottle.'

'Swim out and get me one, then I might call ye me mate.'

'Swim? Ye've a perfectly good boat. Now let's see them skins.'

Brown and I escort the weaving Halfpenny to our boat while Moe and the bairns hang back.

'Black fur, nearly a hundred,' Brown says, handing Halfpenny a folded skin, 'and about three hundred of the brown. What'll that fetch?'

'Plenty if it weren't on the lay,' Halfpenny says.

'You could eat your way round to next winter with this,' I say, showing him the piles. 'So what say we negotiate with your captain? You'll be due a cut and you'll be the toast of all your mates. Imagine their faces when they find out you've brought in upward of four hundred skins without even getting your toes wet!'

'Aye, it'll be worth it for that alone. Four hundred skins. That's worth … I dunno.'

'I don't know myself and that's half the problem,' I say. 'Those thieves can quote whatever figure they like. What did you say his name was, this thief of a captain?'

'William Rook and he is a tight-fisted old bastard.'

Brown and I look at one another and then Halfpenny. 'Now you did say Rook, didn't you?' I say. 'Not Cook or Crook or some other name sounding similar.'

'Aye and I'll say it again, William Bastard Rook. Felt his lash on yer hindquarters, have ye?'

'No it isn't that,' I say. 'It isn't that at all.'

Brown pulls me aside seeking congress and we walk away to have it. 'Ye've gone an' got us proper fucked,' he says. 'Why'd ye have to go mentionin' our abscondin'?'

'I'm sorry, Jimmy.'

Brown looks back up the beach. Halfpenny is standing there.

'Reckon we'll 'ave to do 'im in,' Brown says.

'I won't see a man slain for nothing.'

'Blast ye and yer bleedin' conscience, George. If he turns tattle it's on yer head.'

'I'll deal with him. You go and help Moe awhile.'

I return to the boat, upon which Halfpenny is leaning. Not one grey hair amid the ginger, I can still see the boy within the frame of the man. 'Been in the colony long?' I ask.

'Long enough.'

'Ever knew a lad by the name of Tom Stepney? He'd have been about your age.'

'I don't know no Stepney. Now what's this about?'

'No one's going to hurt you, Joseph.'

'I don't like the way yer mate was lookin' at me. Murderin' eyes he has.'

'Jimmy Brown's about the best mate a fellow would want to have. Look at him messing about with them littluns. They're not even his.'

'That yer woman, is it? An' yer littluns.'

'That's right, Joseph, but forget about that for now. Are you listening?'

'Aye, I'm listenin'. I don't give a damn what ye've done, it's what ye're plannin' on doin' I'm frettin' about.'

'Then I'll lay it out. Rook was our master on *Governor Hunter* back in '09. We ran off, the pair of us in debt to Isaac Nichols. Now we've been five years in the Furneaux and Van Diemen's Land sealing for ourselves. And we don't trust no one, see. Last time we did we were fleeced a boatload of skins.'

Halfpenny thinks before speaking, and for this he climbs in my estimation. 'Rook ain't huntin' absconders. An' he don't work for Nichols no more.'

'I'm glad to hear it.'

'All he cares about is the profit he's makin'. He'll give you a price for yer skins. Prob'ly not a fair price, but a price. Long way from the store here. He don't need to know yer names, not that he'd care if he did. Now I'll trade yer skins on one condition.'

'You'll get your cut.'

'Ain't after no cut, I want off this bastard crew. Why d'ye think I'm out here all alone? They dumped me. Told me to swim back when I was ready to work. But I have been workin' all season, same as them. They've got it in their heads I'm a slugabed. It ain't the first time neither.'

'You'll lose your lay,' I say. 'Of course it's worthless if you're behind.'

'I thought two pound ten was bad. How'd ye end up owin' seventeen?'

'Truth is I don't even know. They tell you a figure and that's just what you owe. You're sure Rook's not hunting debtors?'

'Show me a man who isn't a debtor,' Halfpenny says. 'Some are better thieves than others is all.'

◆

THE LONGBOATS appear just as we are loading the last of the rum bottles. Rook is on the schooner's deck, same as before but fatter, and if he recognises Brown and I he makes no show of it. The man is preoccupied with the return of his boats and the darkening sky. He won't get off today and now he must pray the weather does not turn to his detriment. His heart pines for Kents and safer anchorage but there are not the daylight hours. Five years ago we ran up this coast after Bader and what have we to show for it now?

Halfpenny waits for the final moment before slinking off with us, and when he does the captain calls out: 'Godspeed to you, Joseph. And good luck to you, James and George.'

The old swindler, he knew us after all.

We are underway in the gloom and mist under an enfeebled sun, a hard beat to windward amidst the chink of bottles reminding us of our labour's reward. Halfpenny proves an able oarsman and I am doubly impressed insofar as he turns the fourth and heaviest oar. But is it truly heavier or is it our minds' fiction? If one labours under the misapprehension of the oar's enormous weight, is it truly heavier to lift?

Turn and turn again, a whaleboat in a shroud of mist. The littluns huddle together in the bilge, Daisy ahold of her sister ahold of the littlest. Moe is ahold of all three though not with her arms and I am ahold of Moe, or so I imagine. I wanted to find Brown a woman and instead I have brought home a man.

Night is falling, but perhaps we see a sunset glimmer. I can barely see my wife on the thwart let alone the cove we mean to find, but there are those with sharper eyes. Foremost among them Daisy, pointing and shouting. 'There, there!' she cries. 'We're home!' Her words make it so.

In black surf we run the boat up a black beach.

◆

IN THE fire we are brought back alive, in warmth and crackling light. From modest beginnings the flames climb high and so our spirits. A broad smile on Moe's face and the littluns' shining eyes tell a story – we are still here. Not the first to come to Longtartennerner, but the first to stay.

A feast for the living, Captain Rook's pork and rum, but when we open the barrel of meat the stench turns our guts. No amount of salt can cure such corruption. It is too long in a ship's hold and we are too long living on what we can catch with our hands. Halfpenny proclaims it fresher than we estimate and we tell him he is welcome to it. The latter article, however, is better to my liking and to Brown's. We are months without rum but we imbibe whenever the opportunity presents. The first drink goes down nice and easy and we wonder whether Rook has had it cut with water.

'Wouldn't put it past him, the knave,' Halfpenny says. 'Won't touch a drop himself.'

'Yet for all his knavery he let us go unchallenged,' I say.

'Prob'ly costs him more than he'd be due to ship us back to Sydney,' Brown says. 'And for what? To see us in chains over a debt we might have owed to a man he don't work for no more?'

'You do Rook a disservice,' I say. 'He's a stickler for the rules and yet he turned a blind eye for us.'

'Let's toast his good health then,' Brown says. 'Three cheers for William Bastard Rook!'

In this fashion we begin and long we continue, with huzzahs for all from King and Governor down.

'Dance with me, Moe!' I cry, and I grieve at her naysaying for the woman once won my heart around just such a fire. She draws her littluns close, muttering about rum and karpennooyouhener. I hold out a mug and she slaps it from my hands, four pairs of eyes turned toward me in their aspect of accusation. I raise my hands in surrender and withdraw.

'What's got her goat?' Halfpenny says. 'Doesn't like me being here?'

'She don't like to see us drinkin',' Brown says. 'Reckons we're devils when we do.'

'And ye let her tell ye no?' Halfpenny says. 'If I understand correctly she ain't even yer missus.'

Brown goes quiet and that is the very worst sign. Halfpenny drinks on. For years it was a fraught standoff between Brown and Moe and one I have done all I could to balance. At first she thought him a brute and could not bear his sight, but as the months and years wore on she came to appreciate what I have known all along, that within that thick hide lies a kind-hearted soul. Nowadays it often seems that they are the married couple and myself the other man, except that I am the one to share Moe's bed.

'Let's hear of Kangaroo Island, Halfpenny,' I say.

'Good sealin' on Kangaroo,' Halfpenny says. 'Rook's been back and forth several times. Biggest island I've seen, must be all of a hundred miles long.'

'Folk live there?'

'They do now, Englishmen and native women taken from the mainland. Fireball Bates told me all about it. Must be upwards of a dozen families settled there, and then of course the sealin' crews. They ain't all Englishmen neither. There's a fellow from Otaheite and two or three from New Zealand.'

'Proper little society,' Brown says. 'Ye wouldn't think of settlin'?'

'Naw, it's a touch barbarous. Livin' in bark huts, dogs everywhere at your feet yappin' and caperin' around. On Kangaroo, if a fellow don't like ye he's liable to slit yer throat and carry off yer woman. An' there ain't nothin' like a warm tavern bed for a thousand miles.'

'Seems an awful long way to go for a sealskin,' I say. 'Two thousand you say you took?'

'Will be closer to three with yer lot, but aye. Rook's last trip took four thousand and the one before that was six.'

We're heard this before. It is the story of the Furneaux again. 'He'll never stop, will Rook,' I say. 'Not till he's taken every last one.'

'It ain't just seals he's after, it's salt too,' Halfpenny says. 'In summertime the lagoon dries up and that bastard has us scrapin' it into casks. At the end of summer it crystallises and he had us there the first of Feb. Fifty tons and I must've scraped up half meself. And there ain't no lay on salt, let me tell ye.'

'Scraping salt … bet he makes a killing on that as well.' My mind can barely fathom such a thing.

'If that's civilised society I want nowt to do wi' it,' Brown says. 'The Furneaux might be a backwater but at least it knows how to leave a man alone.'

We drink to that.

The littluns are asleep with Moe at vigil over them. It will be weeks and months before she trusts Halfpenny if she ever does. We know nothing of the man and there is no one to corroborate his truthfulness. He would seek to distance himself from the throat-slitters and rapists, as well he might.

When the bottle is passed again I merely pretend to fill my mug, and next time around I needn't bother with such deception for the pair are well in their cups. I've seen Brown drink nearly a hogshead, pausing only to relieve himself and not always even then. But that was after months of studied drinking, whereas now we have been abstinent by necessity. Meanwhile Halfpenny grows more garrulous. Now he is on about the time he absconded after assaulting the chief officer of the *Trial*.

'How old are you, Halfpenny?' I cut in. 'I'd have taken you for a lad of nineteen.'

'Twenty-four this August if I should live so long. And yerself?'

'Twenty-seven this June.'

I study him in the firelight. Either my eyes deceive or the lad isn't a day over twenty. Is it just that I wanted a surrogate Stepney? How old would you have been now, Tom? No, he ain't no Tom Stepney. Claims to have done three months on the chaingang up in Parramatta. Been to New Zealand, or so he says.

'Why would those fellows on *Elizabeth and Sally* want to strand you?' I ask.

'Told ye before, they reckoned me a layabout.'

'And are you?'

'I do the same work as any man.'

'Then there must be another reason.'

'Ease up, George,' Brown says.

'No, 'tis a fair question and one I'll happily answer,' Halfpenny says. 'Truth is sometimes a fellow just gets it in his head to go after ye, and next thing you know his mates have turned as well. That's how someone ends up gettin' stabbed.'

'You said before that some are better thieves than others. Is that why they turned against you?'

'Ye can't go flingin' around such accusations,' Brown says.

'I ain't no thief,' Halfpenny says, staring me down.

An hour creeps by and my eyelids grow heavy, but I resolve not to turn in before Halfpenny. He is rolling drunk and Brown not much better and between them they make a racket to wake the dead. Moe is silent and liable to be in a foul mood.

'I've a question for ye, George,' Halfpenny says, throwing his arm around me. 'I'm hopin' ye'll not find offence.'

I push him away. 'Best not to ask if you think I might.'

'But I'm askin'.' He skols his drink. 'That pretty dark wench o' yours, is she for sharin'?'

I go at him but he anticipates this and I find myself flat on my back with him pressing down. Then I feel the jab of his knife. 'I'll fuckin' stick yer. Now is she for sharin'?'

'No.'

He presses harder before falling limp atop me, and I have to scrabble out from underneath both he and the knife. Brown has coldcocked him with a musket. Now he resumes his place at the fire. I feel the hot blood at my side as I crouch down alongside Halfpenny, his breathing shallow.

'Don't go thinkin' I did that for ye,' Brown says, raising his mug.

◆

IN THE dark I burrow beneath the skins next to Moe and she murmurs in half-sleep, not quite awake but reproaching me all the same. I whisper that Halfpenny might be dead. She turns away foxing sleep and I lay thinking awhile. I never ought to've brought Halfpenny along but then I never ought to have done any number of things. I can see why Moe is furious because I have brought her into contact with the two things she hates most, rum and Englishmen. It is a mistake and one I must rectify. If we get moving at first light we can have Halfpenny aboard his schooner before it sails.

I whisper some of this to Moe's back not knowing whether she hears and after a while she turns around. 'I ain't scared o' him but it ain't safe for the littluns,' she says.

'Where is it safe then? There's sealers everywhere.'

'Tebrakunna. We go home to Laman.'

'It ain't safe with your old man neither. At least here there's the sea all around.'

'Karpennooyouhener come from the sea.'

'Then we'll go to Norfolk Plains and work for Jacob Garrett. Ain't no sea there. You know how Mrs Garrett took to Daisy, I reckon she'd take her on in a trice.'

Moe turns away.

'One way or another Halfpenny's off tomorrow. I admit I oughtn't to have asked him along.'

'Jimmy protects us.'

'Aye he does. I'd have been stuck like a pig if it weren't for him.' The wound is little more than a nick but I can recall a time when Moe would have doted over it. 'Maybe you'd be better off with him. I can work my way to Launceston or Hobart Town. Make us some real money.'

Silence.

'You'd like that, wouldn't you? The pair of you alone. You know how Daisy adores him.'

'Rum got ahold of you.'

'Then I'll tip it out, every last bottle. I'll do it right away.'

'You'll wake the littluns.'

Moe ain't wrong about rum for it has ahold of me all right. Four hundred skins we traded for a cask of rotten saltpork and a crate of rum, both of which will be gone come morning the way things are going. I'd better get it done while Brown is sleeping or he'll raise hell.

'What do you reckon about Norfolk Plains?' I say.

'We stay Longtartennerner. No more rum, no more Englishmen.'

'I'm an Englishman, Moe. The littluns are Englishmen and subjects of the king.'

'Where is he, this king? Ain't never seen 'im. Reckon you made 'im up to scare us.'

'I might as well have for all the good he does. What about me leaving you with Brown and going to Launceston for a season? I'll take Daisy to work for the Garretts.'

'If you go, you ain't ever comin' back,' she says, though whether she intends this as threat or prophecy I cannot say. 'And you ain't takin' my girl Daisy.'

◆

WHEN I wake, the bad weather has set in and I recall that I have not accomplished any of the tasks I assigned myself the previous night. I had thought to rise with the sun and get to work emptying those bottles before rowing Halfpenny back to his schooner, only today there's no sun. Just a hazing mist, neither fog nor rain. From the grey light I judge it to be mid-morning, the littluns and their mother cocooned in a tangle of furs. Brown snores on.

Halfpenny is missing, however.

No trace of him at the place where he was felled, no scrap of cloth nor drop of blood. The crate of rum remains untouched, as does the pork barrel.

'Brown, wake up,' I whisper, before roughing him a little. 'Jimmy!'

His eyes open, and his breath could slay a hog. 'What is it now?'

'Halfpenny's scarpered.'

'Crawled off to die, more'n likely.' He shuts his eyes again. 'We'll see to it come morning.'

'It is morning, Jimmy. I was going to tip out all those bottles.'

His eyes open. 'Ye won't do that if ye want to live much longer. Where'd ye stow me musket?'

'I never touched it.'

'It were laid there beside 'im.'

'For fuck's sake, Jimmy. He'll be hunting us now.'

'I fuckin' cracked 'im,' Brown mutters, raising the bottle to his lips. 'I'm woozy.'

I get him to his feet but he isn't in fighting condition. Our talking has woken the littluns and thence their mother. I tell her that Halfpenny's nicked off with one of our muskets. I'll go out looking once the weather clears up a bit. If Moe looked surly last night it is nothing compared with her look now.

'I'd go wi' ye but me head's poundin',' Brown says. 'Reckon I'll sit down a spell.'

Moe gives off a deafening shriek. 'Where's Daisy?'

'She ain't wrapped up with the littluns?' I say.

Moe scans the vicinity of the campfire. 'Daisy? Daisy!'

'She might've wandered off,' I say, but I know in my heart it isn't so.

We call and call, to no avail. The beach is shrouded in grey and I can barely see ten yards through the murk. 'I'll get after her,' I say, running to and fro trying to decide whether to bring a musket.

'Reckon ye'd better bring it, George,' Brown says.

'That old thing never fired straight and the other one neither.'

Moe has her knife and a look that's sharper still. 'Guard the littluns, Jimmy.'

'No one's gettin' through.'

'Wollighererperarner.'

She crouches by a patch of mud not far from the fire. 'His boots?'

Footprints in the mud. I try to recall whether Halfpenny had been wearing proper boots or sealskin moccasins like us, but draw a blank. I put my foot in the mud next to the print for comparison. The moccasins leave a more rounded print. 'I reckon they're his.'

There is another such footprint a little further along the bank of the creek. That way lies the path to the hill.

And we run.

◆

WE FIND Halfpenny and Daisy near the cloudlocked summit. I am out of breath, my heart hammering, and yet Moe surges onward. Halfpenny is stooped over the musket he is using for a walking stick, dragging Daisy along with his other hand. Mother cries out to child and the latter pulls away, and they are together on the muddy slope. Halfpenny is fumbling with the cartridge papers but I am upon him.

'Good luck … firing that,' I say between deep sucking gasps. A curtain of cloud atop the dreary summit joins another from my lungs. Moe and Daisy are off back down, leaving me to face Halfpenny.

But he is as infirm as a gent of eighty summers, the only colour on him the ugly gash at his temple. Damp papers fall from trembling hands as I wrest the musket barrel from his grasp.

'We'd best sit down,' I say, and we sit looking over the channel. 'You didn't catch a sight of that schooner?'

'No.'

'A man can barely see the nose on his face in this weather. I can spend hours looking over those mountains. Even on a day like today, I can't see them but I know they're there.'

He looks sidelong at me. 'Ever been across?'

'To Cape Barren? Aye, but I left my climbing days behind me when I was a lad. Reckon you could see Port Jackson from the summit?'

'Not a chance, though ye'd have to go right to the top in provin' it.'

'An idle thought. I think of myself as the first man of these islands and so I ought to be the first to climb that peak.'

'What makes ye the first man and not Brown?'

'First men, then.'

He thinks on this awhile. 'Reckon there ain't no such thing as a first man,' he says. 'It's like that mountain. Just because ye can't see it don't mean it ain't still there.'

'I don't follow you.'

'I reckon there's been men sat on this hill looking at those mountains for a thousand years. For all we know they're buried at our feet. We might be sittin' on their piled-up bones.'

'I'll have to think on that some more, Joseph.'

'See that ye do.'

A chill wind gets up and it goes right through us. 'Now why did you take off with Daisy?' I ask.

'Din't touch a hair on her pretty little head.'

'Maybe you didn't. Last night you would've had me filleted if Jimmy hadn't done what he did.'

'It was the drink to blame.'

'Aye, always the drink. Why'd they put you off that ship?'

'I done stabbed a fellow on Kangaroo Island. Brawlin' over a native wench. Rook was supposed to take me back to stand trial but he didn't want the hassle. That's why they put me off.'

'And here I was thinking Rook did me a good turn, the bastard.'

'So I've come clean. Will ye let me live or no?'

'I'm not much for stabbing fellows. But you can't come back to the camp.'

'Not even if I promise never to touch a drop of rum again?'

'I've made that promise myself for all the good it does.'

'Then I'll die.'

'Maybe you will, but not by my hand.'

And I am off back down, shouldering not one musket but two.

◆

AT CAMP they are eating breakfast, and perhaps the sun will shortly make a belated appearance. Daisy is tearing around as though nothing has happened but Moe won't let her out of her sight, not even to acknowledge my return.

'Is it finished?' Brown says between fishy mouthfuls.

I take my place beside him and reach for a steaming fillet. 'Is what finished?'

He looks at Moe and she at him and the expression they share is one I do not care for.

'Din't hear no shot so we thought ye'd used a knife. At least ye got the musket.'

'I got the musket.'

'But it ain't finished.'

'I won't cut down a man defenceless, Jimmy.'

Brown chews another mouthful. 'He was readyin' to fire, Moe reckons.'

'Very slowly perhaps.'

'Some men are their whole damn lives preparin' for summat, George. An' they never get round to nowt.'

'What's your point?'

He counts off his points on his fingers. 'Man tries to stab ye and threatens yer wife. He snatches yer wee child and makes off to do God only knows what to her. When ye catch up to him he starts very slowly readyin' the musket he stole from ye.' Brown closes his hand into a fist. 'And yet somehow that ain't sufficient grounds for strikin' him.'

'I suppose not, Jimmy.'

He gets up. 'Just sat there, is he? 'Spose ye made 'im nice and cosy.' He commences sharpening his knife on the whetstone.

'He didn't look good to me, Jimmy. Not long for this world, I reckon.'

'Ye got that part right.'

When he is gone I start tucking into breakfast. 'You all right, Daisy?'

The girl doesn't answer, and when I turn to Moe it is more of the same.

'I felt sorry for the man is all,' I say. 'Thought he'd been thrown off by his mates for no good reason. I see now I was wrong.'

I go over to the crate of bottles and hold one aloft. I remove the cork and start tipping out the contents.

'Wait,' Moe says. 'S'good for tradin'.'

I stop mid-pour and re-cork the bottle.

'And besides it's Jimmy's.'

I put the bottle back in the crate and sit down. 'That's not all that's Jimmy's, is it?'

Daisy looks at me and says nothing, and I say nothing back. The littluns gurgle and carry on just the same.

'Brown's a decent man, better than decent,' I say. 'He'll look after you and the littluns. But I'm taking Daisy to be raised by Mrs Garrett.'

'You ain't takin' my Daisy!'

'Next season there'll be two or three like Halfpenny hanging around and they'll think nothing of snatching little girls from their fires. Brown can't protect you from them and nor can I. She'll be safe at Norfolk Plains.'

'You ain't takin' my girl.'

'But I am. And when she's done growing I'll marry her off to a nice gent in Launceston.'

With these words I can feel a vast weight beginning to lift from my chest. For too long have I been trapped in these straitened circumstances and they bedevil my mind. 'I'll not abandon you, Moe. A season or two I'll be gone, and I'll return with my pockets full of coin.'

'No.'

We speak a different language, Moe and I. Perhaps there is no first man of these islands. Just piled-up bones as deep as the hillside.

'Don't look so glum,' I say. 'We might see the sun in a minute.'

What we see instead is Brown trudging down the muddy slope. Daisy runs to his side. 'Look at that smile!' he says. 'Ye'd have thought I'd been away all year.'

'Did you get 'im, uncle?'

He ruffles her hair. 'Never ye mind about that. Now run along but don't go far, for Heaven's sake.' He sits down at the fire and warms his hands. 'See these hands, George? That's yer blood on 'em.'

'Did he say anything?'

'We din't sit around chewin' the fat, George.'

'So it's done?'

'Aye, though I want 'im proper buried so as the girl don't see.'

'I'll deal with that.'

'Aye. Now why the long face, Moe?'

Not waiting to hear Moe's answer, I grab the shovel and head up the hill. Daisy doesn't follow.

Turning Halfpenny over onto his front, I go through his pockets and find only his flask. There isn't as much blood as might have been supposed. I take a long pull but it is nothing more than water. I cap the flask and put it in my pocket.

The mist is lifting, the sun comes out at last. Through a break in the cloud I catch a glimpse of my beloved mountain over on Cape Barren, and my heart soars.

By Christ I shall scale it yet.

JAMES KELLY

1815–16

WHEN I WAS a lad, it was often said I held a certain promise but it was never quite clear what such promise entailed. Now I am just a fellow same as the rest. Maybe not the strongest, maybe not the brightest, but a man who'll do a day's work for an honest wage and drink until dawn if given half a chance. Only one thing makes me different and that is that I've been in Van Diemen's Land since before Davy Collins ever came ashore at Sullivans Cove. Jimmy Brown and the old *Calcutta* lags think themselves the originals but I was on King Island in '02 and there's no one else in Hobart Town claiming that.

My pedigree has landed me a berth working for James Kelly on Mr Birch's whaleboat, *Elizabeth.* We go to the wild west coast in search of the fine timbers so desired by Birch and Gordon for their shipbuilding, particularly the Huon Pine. One day Hobart Town will be a great port to rival Canton and Madras, or so they reckon. I am a man of the north and yet these days the pull of money is south to Hobart Town. When men dream of fortune their eyes rove southward, such chancers endlessly expounding upon the distant isles where a man can hardly walk for wading through blubber. If I am moved by such tales most often it is to silence.

A man who chooses his words carefully eats as heartily as he who does not, however. This man has the same hungers, but whatever dreams he had have died a strangling death. I still owe a debt of seventeen pounds to Isaac Nichols and my soul will not be at peace until I see it repaid.

It is Kelly's intention to continue through Bass Strait and back around to Hobart Town, thus circumnavigating Van Diemen's Land. It is no particular interest of mine but Mr Birch is paying three pounds a month and we will be gone two months or maybe three. It will be still longer before I see Moe again, though I fear not long enough for her to have forgiven me. I told her that taking Daisy to Norfolk Plains was for the best but I nearly broke her heart in doing it. Truth is I was footloose and looking for a way out. Another few weeks and Brown would've buried me next to Joseph Halfpenny.

'What ails ye, George?' says Thomas Tombs, the oarsman sitting next to me on *Elizabeth*'s thwart. 'Ye haven't said a word in hours.'

'I was just thinking upon my wife, Thomas.'

Laughter ahead and behind, a sly smile on Kelly's face at the coxswain.

'I was thinking upon her too,' sneers John Griffiths, reckoning he can lord it over me because he is Kelly's brother-in-law. 'Thinking long and hard was I.'

I exchange a glance with William Jones, the final member of our quintet, a man who speaks even more guardedly than I. There is silence but for the sounds of oars turning and waves lapping as we approach the crumbling cliffs of Whale Head. We must be about as far away from Longtartennerner as you can get and still call it Van Diemen's Land.

'Why don't ye needle the man some more, Griffiths?' Tombs says. 'At least Baggs has a wife. The only wives I've seen ye with were those wi' four legs.'

'Keep pulling, old man.'

'I've been pullin' since before ye were spunked out.'

The oarsmen pull while Kelly directs the whaleboat with the steering oar. Tombs and Jones are ticket-of-leave men, ex-convicts awaiting their final pardon from the Lieutenant-Governor, whereas Kelly and Griffiths are currency lads born to convict mothers. I'm something in between, neither fish nor fowl.

When we round the South East Cape, a nor'easter fills the sails and our arms get a rest from rowing. The grey bulk of the headland juts out into the sea, a finger pointing at the great nothing beyond. There's a mizzling rain and Kelly keeps us offshore lest we wreck on the rocky coastline. After a while the wind swings around and we get a good run along the coast. The South Cape is a wall of grey cliffs where an inopportune gale would see us wrecked but for now our luck is holding. Once we are past the spur of the cape, Kelly changes tack and swings us around to the nor'west. Here we see a series of small beaches cut between rocky promontories, a pair of small rocky islands teeming with muttonbirds. As we pass the islands we catch a glimpse of a larger beach but we are too far gone to leeward to reach it.

It isn't until the sun is low on the water that Kelly has us land. No sooner than we haul the whaleboat up, we see a number of clansmen watching from the edge of the bush. At least ten or twelve, apparently unarmed.

'See if you can make yourself understood, Baggs,' Kelly says.

This is why Kelly sought me out at the Hope & Anchor in Hobart Town. Not because I am especially strong nor especially clever, but because I am reputed to speak the language of Moe's people, the northeast clan. The fact that no one in Hobart Town except me has ever laid eyes on the northeast clan is immaterial. Such intelligence Kelly reckons will come in handy on his expedition.

This clan is far from the northeast and speaks another tongue entirely. We have barely a word in common and yet I am given to understand we are welcome to stay here tonight. The clansmen call to their women and children and soon there is a group of about fifty people on the beach, many with wallaby skins draped across their shoulders. I do not see a single spear or waddy among them and there is nothing in their bearing to suggest the possibility of violence. The clansmen point to a nearby hill and put their hands next to their heads in a gesture suggesting sleep.

'I think they're inviting us to their camp,' I say. 'I reckon they've never seen a white man before.'

'Just as well if they haven't,' Tombs says.

There are smiles and laughter, especially among the children who point and giggle at our jackets and trousers. No doubt they are speculating as to whether any of us are women. In this their focus is on clean-shaven Jones, but he will not drop his drawers to confirm nor deny.

'Tell them we thank them kindly but we're intent on staying on the beach tonight,' Kelly says. I offer the clansmen some sugarloaf and ship's biscuit but they aren't keen on either. By way of gesture I tell them that we will sleep on the beach and they seem satisfied. They wave to us in farewell and vanish into the twilight.

As night falls, we build up a fire and eat heartily of salt pork and damper. Kelly opens the first bottle of Bengal and we begin to make merry, as is our wont.

'If only the Lieutenant-Governor were here, we could have a *Blow Me Skull*!' Tombs says. 'Have you ever partaken with Old Tom, Captain?'

'I most certainly have and a sore head was had by all.'

'Then let us hear of it. Lags like us don't get an invitation.'

'When Tom Davey gets the inclination, which is about every second or third night, he has his servants cook up a pig on a spit. He sits there swirling his noxious mixture –rum, brandy, porter, lemon juice and water – and challenges any who stray within earshot to match him drink for drink, only no one can. "No heel taps!" he cries if his victim leaves even a drop in the bottom of his cup. I thought mine was a stern head but his is immeasurably sterner.'

'If only such a head was any use in governin' he'd have Michael Howe hangin' in the gibbets instead of gallivantin' around the countryside,' Tombs says.

'You'd be the expert on bushrangers, Tombs,' Griffiths says. 'You've spent years running around the interior without them touching a hair on your head.'

'I was never in league with Howe if that's what you're suggestin'.'

'You're as crooked as those teeth is what I'm suggesting.'

'Howe's no mate o' mine.'

'Weren't you a lifer, Tombs?' Kelly says. 'How is it you won your freedom?'

Tombs holds out his mug. 'Pour again and I'll regale ye.' Kelly pours and Tombs drinks and wipes his muzzle. 'Times were I did everythin' asked o' me, and for what? Backbreakin' labour from sunup to sundown and always with the prospect of a floggin'. We were starvin' those first couple o' years till we learned to hunt kangaroo. Ran away first chance I had and there were three hundred lashes waitin' for me when I returned. A man can eat his fill in this country without ever tilling the soil, he just needs one thing and that's a good huntin' dog.'

'So you were a fugitive, a bushranger,' Griffiths says.

'I wanted nowt to do with the settlement nor any man in it. Just to pass my days unmolested.'

'I'm the same,' I say, 'except I did it hunting seals. But how did you win your ticket-of-leave?'

'A few o' us were headin' down the east coast out near the Schoutens when we heard there was a bounty on two lags, McCabe and Townsend. We fell in with the miscreants kiddin' on that we wanted to join their gang, and when they fell asleep we tied 'em up and hauled 'em off to town. I wrote a letter askin' for clemency, and after they swung we got just that.'

'No honour among thieves?' Griffiths says.

'We were bushrangers and freebooters, but never thieves. McCabe and Townsend were brute killers and stupid ones too. Before they were caught, they broke into Parish's house and started beatin' on him and his sons. They made off with all the missus' silk gowns and petticoats and tried to set the place on fire.'

'What about you, Jones?' Griffiths says. 'How did you win your freedom?'

'Only had seven years and I served them every one.'

'And what was your crime?'

'Pinchin' drapery.'

'But it isn't true to say you never once absconded,' Tombs says. 'I could've sworn we made off with a couple o' the Reverend's dogs that one time.'

'That old felon Knopwood,' Jones says. 'Two years labourin' in his garden and huntin' kangaroo for his plate.'

It is a history they share together, these *Calcutta* lags and their old Hobart Town days, whereas mine is entirely different. They do not ask and I do not tell.

◆

THIS DESOLATE coast far from home or hearth is a place forsaken by God and man both. Even now at summer's height the rain comes in blustery squalls that impede our progress at every turn of the oar and each billow of the sail. Long days we spend windbound in some unnamed bay, huddling beside a fire or hunting what meagre game can be had. How the clans make their homes in such frigid climes is beyond my comprehension. I am never sufficiently warm unless I am rowing and not always even then.

One morning we sight the South West Cape and Kelly guides the whaleboat round it in a sou'east wind. The Cape is a triangular marker made of rock and it stands as sentry over this empty corner of Van Diemen's Land. I once saw a sketchbook of the great pyramids of Egypt and this is a sight no less grand. Greenery grows near the summits but the lower reaches are of barefaced granite. Seals loll on the ledges hereabouts and they do so without fear.

But if the south coast is punishing, the west is a sailor's nightmare, a savage coastline made of cliff and rock and spray. The most vicious cliffs I ever saw, and Kelly says the same. No bay visible on the western shore, nowhere to escape the sea's fury should the wind turn to our detriment. And it will.

In the twilight we haul up not far beyond the cape on a grassy island crawling with muttonbirds. The birds are dozy and we feast beneath a crescent moon and a sky full of stars. Soon the fireside is littered with their bones. We are kings of darkness and answerable to none.

'Even the clans stay clear of this coast,' Griffiths says. 'Haven't seen one of their fires in days.'

'There's no grassland, no kangaroo,' Tombs says. 'The clans like the same places we do, where it's warm and dry and there's plenty of game.'

'Places such as the settled districts?'

'Aye, except now they're crawlin' with settlers. No wonder there's been trouble.'

'There's been trouble from the get-go,' Kelly says. 'I remember it when I was a lad.'

'Ye speak of Risdon?' Tombs says.

'I do. I was in Hobart Town back in '04, apprenticed to Henry Kable. One day we heard an almighty boom from where the soldiers were barracked upriver. Those drunkards mucking about and liable to blow themselves to kingdom come, or so we thought. Next day the Reverend took me up in his rowboat. The soldiers told us hundreds of clansmen had come down the hill not knowing soldiers were stationed there, and the surgeon Garrett had ordered the carronade fired. No one could say how many dead. Garrett had a native boy with him, said its parents had been slain. Two, maybe three years old. Where is that child now?'

'Garrett had a native boy with him up in Launceston,' I say. 'Cleveland was his name, as I recall.'

'Likely a different lad,' Kelly says. 'Birch has a boy he calls Black Tom working on his farm and he's not the only one. Even Tom Davey can see the harm it's apt to cause.'

'Are you suggesting these tykes will take up arms when they are grown?' Griffiths says. 'Against the very gentlemen who fed and clothed them?'

'Wouldn't you, Griffiths?' I say. 'If someone slew your mother and father and worked you as a slave?'

'I'd be grateful to my benefactors for the roof over my head.'

'Seen many clan houses, have ye?' Tombs says. 'Them folk can't abide enclosure. They want to see the stars.'

My wife has said this to me many times, that she fears the karpennooyouhener houses and the dead air within. No, these people never asked for rooves nor walls. I think of that time in York Town with the muzzle of Henry Barrett's firing piece poking in the small of my back.

'Didn't I hear Garrett was made to stand trial over his connivance with the bushrangers?' Griffiths says.

'Acquitted for lack of proof,' Kelly says. 'It was the same with that sheep rustler Peter Mills.'

All this is news to me. I never heard a word of it in Hobart Town, but then I never thought to ask. If Garrett has gotten himself into hot water with the powers-that-be, then perhaps it mightn't be the best place for Daisy after all? It's gone a year she's been at Norfolk Plains living under the Garretts' roof. I told Moe it was because the Garretts were childless and would treat the child as they would their own, but how do I know? Its mother a native and its father a man of small reckoning, might not the child be considered a chattel? Moe could not fathom my reasoning. I told her the girl would be brought up in genteel ways and would find a good marriage, but Moe cared nothing for that. All she could see was me taking the child away, and it was all she could talk about when we were together again last winter. I told her to think about the littluns instead. *Will you send these to Norfolk Plains too?* she said, and I replied *Only if the missus should desire it.* Moe didn't like that nor anything else I might have said.

◆

MY HEART is sore, my thoughts adrift. Daisy in Norfolk Plains, Moe and the littluns on Longtartennerner, myself God only knows where. I must have the money for Nichols and then I shall find my peace. *Neither a borrower nor a lender be,* as mam would have said. This sum, this seventeen pounds – *is it a tool, meat or an item of clothing?* That was Moe, straining to understand. No, just marks on a tally or words I'll never learn how to read. Tom Stepney dead, Joseph Halfpenny too. *And where is she, this phantom missus?* So said Henry Barrett. My God, I left her with Brown.

We find ourselves at the mouth of an unknown harbour ringed by great snowy mountains. A lone rock stands at the entrance to this harbour like a shark tooth carved from stone. Entering the harbour, we approach a forbidding wall of cliffs that we soon realise are breaksea islands and not connected to the main. As we get around, we see that the out-facing shores are rocky and barren whereas those facing the inlet are lush with greenery. Kelly steers around and we haul up at the mouth of a river. The mountainside is barren aside from some clumps of grass on the lower slopes and there is a curious stillness in the air. The mountaintop is not snowbound as I first imagined but clad in bare white rock.

Kelly writes in his log while the rest of us make camp. He tells us he's named the harbour Port Davey after the Lieutenant-Governor and the river after Lord Bathurst. Such names mean little to me but each one is worth a huzzah and a tot of rum. We commence hunting the wild fowl so numerous in these waters. The shallows throng with black swans which go down in a flurry of feathers. We wring the necks of some and keep others alive to see us on our passage. For this purpose we have a number of baskets and henceforth we are accompanied by the din of piteous honking.

Jones is the best draughtsman among us and Kelly puts him to work sketching the extent of the harbour. Making our way upstream, we find plenty of Huon Pine and other boatbuilding timber. We determine that the Bathurst is no river but a wide channel leading to a massive body of water. At the southern outlet are a number of small islands wooded with celery-top pine, and in every direction lie thickly forested mountain ranges. I have seen my share of lonely places and this is the loneliest of them all.

'I reckon all the ships in the navy could stand safely in this harbour,' Kelly says.

'Aye, but why would they want to?' Tombs says. 'If this ain't the world's arse-end, I'd like to know what is.'

Here it is, not the world's arse-end but the point of turning back. Like the hands of a clock ticking their way around, there is only so far I can travel outward before I must begin my dutiful return. If Van Diemen's Land were a clockface then Longtartennerner would stand at one o'clock and Port Davey at seven.

Thus I commence my return.

◆

THE SEA is in my blood and yet I have observed a zeal in James Kelly that drives him further than others would dare to try. It is not a matter of fame or riches. He must at all times be the first, the strongest and the best. I remember the day I first laid eyes on him on the Sydney dock in '04. Kable took on a number of boys that season and for the most part they were timid creatures afeared of being shorn from their mother's breast. Not James Kelly, for even at twelve he had the shape of a man. One of Kable's sloops whisked him away to Hobart Town and next time I saw him he'd just returned from a voyage to Fiji in pursuit of sandalwood. Even when telling of sailors eaten by cannibals, the smile never left his face.

The seas of Bass Strait might be treacherous but their trickery is nothing compared with this hellscape of jagged reefs, windswept bays and dangerous riptides. Titanic waves dash themselves upon the shore, throwing up immense drifts of spray, and nothing like a safe harbour appears all morn. Many a sailor would quake in his boots at such a sight but not James Kelly.

In the afternoon we finally chance upon a place of refuge on a low grassy island and even our captain can see the sense in landing. We are unloading in a rocky cove when Griffiths spots a pair of clansmen not more than a stone's throw away. They brandish their spears but I do not think they will loose a volley unprovoked.

'See if you can set their minds at ease, Baggs,' Kelly says.

'We'll be right behind ye,' Tombs says. 'A fair ways behind.'

I take a dead swan under each arm and pick my way along the rocks. The men smile at the sight of such gifts, speaking in their language and pointing to a beach on the mainland. I try to tell them the sea is very rough and the waves fierce. I give them the swans and attempt to explain that we mean no harm. They seem reassured by this. The men would have me come with them and I say I cannot oblige but I thank them kindly all the same. The men seem to accept this and we part on good terms.

'The rest of their clan must be camped over yonder,' I say to Kelly and the others, indicating to the beach across the water. 'I reckon they've invited us to dinner.'

'You've a knack for inspiring their trust,' Kelly says.

'Not pointing a musket at them's a good place to start,' I say. 'No different from an Englishman, start waving your knife and he'll show you the glint of his.'

'What if they come back in the night and slay us in our sleep?' Griffiths asks.

'They don't go around ambushing folk after dark. They leave that to the English.'

Cosy and snug by the fire, even Griffiths loses any fear he had. 'Tombs, I want to hear more about your run-in with Michael Howe. Did you not say the reprobate fired upon you at New Norfolk?'

Tombs spits. 'It were a bad business and one I lay at the feet of Governor Macquarie and his stinkin' amnesty. Howe and Whitehead were cock-a-hoop thinkin' they had time for pursuin' their spree. They set the district constable's farm ablaze and the man found a note sayin' "For injustices we begin and the next is death to you all." I was at New Norfolk when I heard McCarty was gettin' a party together. I'm nowhere near daft enough to sign up for such a venture but suddenly it became a condition of me employment. Some of the men had fowling pieces but all I had were a pair o' pistols. Howe's gang were said to be camped near Triffit's so of course the fools went blundering in. It were a bloodbath. Carlisle were shot up so badly he croaked within the hour, Jemott caught a ball in the leg and O'Birne one in the neck. Murphy lay gutshot cryin' "for God's sake don't use me ill for I am a dead man already." Whitehead went up to Murphy with the aim of finishin' him off except Howe wouldn't allow it. The gang cleared out and McCarty sent up a barrow for the dead.'

'And Thomas Tombs never fired a single shot, did he?' Griffiths says.

'No, he never.'

'Whitehead got his just desserts though,' Griffiths says. 'Was it you who did him in?'

'It was not and nor was I there precisely.'

'Laying low again?'

'The miscreants were after revenge on McCarty, but when they besieged his house they came upon a party of the 46th Regiment. Whitehead was shot clean through and Howe took off his head so no one could claim the bounty. Din't stop the redcoats stringin' Whitehead up in the Hobart Town gibbets, what was left o' him. Been there six month and lookin' prettier than he ever did.'

'And where were you precisely?'

'Let's just say I was in the district.'

'The aptly-named Thomas Tombs,' Griffiths says. 'Always at graveside but never in the grave.'

I could say the same for myself. More dead men than living have I known, my nights besieged by the former. Latterly it has been Joseph Halfpenny spoiling my rest, pleading that he never meant nothing taking Daisy like he did. *Is it finished?* Brown says and I tell him nothing is ever finished, especially not this.

◆

IT IS days before we see clansmen again. One morning we catch a whiff of smoke, and before we know it the coast we are passing is afire, black plumes drifting inland on the breeze. The smoke is so thick that we cannot see anything beyond the channel leading into what appears to be a vast harbour to rival Port Davey. And we can hear the cries of clansmen at their hunt. Coughing and hacking, we make hard work of rowing against the current, the hidden sun beating down upon us. I have seen a man speared and it left an injury no less grievous that a musket ball.

When we clear the heads, the smoke thins and we find ourselves on an immense sheet of water. Never have I seen such a gloomy sight, a nightshade world of tannin-dark waves and stunted vegetation. Kelly steers us toward a wooded isle and we haul up in a rocky cove. Hundreds of swans nest nearby, but there is no sign of clansmen. Kelly writes in his log while the rest make camp. When the smoke lifts further we find we can see right across the harbour. Stands of Huon Pine grow on the silent banks but otherwise it is a hostile and arid landscape. Something about this place inspires not awe, as Port Davey did, but a sinking horror.

'Two rivers and perhaps a third,' Kelly says, his eye to the spyglass. 'One south of us and the other sou'east. It is an excellent harbour and one befitting of being named after Governor Macquarie.'

What Kelly's eyes see is not the same as mine. Where I see terror, he sees opportunity.

'And the island?' Griffiths says.

'The island I shall name after Mr Birch's wife, Sarah.'

She will never see it, Mrs Birch, and good that she does not for she would hardly consider it a fitting testament. Nor is the Governor likely to visit the sinister harbour Kelly would honour with his name. Perhaps Macquarie's supposed talent for governing is no more than the liberal application of names.

The afternoon is spent exploring the eastern reaches, beyond which lies even more inhospitable terrain. Kelly names the southern inlet after Mr Birch but the southeast river proves the true leviathan. This Kelly names after James Gordon, the man who lent him *Elizabeth*, and it is a fine and fast flowing river with stands of Huon Pine growing on its banks. I can well imagine the saws of the woodcutters who will come here, and their camps. And we are their advance guard, ticket-of-leaver William Jones their map-maker and guide.

After dinner, Kelly tells us of how he came to be wrecked on a far-off island which is also named after Governor Macquarie:

'I was nineteen when Captain Siddons made me Chief Officer of the *Campbell Macquarie* and a fine boat she was. We took two thousand skins on Kangaroo Island but the real prize lay eight hundred miles sou'east of Hobart Town.'

'And that would be Macquarie Island?' I say.

'Aye. It was June and fearful cold when we caught sight of land, snow on the ground and drifts on the mountains. Our ship struck a reef and started to break up in the surf, but somehow we got ashore. We were obliged to build huts, the walls of which we covered in the skins of the sea elephants we slew night and day. Blubber to light our lamps and fuel our fires. We had plenty to eat, even a wild cabbage for the scurvy.'

'We'll be wantin' a cabbage soon enough,' Tombs says.

'We were all winter thinking we'd never see spring,' Kelly says, 'but then we were picked up by *Perseverance*. A month later we were windbound in Broken Bay when I got it into my head to trek overland to Sydney. That's how I came to be the first to inform Underwood of the fate which had befallen *Campbell Macquarie*. I had my reasons for not putting my name forward for sailing to its rescue, however.'

'Such as marrying my sister,' Griffiths says.

'Elizabeth is a fine woman, John, but no woman could keep me in port long, not with the prospect of captaincy in the offing.'

'And so ye took yer brother-in-law along?' Tombs says. 'Daft bugger that he is.'

'Aboard *The Brothers*, aye. There was a great rush for any supply of seals that could be found. Macquarie Island was one such place, as were the isles of Dusky Sound, but it was not my intention to venture so far afield. I thought to try Bass Strait once more. It proved a mistake.'

'From memory, twelve skins we took at the Stacks and only three at King Island,' Griffiths says.

'Three at King Island?' I say. 'My old captain Rook beat you to them all.'

'A pitiful harvest and one ill-fitting of my first command,' Kelly says. 'We took seven hundred skins at Western Port but the real bounty was at Seal Rocks off Philip Island. No matter how many seals we slew, next day there were hundreds more. By the time we were satisfied we'd taken more than seven thousand skins.'

'Won't be seven thousand there next time,' I say.

'But enough of this,' Kelly says. 'Mr Birch will be pleased to hear of our endeavours, as no doubt will Messrs Gordon and Lord.'

'It's a miracle Edward Lord still has a head on his shoulders,' Tombs says. 'Only in Van Diemen's Land could such a cur as he make good.'

'You speak of his alleged connivance with Michael Howe?' Kelly says.

'Nothin' alleged about it,' Tombs says. 'It is a club they are in together, bushranger and magistrate.'

'Such rumours aside,' Kelly says, 'the landed gentlemen are certainly in league in terms of their trading endeavours. Davey pays Lord twelve shillings a bushel of wheat when the price Sydney pays is only ten. Then there's the business of Lieutenant Jeffreys and the *Kangaroo*. Macquarie sent him from Sydney expecting him back in two months and the man took six. And what was he doing? Landing spirits right under Davey's nose. Meanwhile Gordon demanded payment for percentages on spirits landed while he was Naval Officer, a sum totalling more than three hundred pounds. Now Davey finds himself obliged to levy a higher impost on spirits to replenish the much-depleted Police Fund. At this rate the church and gaol will never be built. If there's an honest man in Van Diemen's Land, you'll find him face down with a knife in his back. No, the roguery which has been carried on in this place is beyond all calculation.'

◆

NORTH OF Macquarie Harbour lies an immense white sand beach and if there is a longer stretch in Van Diemen's Land I have not seen it. We run full sail through a tunnel of wind and wave alongside this neverending beach, praying that Kelly can steer us true. It is in these moments on the precipice of life and death that the trappings of everyday existence are shorn away. I put my life in Kelly's hands, but for all his risk-taking the man has uncanny luck and the rest of us are only riding on his coattails.

By dusk we have been running nor'west the whole day, rising and falling amid forty-foot waves, and still Kelly does not seek shelter. With no safe cove on offer, he finally steers us coastward in the vicinity of a rivermouth where we are very nearly wrecked on the sandbar. He thinks nothing of it, our captain with the soul of a gambler. Waves crash over the side and we are set to baling with the buckets fastened to the thwarts while Kelly steers us into deeper water. He orders that the boat be heaved-to, which we do by setting the jib against the mainsail and making a raft of the oars lashed with rope. Thus the boat is made to stand. The only dry thing is the ammunition in Kelly's watertight box along with his precious journal.

'Sing us a song, fellows,' Tombs says when Kelly is done writing. 'I don't think I can sleep a wink.'

'Griffiths and I heard a new ditty when we were last in port,' Kelly says.

'You mean the one about the sailors of the *Active*?' Griffiths says.

'Aye, the Davy Lowston song.'

Kelly and Griffiths sing and the rest of us join in where we can:

My name is Davy Lowston, I did seal, I did seal,
My name is Davy Lowston, I did seal,
Though my men and I were lost,
Though our very lives 'twould cost,
We did seal, we did seal, we did seal.

'twas in eighteen hundred and ten, we set sail, we set sail,
'twas in eighteen hundred and ten, we set sail,
We were left we gallant men,
Never more to sail again,
For to seal, for to seal, for to seal.

*We were set down in Open Bay, were set down, were
    set down,*
We were set down in Open Bay, were set down,
Upon the sixteenth day,
Of Februar-aye-ay,
For to seal, for to seal, for to seal.

Our Captain John Bader, he set sail, he set sail,
Our Captain John Bader, he set sail,
I'll return men without fail,
But she foundered in a gale,
And went down, and went down, and went down.

We cured ten thousand skins, for the fur, for the fur,
Yes we cured ten thousand skins for the fur,
Brackish water, putrid seal,
We did all of us fall ill,
For to die, for to die, for to die.

Come all you lads who sail upon the sea, upon the sea,
Come all you jacks who sail upon the sea,
Though the schooner Governor Bligh
Took on some who did not die,
Never seal, never seal, never seal.

'Bader's dead?' I say when they are done. 'I did not know.'

'Dead and gone. Those men were stranded three years and I could've been one of them,' Kelly says. 'I sailed under Captain Grono on *Governor Bligh* and we took ten thousand skins at Foveaux Strait. Those *Active* sealers were set down the following year.'

'Could've been me as well,' I say. 'I was supposed to go aboard *Active* at Kents Bay, except that three of us absconded so as not to pay our debts. That could have been me stranded with Davy Lowston or maybe drowned with Bader.'

Another thought occurs: *maybe Tom Stepney would've drowned too.* Could it be that the boy would have met his death either way? I wonder whether Jimmy Brown has heard the Davy Lowston song and if so whether it gladdens his heart? All these years I thought it a mistake not to have gone with Bader and now I discover that the man is dead and *Active* lost. I can still picture it standing proud at Kents that fateful day.

'I never figured you for an absconder, Baggs,' Kelly says. 'You've kept this card close to your chest. I wonder what other cards you've been holding?'

I have spoken out of turn in thinking myself absolved for Tom Stepney's death and now I must make amends. 'It is my intention to repay Isaac Nichols the debt I owe, but it is a matter of seventeen pounds,' I say.

'Seventeen pounds might seem a fortune to you but it is a pittance to Nichols,' Kelly says. 'I think you'll find he can afford to be generous.'

'Then I shall appeal to him,' I say. 'I've been as good as vanished for years.'

'Ye wouldn't be the first to've upped and vanished,' Tombs says. 'Weren't all ye sealing men supposed to be workin' for George Bass by now? It were him asked Governor King for a monopoly over the waters of New Zealand. Then he sailed off in *Venus* never to be seen again. Grand plans had George Bass and what is he now? Food for fishes.'

My plans are not so grand. Too long I have lived the life of an outcast, but perhaps it is a curse upon my head for the debt I owe. Should Nichols forgive it as Kelly has convinced me he might, then I would truly be free. Perhaps six pounds might be enough to make him forgive the rest? But there is my mam nagging me to pay back every penny. I'd have to go right way round Van Diemen's Land again in pursuit of such a sum.

During the night, we take our turns at the steering-oar ensuring that the whaleboat does not turn to windward, and otherwise we try to find what sleep might be had. In my dream I find myself twelve years old and mudlarking on the Thames again. Thousands of ships crowd around London Bridge, some waiting months to unload their cargo, and boys like me pilfer what we can in the hope of a crust of bread. The smallest boys are given the filthiest jobs scouring the mud for lost coins or trinkets. Then I am beside Tom Stepney and this time it is I the wave crashes over and he who stands in judgement.

Do not think I shall absolve you yet.

◆

AT FIRST light we ready the boat and make good running with a sou'easter at our backs. By midday we have reached Cape Grim, the north-western tip of Van Diemen's Land. If Port Davey was seven o'clock, then Cape Grim is closer to ten. There is still the length of Bass Strait to navigate between us and Longtartennerner, however.

'Those islands are called the Doughboys on account of their shape,' Kelly says.

'Just hearin' the word makes me hunger for bread,' Tombs says. 'A whole fresh loaf to meself.'

Kelly steers us between the islands, low cliffs forestalling any thought of a landing. As we pass between the rocks, a strong riptide sucks at us and waves slop over the side.

'Fried dumplings dipped in sugar,' Tombs says. 'Glazed ham hocks and green cabbage.'

We pass a low rocky island known as the Trefoil and by mid-afternoon we haul up on a pebbly beach in the Hunter Isles. We go about collecting firewood, managing to scavenge a few miserable boughs from the windswept shore. We have just got the fire going when we realise we are being studied by dozens of clansmen armed with spears and waddies. We scramble for our muskets knowing them likely useless from the wet. We level them at our foes, hoping for the best.

The warriors are closing in when they stop and burst out laughing. They jeer, pretending to ready their spears for throwing and clapping each other on the back. They make a show of putting down their spears and waddies, raising their hands. They speak a language I do not understand but plainly they wish for us to put down our weapons. I place my musket on the ground and the others begin to do likewise. Two of the clansmen appear to be leaders, one around thirty and powerfully built and the other older and slighter. Both are scarified and painted in red from the waist up.

'I think the younger is the bunganna, the chief,' I say. 'Look how he commands them. The other's a cleverman.' I know something of this from my time spent with Moe's father, Laman. The chief orders his warriors to take up sitting positions by the fire and the cleverman commences a song and dance. The cleverman contorts his body and pulls horrible faces, but whether to amuse or intimidate I cannot say. He is hunter and hunted, friend and foe. From what I understand it is a story filled with ghouls and spirits, a shadow-play of dark deeds. The cleverman falls down theatrically and jumps up again with his eyes bulging and his tongue sticking out. He circles toward us, malice written across his face, and he stops to direct his fury before me.

We watch until Tombs cries out that the warriors are gathering stones to hurl at us. Sure enough, they are collecting pebbles between their toes.

'Baggs, go grab a pair of swans and be quick about it!' Kelly says.

I hurry back to the whaleboat and take a dead swan under each arm. As I make my way back, the chief comes up to me. As I go to hand him the swans, he pushes me down to the stones where I bang my knee. The chief says something to his men and they commence pelting us in time to his cry of 'Yah! Yah! Yah!' One stone hits me on the point of the elbow just as I am bending down to rub my knee. I hear a pistol crack and another and then the clansmen are in flight. Kelly stands among them, a pistol in each hand, firing a third and a fourth time. It is a general retreat except for the cleverman who lays flat on his back near the fire. We go to examine him and he jumps up just like he did in his dance. We recoil in fright. The cleverman walks a few steps, glances back and dashes off into the scrub. We hear the cries of women from beyond the rise.

'Let's get out of here,' Tombs says. 'This old musket's wet through.'

'This one as well,' Griffiths says.

'Agreed,' Kelly says.

We heave the whaleboat down to the water and row for all our worth. My elbow stings with every jar. Kelly steers us into a cove on a nearby islet swarming with seabirds. Our bellies growl for we have not eaten all day and we eye the birds' nests hungrily. Jones and Tombs go ashore with buckets and return promptly with a haul of eggs. We can see the clanswomen coming down to the point of the larger isle to hurl abuse across the water. Though the words are unintelligible, their opinion on our conduct is plain for they rant and rave and shake their fists.

Never darken these shores again.

We cast off and Kelly steers us nor'east in the direction of an isle further removed. Though none will admit to it, we are shaken by the morning's events. This island abounds with birds and penguins but there is precious little fuel for our fire. Finally we get a fire started in the tussock and we boil up a vast quantity of eggs.

'Will those clansmen come after us, Baggs?' Kelly says.

'I didn't see if they had any canoes.'

'Then let us pray they do not come.'

'I can't make out why the chief charged me when he saw those swans.'

'I imagine he thought they were his swans ye'd thieved,' Tombs says. 'Ye can't give back what ain't yers to give.'

◆

BY NOW we are three weeks between ports and much dishevelled for it. The unruly state of Tombs' beard marks him as a saint or madman and even Kelly has abandoned his attempts at shaving. We are running low on every provision and there is the stench of something rotting in the whaleboat.

Kelly guides us into Robbins Passage and all the while we are on the lookout for hostile clansmen. Robbins Island is named after the same Lieutenant Robbins who flew the Union Jack upside down on King Island all those years ago. He later went down with all hands aboard the *Integrity*. I can still see his face turning red at the taunts of a cheeky boy. Another of Tombs' vanished men is Charles Robbins.

By midday the breeze has swung around and we make heavy work of leaving the passage behind. We are hours getting through the passage before Kelly finally lands us on a sandy beach to the west of Circular Head, a massive round rock that looks to be have dropped from the sky. It is a perfect natural fort and yet there are no fires up there nor other signs of life. Ducks and geese abound in the bay and our hunger goes in advance of any common sense. We fire among them freely, not caring who we might disturb.

That evening we gorge ourselves on roasted fowl. 'How many articles of refreshment remain, Mr Kelly?' Tombs says. 'Enough to see us through our voyage?'

'Not at the rate you lot drink it,' Kelly says, 'although we may chance upon a cache ahead. Lieutenant Jeffreys landed a goodly shipment in Launceston but those marines are thirsty men.'

'Jeffreys is more privateer than His Majesty's,' Griffiths says. 'He lands more liquor than even the thirstiest marines could quaff in a given year.'

'Indeed. Macquarie called him a timid man and one ignorant of his duties.'

'Ignorant he may be, but timid never,' Tombs says.

We eat and drink and I grow weary of these men. I prefer Jones to all the rest and that is because the man seldom speaks. I have been so long away that I have lost the habit of talking freely among men.

'Ye say ye went to Macquarie Island a second time?' Tombs says when the night is well advanced.

'Aye, aboard *Mary and Sally*,' Kelly says. 'Griffiths and Jones sailed with me.'

'And were ye not afeared of another shipwreck?'

'Of course, but Macquarie Island is one of the only places where sea elephants might reliably be found.'

'A perilous journey just for a cask of oil. It must be miserable cold so far south.'

'There's a freezing rain even in summer. Snow, sleet and seas so heavy that many a sailor's face turned green. You were among the shore party, weren't you Jones? Tell Tombs and Baggs of it, if you will.'

'We didn't see any fur seals but a great many elephants and we slew them where they lay,' Jones says in a quiet voice. 'By the time we'd been there a fortnight we were swimming in oil. I'll never forget that stench.'

'A vicious gale set in and we had to leave the anchorage to ride out the storm,' Kelly says. 'When we contacted the shore party again, they'd killed most of the elephants. We were in desperate need of firewood and the only place where it might be obtained was the wreck of the *Campbell Macquarie*. Men were sent out to retrieve timber, but then we started running low on victuals and were obliged to go on short allowance for the return voyage. By the time we sighted port we were shipping water like you wouldn't believe.'

'Ye'd return to Macquarie Island a third time?' Tombs says.

'Only if I thought there were sufficient elephants to make it worthwhile,' Kelly says. 'It is to New Zealand I return next season with John at my side. You are most welcome to sail with us, Thomas.'

'Not bloody likely.'

'What about you, George?'

'No thank you, Mr Kelly.'

'Those clansmen have you spooked,' Griffiths says. 'You've the wrong attitude toward them, trying to converse with them as you do. The only thing they understand is in our musket fire.'

'The language of the musket they're learnin' to appreciate,' Tombs says, 'but let us pray they remain ignorant as to the means of its operation.'

We eat our meat and drink our rum and finally lay a'bed. Such men as these are a plague of locusts upon the earth and they will not rest until they have despoiled it entire. I look about us and see a trail of bones there strewn, imagining a day when the world is all bone and no meat.

◆

FINALLY WE arrive at what passes for the settled districts of the north. When we reach the entrance to the Tamar, the pilot has us go to George Town and give an account of ourselves to Major Stewart of the 46th Regiment. It is years since Governor Macquarie put those boards up proclaiming George Town and yet the bulk of the settlers are still forty miles upriver. The Governor is a man accustomed to getting his way, but Van Diemen's Land has a way of making you bend to it. We find George Town no more than a handful of huts on the muddy bank. When we land, musket-wielding men dressed in skins rush out to accost us. The only man more formally dressed is toting a double-barrelled gun. 'Have you firearms in the boat?' he says.

'Of course,' Kelly says.

'Sergeant, disarm and handcuff these men.'

'Certainly, Major.' One of the men approaches the boat and we pass him our muskets. He handcuffs us in twos and I find myself paired with Tombs on the muddy beach.

'Now my lads, what have you to say for yourselves?' the Major says. 'You are accomplices of Michael Howe and if you do not tell me where he is I shall have you sent to Hobart Town in double irons.'

'We aren't bushrangers,' Kelly says. 'We're in the employ of Mr Birch of Hobart Town.'

'I'm afraid that story won't do for me. Six weeks I've been hunting that scoundrel Howe and I won't have him slip through my fingers.'

'You are Major Stewart of the 46th Regiment?' Kelly says, reaching into his pocket. 'I can have this cleared up in a trice.'

'Sergeant, he's reaching for his weapon!'

The sergeant grabs Kelly by the arm and Kelly shows him the key in his hand. 'This is the key to the ammunition box. You'll find our port clearance there.'

The sergeant takes the key while the others keep their muskets trained. A chill wind blows across the bay. The sergeant unlocks the box and retrieves the necessary paperwork.

The Major reads aloud:

*'This is to certify to all whom it may concern, that
the boat* Elizabeth, *commanded by Mr James Kelly,
was cleared out for the West Coast of Van Diemen's
Land, on a voyage of discovery, after having paid
the accustomed dues. Given under my hand this
11th day of December 1815 – in the absence of the
Lieutenant-Governor, William Nairn, Captain,
46th Regiment, Commandant.'*

'Why was the Lieutenant-Governor not called upon to sign this?' the Major says.

'I believe he was incapacitated,' Kelly says. 'That is not an unusual occurrence, I might add.'

'James Kelly, is it? I believe we've had the pleasure of dining at Tom Birch's.'

'That's right, with the Reverend Knopwood.'

'Then you have my sincere apologies. How long out of Hobart Town are you?'

'Upwards of a month and we're in need of a great many provisions.'

'I'll have you issued with fresh slops immediately. Have you seen any military parties in the course of your voyage?'

'No, we haven't seen a single Englishman until your pilot.'

'Is it normal for port clearances of this nature to be granted at Hobart Town?'

'It is. We are searching for fine timber, especially the Huon pine, and have made several such discoveries along the way.'

'Splendid. Sergeant, you can remove the handcuffs.'

The sergeant frees us from our restraints and our muskets are returned to our possession.

'I am very sorry for the inconvenience,' the Major says. 'The Governor asks for this place to be improved and yet we find ourselves critically short of labour. We are but a handful of men to defend ourselves against Howe's depredations and there is dim prospect of getting a message through as the malefactor has a stranglehold upon the interior.'

'I'm sorry to hear it, Major. Do we have your permission to continue up to Launceston and draw upon the King's Stores?'

'I would have you take a knife and fork in my quarters, but as you can see we possess only rude dwellings here at George Town. Yes, I will issue you a ticket to give to the acting commissary at Launceston. He will issue each of you a blanket, a fresh set of slops and all the fresh provisions you should require.'

'Thank you, Major. I will write out a draft on Hobart Town for the full amount.'

'I shall account for all expenses incurred. And now I must bid you farewell.'

The Major and his men commence slopping through the muck back to their huts.

◆

IT IS long past nightfall when we finally reach Launceston. We anchor by moonlight before stumbling toward the barracks and the raucous hubbub emanating from within. Kelly thrusts our paperwork at the nearest soldier and we are swiftly admitted. The room is dim and smoky but we have come in time for a late supper. We commence loading our plates with beef and pork and bread.

'And who might you rascals be?' a soldier says. 'Scoffin' our meat and guzzlin' our grog!'

'We brought our own grog and have plenty to share,' Kelly says, handing the man a bottle.

'That's different then. To the King's health!' the soldier says, raising the bottle high.

'To the King!'

Kelly and Griffiths go off in search of the commissary while the rest of us commence drinking. No one gives a thought to Howe and his ilk and the watch is lax. The soldiers seem to be celebrating something in particular and we ask them what it is.

'Why, the armies of Napoleon are defeated,' another soldier informs us. 'The Duke of Wellington routed him at Waterloo. They say the war is won!'

A great roar goes up among the soldiery and we find ourselves cheering too. The soldiers show us an edition of *The London Gazette*. All I can make out is the newspaper's date: Thursday, June 12, 1815, which is nearly seven months ago.

'I believe this calls for further refreshment!' Tombs says.

Talk of the French reminds me of Pierre Faure, as it always does. It was he who told me of the Treaty of Amiens all those years ago. Now his nation is defeated and mine the victor but what business is it of ours? It would mean the world to me to speak with him again.

Amid the scenes of merriment, I see a familiar face in the corner of the room. He is a man about my age, dressed not in a soldier's coat but in a grimy tunic with holes at the elbows. His hair is lank and his manner forlorn but it is the harbourmaster Peter Mills all the same. I go to him bottle in hand.

'How long has it been, George?' he says, refilling his mug from my bottle.

'I heard you'd been arrested and yet here you sit amidst the soldiery.'

'It is a tale of unremitting woe although I daresay you are apprised of it already.'

'Sheep stealing, was it?'

'I am brought low by rumours unfounded and malicious and I find myself removed from my positions as a consequence. That cur Garrett has much to answer for.'

'And yet Governor Macquarie is said to hold Garrett in contempt also.'

'Those vipers had the temerity to label me a bushranger. Preposterous! If I am a bushranger then why, pray tell, did I surrender myself to the Guard House? Even Howe has fallen for this rot, boasting he would break me out if only I were worth the trouble. In fact I had no need of his assistance, my dear wife Jennifer providing more than amply.'

'They say you were discovered in a stable hiding in a bed of straw.'

'That part is accurate, I'm afraid. Justice was served at my trial, however. Major Stewart neglected to send up the incriminating documents and I was thusly acquitted. Between you and I, Baggs, this was no mere oversight, for The Major and I are on splendid terms. He even volunteered to intercede with the Governor on my behalf, for which purpose I am penning a missive.'

'And what will you ask?'

Mill leans closer. 'There will be a settlement at George Town requiring a naval officer and storekeeper. I have three children to consider and I find myself financially embarrassed. The Governor cannot but accede to my entreaties.'

'I wish you all the best, Peter. What news have you of your accuser Garrett?'

'He too is acquitted, the Judas.'

'Is he up in Sydney? I am given to understand his wife is at Norfolk Plains.'

'Bridget is indeed at Norfolk Plains, each night drinking herself into a stupor. What business is it of yours?'

'My girl Daisy has been with them the past year. If only I had some news of her.'

'Ah yes, young Daisy Garrett. The girl is but a sprite but I gather Bridget puts her to work. I did not know it was a child of your issue, Baggs.'

'Surely you have not forgotten my wife Moe? I once brought her up here, as you'll no doubt remember.'

'I recall your native woman but I must confess to scant recollection of the child.'

'She was a bairn then and nameless besides, but I assure you it is the very same child. You say you've seen her?'

'I saw the child some months back and she was the picture of good health. The same cannot be said for her mistress, however. Bridget remains in no small state of distress on account of her husband's ill-doings. This I know for Jennifer has oftentimes been called upon to act as her interlocutor. I am given to understand that, for all her husband's wealth, Bridget is a bitter woman.'

'I never ought to have left Daisy with her. I would have thought twice had I known of Garrett's woes. There's a road through to Norfolk Plains?'

'It is but a rough track and you would not return inside three days at the earliest. Surely your captain will not wait as long as that?'

'I very much doubt he would. I would be in breach of my contract and obliged to forego any payment. But you say the child is well?'

'The child is safer with Bridget Garrett than gallivanting with her rogue of a father. I will look in on her when I am able.'

'You give your word, Peter?'

'Yes, I give it freely.'

I pour us another drink. 'Then let us celebrate threefold. To my Daisy, to your rehabilitation in the eyes of Governor Macquarie, and to the King!'

◆

IN THE morning we rise worse for wear amid the soldiers in their disorderly barracks, the revelry having long continued into the night. After breakfast, the acting commissary issues each of us a suit of slops to replace our filth-ridden garments, but the only bath on offer is down by the jetty. Tombs will not consent to bathing despite Griffiths' taunts that he stinks worse than one of his hunting dogs. The old ranger sits impassive on the wharf smoking a clay pipe while the rest of us freeze. Once we are shaved and dressed, the whaleboat is loaded with enough flour, tea, sugar, beef, pork and spirits to see us through to Hobart Town. We are thankful for the ebb tide but even so it is mid-afternoon before we are able to furnish the pilot at Low Head with his wretched port clearance. Then it is eastward ho.

Two days later, an hour before sunset, we see smoke rising on the shore ahead. 'Clansmen, but whether friend or foe I cannot tell,' Kelly says, his eye to the spyglass. 'Baggs?'

He passes me the spyglass and I observe a band of ten or more walking on the beach. 'I can't be certain who they are.'

'Then we shall make camp on Waterhouse Island and leave such parley for the morn.'

We haul up on a beach on the protected side of Waterhouse. A few miserable trees stand in defiance of the wind but the vegetation is low and sparse. A clear night is in the offing and the stars make their welcome return. If it is clear in the morning, I will be able to see the curve of Cape Portland and Moe's father's country, Tebrakunna. And if my eyes were as sharp as they once were, I would be able to see Longtartennerner and the blue hills of Cape Barren.

At dinner, Griffiths asks me how one might obtain a clanwife without resorting to kidnapping, which has become an all-too-common practice.

'The clans make alliances just like the English, but first you must show them that you mean no harm,' I say. 'Never carry a musket and if you must then for God's sake never fire it.'

'But then you are defenceless against their spears.'

'Your best defence is their goodwill, John. They're often-times twenty to your one. They'll kill a man if given sufficient reason.'

'And what do they consider sufficient reason?'

'They don't take kindly to us hunting game they consider to be theirs, and they don't like finding huts at places they want to camp. Meanwhile, Government grants the settlers land and furnishes them with convicts to toil upon it. The clans find themselves forced into competition with their neighbours because of the land taken from them.'

'I do not believe they have such notions of ownership,' Griffiths says. 'To their way of thinking, one place is as good as another.'

'Not true,' I say. 'They are no less civilised than ourselves but the problem is we fail to comprehend their outrage. Take that fellow killed at Grindstone Bay. Five men go out in a whaleboat to the Schoutens. They take a great quantity of swans as well as kangaroos and sealskins. Four go back a second time, leaving one behind at Grindstone Bay with a few dogs and hundreds of skins. When the others return, they find their fellow slain and the skins taken. One of the dogs has been killed and the others are missing. Isn't it obvious why the man was slain?'

'The clansmen wanted the skins and they had that unlucky gentleman outnumbered,' Griffiths says.

'No, I'll wager he set the dogs to barking and fired his musket.'

'It sounds as though you're condoning what can only be described as murder.'

'You wanted to know how a man goes about obtaining a wife, John. There's a right way and a wrong way. The wrong way is getting together a party of six or seven muskets and catching a clan unawares.'

'Tom Davey might be an old sot but even he can see the folly in that,' Kelly says. 'Said it ignominiously stains the honour of his country.'

'And the correct way is?' Griffiths says.

'The clans are often desirous of seal meat and they're partial to the dogs employed by Tombs and others of his ilk,' I say.

'So you give them dogs and they give you a wife?' Griffiths says.

'The island women have a word for themselves, Tyereelore,' I say. 'I don't believe these women consider themselves property of the sealers even though many are ill-used as such. I know of men who tie up their women and flog them for failing to procure sufficient skins. People want to know why the Oyster Bay clan slew that fellow at Grindstone and here's your answer. That clan has had the most exposure to our ways, ways which even Tom Davey saw fit to admonish. Each year the settlers move further into clan lands, and they come with their sheep and their stockkeepers and their muskets. Soon every clan in Van Diemen's Land will learn to despise us.'

◆

THAT NIGHT my dreams are filled with ghosts and visions of the departed. In my confusion I go to the graveyard to look upon the headstones and I do not fail to recognise my own name. When I wake the morn is clear and I can see that we have arrived in my wife's homeland. We spot several fires throughout the morning's sail and at midday we haul up at the beach just short of Cape Portland. We are only a few miles away from the place Brown and I first landed on these shores back in '09, on the far side of the cape.

'What do they call this place?' Kelly asks me.

'The river they call Ringarooma and the country Tebrakunna,' I say. 'It is my wife's country.'

There they are, a dozen or more huntsmen coming down to meet us. I recognise Chief Laman, Moe's father, from his grey beard and the red paint adorning him. 'Laman Bunganna,' I say. 'It's good to see you again.'

Laman comes forward grinning. 'Yah peulinghenar, Baggs. Kannowner lillerclapperlar?'

'Lillerclapperlar, a fine whaleboat. And these are free men, not prisoners.'

'Kartummeter partroller Longtartennerner.'

I turn to Kelly. 'He says he sees my wife's signal fires every day over on Longtartennerner, Clarke Island.'

'Ask him if he's seen Michael Howe,' Kelly says.

'Laman, have you seen the bushranger – perringye – Michael Howe?'

Laman frowns. 'No perringye. Baggs larngerner Tolo Bunganna. Partrollarne Tolo.'

'Tolo Bunganna? Isn't he your brother?'

'What does he want?' Kelly says.

'I think he wants us to fight his brother Tolo, a neighbouring chief,' I say. To Laman I say: 'Larngerner Tolo Bunganna? Where is he?'

'Tolo Tangumronener.'

'Tangumronener, the Eddystone?'

'Tangumronener, Eddystone.' He speaks so fast I can barely follow, but I pick up the words parkutetennar and partrollarne.

'Soldiers firing muskets? Surely you mean bushrangers, not soldiers. There's no settlement near there.'

'Soldier, bushranger, kartummeter karpennooyouhener.'

'It might be Howe and his gang,' Kelly says.

'Kartummeter partrollarne lillerclapperlar?' Laman says.

'Plenty of muskets, but we don't plan on firing them unless we need to,' I say. 'No partrollarne.'

Laman's smile fades. 'Warrander larngerner kartummeter loonner, Baggs. Kartummeter loonner. Baggs partrollarne Tolo.'

'He's saying he always helped me before so now I have to help him fight Tolo.' To Laman: 'Howe lillerclapperlar? Does he have a whaleboat?'

'No lillerclapperlar, kartummeter partrollarne.'

'No whaleboat but plenty of firepower. We'll go get some straitsmen from the islands. We'll need more men if we're to fight Tolo. Kannowner pleengenner, kartummeter partrollarne Tolo Bunganna.'

Laman seems pleased. 'Lillerclapperlar larngerner pleengenner. Kartummeter partrollarne.'

'We'll go to the islands and return as soon as we can.'

Laman claps me on the shoulder, satisfied that our business is thus transacted. His warriors stand back and no one says a word until we are well clear. We would have to sail north from here to reach Longtartennerner and Cape Barren but it is to the east that Kelly steers us. The wind is favourable but the sky is dark with coming rain. Though they are hidden from us, I know that Laman's men will be watching. They might think us intent on clearing Swan Island before turning north and if so they would not be surprised to see us running along the coast. But what of tomorrow and the day after that, when Laman stands atop the highest hill and sees his daughter's fires? Perhaps he will think us shipwrecked. It is six years since Brown and I first landed here, dead men that day but for the goodwill of Laman and his people. Now I find myself poised to deceive him. How could I make him understand that his son-in-law is not truly kannowner, free man, but a servant to James Kelly? I should have told him that Chief Kelly has no desire to make war on Chief Tolo. I could have told him I must return to Hobart Town for the wages owed me. What would Laman think of that?

'You're brooding, Baggs,' Kelly says.

'I'm just thinking upon my future.'

'A dream of riches perhaps?'

'Not for me.'

'One requires a certain daring to have a chance of becoming rich,' Kelly says. 'Not all men possess such daring. I shall be rich or in my grave whereas men like yourself are content with considerably less.'

'Baggs dreams of his wife and not of riches,' Griffiths says. 'He owes his melancholy to their continued state of separation. Isn't it so?'

'It is, John.'

'And you grow especially heartsore on account of our comparative proximity?'

'I do, damn you.'

◆

WE ARRIVE at George Rocks two days later, an archipelago over which a million seabirds swirl. We haul up on a small beach on the western shore of the largest island, no more than a patch of green against the ocean blue. If the southwest corner of Van Diemen's Land has the foulest weather then the northeast has the fairest.

'Plenty of seals here,' Griffiths says. 'Look at them, not a care in the world.'

'I'll give 'em a care,' Tombs says.

We set to work, falling upon three bulls and their clapmatches. They are dozy and incurious and make no move toward flight. We raise our clubs and smash them down on whiskered snouts. Those seals that are still able begin to flop away but with pitiful slowness. These too are swiftly clubbed. We commence cutting with our knives, blood and gore running freely, the air filled with a putrid stench. Now there is a general alarm of barking, shrieking and a panicky stampede to water's edge. In their fright the seals try to bite or crush us, but we are all old hands and have felled their like before. One blood-soaked clapmatch tries to push past me but I bring the club down on her head and it cleaves in two like an apple. Pups mewl piteously nearby.

Once the killing is done, the butchery begins. We hack at the carcasses, rending them neck to flipper and sending forth fresh torrents of blood. Cutting our way through, we peel back the silky blubber, gutting the innards. We are soon surrounded by stinking offal, squabbling seabirds, and slimy fat slopping into the water. We turn the hides inside out and commence flensing to the birds' delight. Then we peg out the skins to dry. There are still hours left in the day so we repeat the dose and soon find we have taken thirty skins. It is not a patch on the old days but an honest labour nonetheless. We take four live pups which we give fresh water and put into a basket.

'What does a skin go for these days, Mr Kelly?' Tombs says. 'Enough for a bottle of Bengal?'

'You're all on wages, not the lay,' Kelly says.

'Aye, three pounds a month. I'll make me packet yet, will I?'

'It's a fair sight better than a hundredth lay,' I say. 'That's how I ended up owing as much as I did.'

'Perhaps there may even be a bonus from Mr Birch,' Kelly says.

'I won't go holdin' me breath,' Tombs says.

My wage will be dwarfed by Kelly's and his in turn will be dwarfed by the profit Birch will make, but on the other hand the Tyereelore work for nothing. I have observed that the higher a man finds himself in the scheme of things, the less of his toil he is obliged to spend. Six pounds is a sizeable down payment on the seventeen I owe Nichols and I would give every penny if it will release me from a life of skulking in the margins. Perhaps I ought to offer my services to Mr Birch as a woodcutter but I cannot face the thought of wintering on that hostile western coast. Besides, there will be men by the hatful clamouring for such work. Let them be the ones to drown out there in the inky darkness of Macquarie Harbour.

◆

BY THE third day at George Rocks, the seals are getting shy of coming up and we take just seven skins. The wind is a strong sou'easter and one we do not fancy, and perhaps we are enjoying our sojourn here after weeks under sail. We find ourselves in want of fresh water, however, our kegs fast running dry. There is a signal fire on the mainland near the Eddystone and through the spyglass we see a group of clansmen walking on the beach.

'That'll be Tolo and his band?' Kelly says, handing me the instrument.

That they are clansmen is all I can say for sure.

'Known to you, this Tolo? He won't attack us?'

'I've met the man. He won't attack us if we come with plenty of seal carcasses for sharing.'

'What about this business with Laman?' Griffiths says. 'Do you think they're truly at war, these brothers?'

'It's possible that I misunderstood,' I say, 'but what I cannot fathom is the thought of Tolo in league with a man like Michael Howe. They would rather slit the other's throat, but even so I think it better to keep Laman's name out of it when we see Tolo.'

We launch the whaleboat and steer between the rocks, all the while scanning the beach for sign of Howe. As we approach the shore we see plenty of clansmen but nary a bushranger. The Eddystone juts out into the sea and it is a familiar marker for any mariner, but the swell is not excessive and Kelly steers us safely past the orange-furred rocks so prevalent on this coast. The main beach is on the far side of the Eddystone and it is here that the main body of clansmen is grouped. Kelly has us stand off from the shore and I stand up in the whaleboat and call out: 'Yarnenner legana! Swim to us! Yarnenner legana!' The clansmen make no move to approach, so I try again. 'Meena George Baggs! Yarnenner legana! Meena George Baggs!'

This seems to have the desired effect and one of the clansmen starts wading out. He is a similar age to Tombs and similarly bearded. The whaleboat is in deep water and thus he is obliged to swim to us. We haul him up and my suspicions are confirmed. 'Tolo Bunganna!'

'Yah peulinghenar, Baggs.'

'Thank you,' I say before introducing my crewmates. Knowing our custom, Tolo shakes hands with every man.

'Baggs larngerner Laman Bunganna Ringarooma?' he says.

'No Tolo, we didn't see Laman at Ringarooma. We sailed from Cape Barren.'

'Nummerwar larngerner Laman Bunganna?'

'No, we saw some fires along the coast but we haven't seen him.'

Tolo seems satisfied and, cordial relations thus established, Kelly steers us closer to the shore. I explain to Tolo that the seal carcasses are intended as gifts.

'Warrander kueberrenner!' he says, then something about celebrating on the beach.

Kelly has us linger in the shallows and this lack of faith is not lost on Tolo, who points to the welcoming party on the shore. We row a little closer without beaching entirely. As we watch, six women come up from the bush, each hauling a kangaroo carcass on her shoulders. The kangaroos are given in exchange for the seals and are loaded onto the boat. Tolo explains that his people will hunt more kangaroo for trade with us tomorrow.

'Thank you, Tolo Bunganna.'

'Ask him if he's seen Howe,' Kelly says.

'Tolo Bunganna,' I say, 'larngerner perringye Michael Howe? Kartummeter partrollarne, much musket fire. Karpennooyouhener, a bad man.'

'Howe larngerner Baggs?'

'He's not hunting us, but do you know where he is?'

'Kartummeter pleengenner.'

'Many white men. Are they near here?'

Tolo points along the coast in a southerly direction. 'Parkutetennar larngerner Howe.'

'The soldiers are chasing him?'

'Kartummeter parkutetennar.'

I explain to Tolo that we need fresh water for our kegs. We pass the empty kegs out and the clansmen take them away to refill.

'Tell him if he wants those pups we'll happily trade them for kangaroo skins,' Kelly says. I reach into the basket and hand a pup to Tolo, who holds it aloft to show his people. I explain that he can have the lot for any kangaroo skins he might have, and he asks if we will bring more carcasses for trade tomorrow. I convey this request to Kelly.

'Tell him we're on our way south just as soon as this wind changes,' Kelly says.

I explain this to Tolo and he thinks about it for a moment. 'Loonner larngerner kartummeter kueberrenner,' he says.

'Kueberrenner? I don't doubt that your women are excellent seal hunters, Tolo.'

'Pernickerter legana!' he says to the six women who delivered the kangaroos, and they start wading out again.

'What's happening?' Kelly says.

'He's sending those women a'sealing with us.'

'Tell him we're much obliged but I don't think it'll be necessary.'

'Too late for that,' I say. We make room for the women and it is a tight squeeze on the thwarts. I tell Tolo we will return tomorrow.

The women are eager to get to work when we return to George Rocks and we watch as they creep down to water's edge. Laying on the rocks, the women wet themselves all over with seawater.

'What are they doing, George?' Griffiths says.

'Masking their scent,' I say. 'Look.'

The women slip down into the water and swim out to the offshore rocks, where a group of seals lay basking in the sun. The women creep up to the dozing seals, but instead of commencing their attack they lay on the rocks amid them. Some of the seals lift their heads to inspect the newcomers but soon subside. The sun beats down and waves wash over the rocks. Suddenly the women spring to their feet and start clubbing the seals. We watch as they kill half a dozen. The women each drag a seal into the water and swim over to us with seal in tow. They repeat the trick and before we know it we have twelve dead seals piled up before us. The women stride past us and climb the hillock in the middle of the island, where they start building a signal fire to communicate their success to Tolo. Not long after, we see smoke rising from near the Eddystone. Meanwhile we skin the seals and peg them out. The women ask for knives and start butchering the carcasses.

That night we have a fine cook up, although the kangaroo meat is more to our liking than the seal. The women devour the latter with gusto and rub their oily hands on their skin. They will not partake of the Major's rum and they sit off from us in a phalanx that will broach no intrusion. When the feast is done we ready ourselves for bed.

'I'll take the first watch and yourself the second, Baggs,' Kelly says. 'There may not be time for a third, you understand?'

'I do.'

'Then to bed with you. And George? We'd best take them back tomorrow.'

◆

THE NEXT day, the women again show their worth in the sealing endeavour. They will not take breakfast, preferring to storm the seals at low-tide, and they kill and skin more than two dozen. In the afternoon they rest awhile before assisting us in bundling up the dry skins. Then they dive for oysters. Throughout the day I keep expecting Kelly to announce it is time to return the women to Tolo but on this score he remains silent. No doubt he is thinking of the profit he will make on the skins.

The second evening passes in much the same way as the first and Kelly makes free with the rum. Although the women will not drink, there is not the same defensiveness in their postures. Tombs is stumbling drunk and Griffiths not far behind and Kelly announces it is time we were all abed. He assigns Jones first watch and Griffiths second and it is clear he trusts Tombs not at all. I try to stay up with Jones but he is a hard man to engage in conversation. I crawl into the tent and into my dreams.

'Nummerwar pargonee meenar myhena!'

I jump to my feet amid the shrieking of the women. There is an ugly scene at the fireside, two Tyereelore grappling Jones while a third approaches with a knife.

'Wongherne! Nummerwar!' I say to the knife-wielder. 'Give me the knife!'

The knife-wielder circles closer. 'Nummerwar pargonee meenar myhena,' she repeats. 'Meena oongurlerpooler pleengenner. Karpennooyouhener!'

'Nummerwar,' I say, stepping between her and Jones. 'Crackena!'

The women relinquish Jones and he shuffles away shamefaced. Kelly and Griffiths have joined us at the fireside but nothing will rouse Tombs. The knife-wielder is not disarmed but thank God she does not try to get to Jones.

'What happened?' Kelly says. 'What's she saying?'

'"Don't touch my body."'

'He's lucky she didn't slit him ear to ear.'

'Karpennooyouhener!' the knife-wielder says.

'Pernickerter, give me the knife,' I say. 'Crackena.'

She glares but hands it over.

The women sit down in their phalanx and none will speak. It is at least an hour before they lay down to sleep again, and when they do they sleep practically atop one another. We will begone to the south tomorrow even if we have to row into the teeth of the wind.

◆

THEN IT is mid-morning the next day and the camp is being dismantled. The whaleboat is packed with skins and the women have returned from their final sortie. Smoke again rises from the Eddystone.

Leaving George Rocks, we haul up on the beach past the Eddystone as before. I thank the women for their labour and they return to their people who are beginning to come down from the dunes. Tolo is among their number.

'Thank you, Tolo Bunganna,' I say.

'Kartummeter seal,' he says.

'It's time we were back in Hobart Town,' I say, pointing south. 'Your women are mighty sealers, Tolo. Loonner kartummeter yarnenner, kartummeter larngerner.'

He turns to his people and orders that they bring down more kangaroo skins to load into the whaleboat. By this time the entire clan seems to be on the beach and for the most part they are in a festive mood. Only the Tyereelore remain subdued but I do not think they will raise a fuss. Tolo informs me that before we leave we must first watch his people in their dance. I explain this to Kelly and the others and we sit on the beach. Jones sits between Griffiths and Tombs and will not raise his head. Tolo barks out instructions and the clan splits into groups of men, women and children. The women make a ring around the pile of seal carcasses while the others form a ring around them. The women commence their singing and dancing, and while many of the words of the song are lost on me, I know that the intent of the song is celebratory. The women throw themselves to the sand and lay sprawled out in mimicry of the slain seals, then spring up and adopt a warlike pose, baring their teeth. The dance continues and the women beat upon their calves and kick at the sand. The women fall to the ground and their part of the song is at an end.

It is the turn of the men. Spears and waddies in hand, they dance around the pile of carcasses and engage in a sham battle, pretending to slay the seals by hitting them with waddies and sticking them with spears. All the while they whirl around uttering war cries, the cumulative effect a deafening din. They sing of the sun, the sea and the birds in the sky. They sing of their wars and of the coming of the English, and when it is done they return to their places.

Tolo comes over and tells us the ceremony is over. He wishes us a safe journey. Kelly is eager to be off, but my heart lingers hereabouts even if my body cannot stay. Clansmen call this place Tangumronener and on a sunny day it is as good a place as any to look upon the faraway isles. I can see the smooth rocks of the Eddystone before us, George Rocks a good distance behind and the distinctive outline of Cape Barren on the horizon. Today I am headed south and tomorrow I shall be further from my wife than today. In my heartache my soul would leap across the water and bridge that gap and we would be together.

It is only then, in a moment fleeting and then vanished, that I begin to understand what this place means to these people.

HOMECOMING

1819

BY THE HOSPITAL Wharf in Sydney lies the house of Isaac Nichols, erstwhile sealing master and latterly postmaster to the colony. Here the sandstone townhouses of the affluent traders speak of riches won and of the ill-fortune of transportation respun to best advantage. This mercantile class were all convicts, some First Fleeters, and it has made them cannier for it. They have known the bite of the lash and what it is like to be chained in the bowels of a ship. Some have cheated a sentence of death and others survived shipwreck on hostile shores. A generation ago they were banished to a place beyond the sea and they have been hustling ever since. It is the same tale told a hundred times in the lives of Henry Kable, Simeon Lord, James Underwood and Mary Reibey.

Now they are infirm, their days of adventure long passed. With rheumy eyes they lie abed, their minds scheming of further profit, but for all their wealth they cannot buy their youth to have again. Nor can I. They know that the moment the final breath escapes their rattling lungs, a plague of unworthy descendants will squabble over their empires with no greater decorum than seagulls on the very same wharf.

Death might linger in the Nichols' doorway but he does not demand admittance this day. It is I, the honest absconder, who would knock instead.

A muffled voice from within, a woman's. 'What do you want?'

'I'm here to see Mr Nichols, ma'am.'

'He's poorly, you'll have to come back.'

'That's what you said last week, ma'am. Tell him it's about his schooner *Governor Hunter*.'

I wait awhile, the coinpurse heavy in my pocket and on my conscience. Seventeen pounds I have acquired and I will put it in Nichols' hand or count myself damned. I mean to pay him in the currency of the colony and those are the holey dollars. Five shillings to the dollar, four dollars to the pound, and thus sixty-eight dollars will repay the debt in full. Strange currency cut from Spanish reales, the words NEW SOUTH WALES 1813 and FIVE SHILLINGS on the reverse side.

The door opens to reveal a handsome woman about my age.

'I'm George Baggs and you must be Mrs Nichols.'

'I am. Isaac will see you presently.'

The lady of the house leads the way past a ballroom that has seen its share of grand dinners and soirees, a fine hall which had seated Governor Macquarie and assorted dignitaries. Following Mrs Nichols upstairs, I come to the closed door of the master bedroom. 'Isaac's weak with dropsy so you won't upset him,' she says. It isn't a question.

'I won't upset him.'

'Ring the bell should he require anything. The maid is on an errand so it shall be I who attends.'

It is dark and draughty inside, ghost-grey Isaac Nichols propped up in bed.

'Shall I close the window?' I say.

'Doctor says not ter,' he says, his voice thick with phlegm. 'Don't reckon I've had ... the honour ... of makin' yer acquaintance.'

'I'm George Baggs and no we haven't met, although I worked for you ten years ago aboard *Governor Hunter.*'

'Aye, she were a ... fine vessel ... Rosanna said ... you wanted ter speak ... about that.'

The man can barely draw breath let alone engage in conversation and there is the whiff of carrion about him. 'I'll be brief so you can get your rest,' I say. 'I've owed you a debt for many years and I've come to repay it.'

'What debt?'

'Seventeen pounds.' I put the heavy purse in the grasp of trembling fingers that could not hope to lift it.

'What debt?' he repeats.

'Seventeen pounds I owed you when *Governor Hunter* ran aground. I absconded.'

'You're ... a survivor?'

'I am, myself and Jimmy Brown. The boy Tom Stepney sadly drowned off Clarke Island.'

'They told me ... no survivors.'

'Then they told you wrong. Some of the others might have been lost with Bader on *Active.*'

'*Active?* That's ... long ago.'

'April 1ˢᵗ 1809 was the day *Governor Hunter* ran aground on Badger Island. That's even longer.'

'Wait, you're ... talkin' about that? ... About Badger? ... That's ancient hist'ry ... You don't know ... about the wreck?' Nichols sounds worse than ever, his breath hoarse and ragged. 'Ring ... the bell.'

I ring it and Mrs Nichols – Rosanna – comes promptly. I told you not to upset him.'

'Your husband is trying to tell me about a shipwreck.'

'He mustn't. Best you take your leave, Mr Baggs.'

'Wait,' Nichols says. 'Get … the newspaper.'

Rosanna is plainly furious but does as her husband commands, retrieving an old copy of the *Sydney Gazette* from the sideboard. She hands it to me. 'Go on, he wants you to read it.'

All I can read is the date, Saturday 17th October 1818, just over a year ago. The letters swim before my eyes and will not cohere into the words I know are there.

'In the Ship News,' Rosanna says. 'Page 2.'

The first word in large lettering is *Ship*, the second no doubt *News*, and I recognise the word *Sydney* printed further down. I stare at the lines of smaller text, praying in vain that this one time they will sit down and behave. Mr and Mrs Nichols are waiting, Rosanna pointing to a jungle of words in the third column, and my heart sinks in the knowledge that I will never learn to untangle them. The first word is *By*, the second probably *His*, but beyond that I am lost.

'Give it here,' she says. She reads aloud as if from memory, and I wonder how many times she has been called upon to perform this task:

> *'By His Majesty's armed brig* Lady Nelson, *Mr Isaac Nichols learns the fate that attended his schooner* Governor Hunter, *which sailed hence for Kangaroo Island so long ago as three years. The discovery of the vessel's wreck was made in a small branch leading inland out of an extensive bay about 45 or 50 miles north of Port Stevens.'*

'And … the rest.'

> *'In the lagoon the almost buried hull of the* Hunter *was found, and the small figurehead is restored to*

its owner. Mr Murrell and his ill-fated crew there can be little doubt were killed by the natives; the foremast has been cut away, and her sails are gone. Mr Murrell and his people are much to be lamented, as the melancholy catastrophe which involved them was the act of Providence, and not of that species of temerity which has plunged offenders in numberless instances into the vortex of destruction which every part of this coast presents inevitably to them. That any should escape the dreary destiny of perishing by famine or the spear, would at least appear a miracle, and the greatest of absurdities for any man to expect or hope for.'

They are waiting for me to speak and I do not.

'Show him ... the figurehead.'

In the corner of the room stands a mottled likeness of the former governor, except that he is shrunken to half his proper size. With unseeing eyes, the gnomish figurehead stands warden over the sickbed.

'So that is all that remains of *Governor Hunter*,' I say.

'Poor Isaac thinks you're a survivor of the wreck,' Rosanna says. 'If only it were so, it would mean the world to him.'

'I owe ... Hunter... me life ... I'll never forget.'

'Hush, Isaac, and I shall fill in the rest,' Rosanna says. 'Know you the tale of how John Hunter came to save my husband from the hangman's noose?' she asks me. 'Must be all of twenty years ago.'

'Aye in ... '99.'

'It was before my time,' I say. 'Yours too, Rosanna, if I may be so bold as to say.'

'Not true, I remember the saga well, although I was but a girl of twelve. Macarthur had my poor Isaac sentenced to fourteen years hard labour on Norfolk Island for supposedly receiving stolen goods, but Governor Hunter suspended the sentence and Isaac walked free. That's why he named his prized schooner after the man.'

'I see, but I never said I sailed on *Hunter*'s final voyage.'

'It is a misunderstanding and nothing more. You said *Governor Hunter* and it is only natural that Isaac's thoughts should turn to its final journey.'

I explain to her the circumstances by which I came to abscond from her husband's employ, of Badger Island and *Active* and Tom Stepney. Isaac might or might not be asleep.

'I have but dim recollection of these events,' Rosanna says. '1809 was the year I bore Isaac his second son. Just last month we sent the eldest two home to England to complete their education.'

'I'm sure they are fine boys who will do you both proud,' I say. 'I'll take my leave.'

'No.'

'No what, Isaac?' Rosanna says.

'No … money.'

'Mr Baggs simply wishes to repay his debt to you.'

'Take it … back.'

With a sigh, Rosanna retrieves the bulging purse and hands it to me. I am torn between tucking it away and throwing it back on the bed, so for the time being I do neither. 'I wanted to repay you, Mr Nichols, for the debt has been ten years on my conscience. Four months I've been in Sydney and I barely recognise it now. It has grown up into a right proper town.'

'Aye … it has.'

'All I wanted was two things and I've managed neither. I wanted to find Tom Stepney's relations or anyone who might remember him. You don't recollect a boy of that name, Rosanna? Taken on back in '08.'

'There have been oh so many boys, Mr Baggs.'

'And yet only one lost by me. I asked everywhere around the Rocks for him, even went up to Parramatta. It's like the boy never lived.'

'But you remember him, and you won't forget.'

'Not in this life, no.'

'I can see the sorrow written in your face, Mr Baggs. The boy is with God now.'

'Bless you, Rosanna, for yours is a gentle soul. I suppose I thought repaying this debt to be compensation of a kind. If only you'd accept it.'

'No ... compen ... '

'Do you have a wife, Mr Baggs? Children perhaps?'

'Yes I do, in Van Diemen's Land.'

'Then I suggest you might more properly focus your investment there. Isaac is a wealthy man and he simply has no need of your money. He has forgiven the debt and thus you can go with your head held high.'

'Is it as your wife says, Mr Nichols? I don't imagine we'll be seeing one another again in this life.'

'It is ... forgiven.'

◆

I AM in a whirl, my pockets heavy with coin I had meant not to have. Thirty-two years am I and I have never possessed such money, not only the seventeen pounds meant for Nichols but the other six left for myself. Not far shy of a hundred holey dollars all told, no fortune but perhaps the beginnings of one. How many seals have fallen to my blows in pursuit of such a sum? How many skins flensed? How many gallons of blubber tried? It has taken me years and years to amass such a sum and now I am at a loss as to what to do with it.

Truth is I grow weary of the sealer's life and pine after one less arduous. Sealing is a young man's game and the colony is latterly flooded with such chancers, many of whom will find their deaths soon enough. Men like James Kelly turn their thoughts to the pursuit of the right whale while Jacob Garrett thinks to turn all Van Diemen's Land into a sheep run, but I will emulate neither. Let them spend their days imagining ways of doubling their money and doubling it again for the grave will find them too.

Twenty-three pounds, the very thought of which makes me heartsore. Some men are born into money and others born into the winning of it, whereas men like myself are happier with little. That I must turn my attention to settling accounts with myself is self-evident. All this time I had thought to put the money into Nichols' palm and thence to wash my hands. As if by paying this obscure debt I might absolve myself of debts less tangible, debts not only to the dead men I carry at my side but to the wife and children still living.

How easily I might allow the gloom to take my legs, to make the oft-repeated pilgrimage up Brown Bear Lane to the top of the hill overlooking Sydney Cove. To Gloucester Street and the Black Dog Hotel where many an eager sailor lost his coinpurse laying with the scarlet women and imbibing the noxious brews strong enough to slay horses. Now that he has been removed from his position of Lieutenant-Governor of Van Diemen's Land, one might expect to see Old Tom Davey slurping from a dish of *Blow Me Skull*. Only here, where the Cape wine is cut with opium and cayenne pepper, might he hope to find a head as hard as his. Twenty-three pounds would not last long in such a place. When the money was spent or stolen I would find myself obliged to ship out on a sealer as though it were 1809 again.

Not to the *Black Dog* then. I shall repair to my lodgings on Cumberland Street and thereupon lay my head with the intention of waking tomorrow a man in possession of a tidy sum. Come break of day, when all but the spriteliest of pickpockets are snugly abed, I will make my way down to the wharf for what I pray will be the last time. It is a cruel town Sydney, as I have often said, and I find the years do not improve its countenance.

I am going home to Van Diemen's Land.

◆

GLORY IS a handsome two-masted brig of eighty-five tons and a finer vessel I have seldom seen. Newly built on the Hawkesbury by Jonathan Griffin and sons, she is altogether too cumbersome for the Parramatta run and intended as an oceangoing vessel. Stout enough to brave the worst of Bass Strait yet sufficiently nimble to navigate the islands, her primary function will be to service the burgeoning shipping trade between Sydney and Launceston.

'The old man reckons we'll be movin' down there in a year or two,' eighteen-year-old John tells me as we get underway. 'Says we'll build a shipyard on the banks of the Tamar.'

'I've thought of settling in Launceston myself,' I say. 'If you can establish yourself there you shall be to Van Diemen's Land what your father's generation was to Sydney.'

'That's just what he says, says that there's a fortune there for the makin'.'

It seems there is always a fortune for the making and I am never the one making it. So says the man with twenty-three pounds in his pocket. These weeks in Sydney have corrupted me but no sooner than we clear the heads such pecunious thoughts are left in *Glory's* wake. It is good to feel the sea beneath my legs.

'Remember me when your shipyard's built, John. I daresay you'll find me a job.'

'Sailed around Van Diemen's Land with Kelly, din't you?'

'Reckon I've sailed these waters since before you were born, not that the sea's any more forgiving. It does for good men just the same as bad.'

'You sound just like the old man.'

Standing at the bowsprit as the brig tacks into the wind, a glorious sensation of homecoming begins to bubble up inside me. My heart pines not for Launceston but the Furneaux where I was happiest. Unfinished business awaits me there, but it is business of a family kind. Moe ought still to be on Longtartennerner with Jimmy Brown unless she has finally made good on her threat to go back to her people. I do not know if she will have me back, but I know of something – or rather someone – who will sweeten the deal.

'You'll seal with us this season?' John says. 'Dad means to try Kangaroo Island and Western Port.'

'Don't think I will, John. Reckon I might take myself to Norfolk Plains first of all.'

'Family down there, is it?'

'You might say that.'

I ought to have listened to Moe and never taken Daisy to the Garretts. I see now that I wrecked the family life we might have had. Truth is and always was that I couldn't abide enclosure. And the sea was always calling.

That evening I dine with Griffin, his sons and all the eminent gentlemen aboard *Glory*. It is a feast of pork and greens and bread accompanied by freshly brewed beer. Seated at the captain's table are notable personages such as Richard Lawson, Robert Atkins and James Cox, Esquire. I am known to none of them and eager that it might remain so. Meanwhile the ordinary sailors take their repast in the mess and I know I would be more comfortable among them. The crew includes a pair of Sydney clansmen and a New Zealander by the name of

Jacky Myty who knows something of James Kelly's ill-doings in his homeland.

'October thirtieth and we're shot of port in the nick of time,' Griffin Sr. says, presiding over the assembly.

'And why, pray tell, is that?' James Cox says.

'Muster's tomorrer, int it?' Griffin says. 'I expect some of ye are considered free men although in several instances I couldn't say why.'

'Is that why you were so insistent on having us sail on a Sunday?' Cox says.

'Ye currency lads don't know what it's like bein' sat on t'other side.'

'I strongly doubt that the Governor would think of sending you back to Norfolk Island at this late stage, Captain.'

'P'raps not, but I'll sleep easier at sea all the same.'

'It is Governor Macquarie who must watch his step now that Commissioner Bigge is in town,' Atkins says. 'The colony's well overdue for a shakeup.'

'Best steer clear o' that bonfire lest yer fingers get burned,' Griffin says. 'Who knows what the man'll turn up once he commences pokin' around.'

'No doubt the Commissioner will find his way to Hobart Town eventually,' Cox says. 'I daresay he'll find plenty there to engage his energies.'

'Get yerself clear is my advice,' the captain says, and he might as well be speaking directly to me.

The conversation moves on and I am barely listening to these braggarts and their grandiose imaginings. No doubt they shall remain at their meat and drink long into the night, regaling one another with tales of their fabricated fortunes and of tracts of land dubiously granted. I am no more than a servant to such men. Evidently some of them have not set eyes on Van Diemen's Land, but it does not stop them from discussing the merits of the districts over which they mean to preside. I keep my mouth firmly closed and, citing a bellyache, retire as soon as decorum will allow.

I am in the bunk but I pine after the night sky and an open fire. Living amid Moe's people, I have learned to distrust the English and their duplicitous utterances and to flee from soldiers on sight. I am between worlds now, neither pannerkarner nor pleengenner, a ghost of days long past. *I am numbered among the first*, I might declare to those wretches upstairs, *and I have known the places you think to name after yourselves.* They would roar and laugh, demanding to know what I have to show. The answer is nothing save for a bag of coins and a hatful of littluns scattered to the wind. If I had a certain promise it remains unfulfilled but by God I am not dead yet.

Nichols might have elected in his dotage to forgive the debt owing him, but there is another and it shall not be so readily expunged. Long have I thought on Tom Stepney and the manner of his passing but it was cruel mischance which befell him. This is not the debt to which my thoughts address, nor is it toward that fool Joseph Halfpenny who was the agent of his own downfall. I might claim to distrust the English but the truth is I am he and it is my own sordid actions I fear the most. Chief Laman's men could have struck me down in '09 or several times since but they came to me in friendship. *Warrander molookener kartummeter loonner*, Laman said when I told him I wouldn't help him fight his brother. *I always went with you before to fight other clans when you wanted women* is what he meant, and when called upon to reciprocate I fled.

Now a new generation of Englishmen approaches these shores in perfect ignorance of and contempt for all that has gone before. Whatever deals I made, whatever half-intended assurances I gave or did not give, are null and void. Not spirits of departed ancestors these karpennooyouhener, but ghosts of an onrushing future.

◆

IT WAS winter when I last saw Launceston and it is not much warmer today. If there is a muddier place for disembarking I cannot think where it is, rich men and poor liable to fall on their arses and slide down the goat track the locals call the street. Everywhere is the stink and bleats of pigs and sheep and even a fine thoroughbred horse with a dark glossy coat being corralled along the dock. On the opposite corner, a greengrocer displays fresh turnips and carrots but it is the tavern I desire.

The public house is called the Cornwall although there is no sign proclaiming it so, its floor not much less muddy than the street. Familiar faces I am apt to see but what I desire is a quiet place to rest. It would not do well to show my coinpurse and thus I have a single dollar to proffer as coin of the realm. It is to rum my thoughts turn, to rum and rum again.

'If it isn't George bleedin' Baggs!'

A familiar voice, a bearded scowl. 'Thomas Tombs! What are you doing above ground?'

'Might ask ye the same, George. Come an' share the news.'

I throw the first rum down and find it a potent firewater. Tombs drinks no differently. 'Arrived on *Glory*, did ye? I heard ye'd gone north for good.'

'I'm a van Diemener same as you.' Tombs' second drink is gone while mine is still untouched. 'Drink that one if you've a mind to,' I say. Only after he has knocked it down does he confess to being penniless. 'Thought you'd news to share,' I say, reaching into my pocket.

'Thankin' ye.'

He returns forthwith with a bottle in hand, my change not even a penny. 'What has it been, three years?' he says.

'Would've been in Hobart Town last time I saw you, fresh off *Elizabeth*.'

'Plenty gone to their maker since then. Ye heard about the harbourmaster, the old ruffian?'

'Peter Mills? Next you'll be telling me about the demise of Michael Howe.'

'Saw off Tom Davey though, din't he? Speakin' of Kelly, did ye hear of his New Zealand exploits? Got his brother-in-law good and killed.'

'Not John Griffiths?'

'Eaten by cannibals! Kelly razed their village to the ground, or so he says.'

'Kelly told you this? I wouldn't trust his tall tales in the slightest.' I heard something of Kelly's exploits from Jacky Myty but nothing like this.

'It were in the *Gazette*,' Tombs says. 'Never liked that smarmy sod Griffiths.'

'Nor I, but *eaten*? How many men have we known that went to an untimely grave, Thomas?'

'I could not count as high. A life of misery, but for the most part blessedly brief.'

'But not so brief for you, Thomas. I've felt myself an old man recently but next to you I am a youngster.'

'Measure a man not by his years but by those remaining to him,' Tombs says, downing another glass.

'And how would you measure that?'

'S'easy. Some men don't think of death until the moment it is upon them. Such fools are lambs to the slaughter and seldom live long lives. Others see death well enough but run straight towards it, men like James Kelly. They think to tame death, to ride its crest, and for a while they nearly do. Such daredevils are to be admired but from a suitable distance. Wilier are those who spend their days in flight of death. They see it on the streetcorner or in the whites of a fellow's eyes.'

'What kind of fellow am I?'

'I take ye for a bolter.'

A man who has bolted once without ill consequence is liable to bolt again. All Van Diemen's Land has been a haven for rogues and ne'er-do-wells and I would be wise to avoid them one and all.

'I understand there's a road through to Norfolk Plains these days?' I say.

'If ye could call it that. Cart goes twice a week. What's in Norfolk Plains for ye? Pack of scum down there.'

'My daughter Daisy living with the Garretts.'

'Garrett? Now there's a feller gone to seed. If yer in Norfolk Plains ye might want to call on Jennifer Mills, the harbourmaster's widow. Near about destitute, what with all that brood.'

'I may just do that, Thomas. And how have you been keeping?'

'I've been out in the interior ever since me pardon came through. Such lakes as you've never seen, George, one of 'em no littler than the sea. I've been ramblin' all over and shearin' too.'

'The clansmen don't bother you?'

'I try to stay well clear and turn a blind eye when they're spearin' sheep. Don't reckon they much care for stock runnin' across their huntin' grounds, but they won't harm a man if they judge him to be of reasonable character. I try not to get close enough for them to judge mine.'

'I'd have thought you too old for such a life. You must be ready to settle down.'

'Don't think I ever could, George. Only come int' town when I'm feelin' thirsty.'

'Well, it seems you're thirsty today.' Slumped back, Tombs might fall asleep at any moment and I do not wish to be responsible for his wellbeing if he does. 'Are your lodgings here, Thomas?'

'Upstairs.'

'Then I shall assist you.'

I take the last mouthful of rum and get Tombs on his feet. Grizzled he might be but his is a spritely frame and I could all but carry him. Upstairs it is dark and rank. I grope around in the gloom for the bucket.

'Back corner,' Tombs says from his cot, and passes out.

◆

NINE BUMPY miles through thickwooded country to Norfolk Plains and it is on the very last that the cart sinks wheel-deep in mud. I am sore from a thousand jolts and not best pleased for the day is waning fast. The horses will not pull and the driver disinclined to whip them and thus we abandon the cart and proceed on foot. As I am the cart's sole passenger, I am obliged to lead one heavily laden horse while the driver handles the other. Thankfully my charge is too weary to give much nuisance beyond the occasional tossing of the head, complacent in the knowledge of where bed and feed might be found.

'Ain't handled many horses in yer time, have ye?' the driver says, whose name is Clements.

'First one I ever saw in Van Diemen's Land was belonging to Dr Garrett, the man I'm hoping to call on now.'

'Friend of yours, is he?'

'Hardly, but he has something of mine.'

'Then ye ain't no orphan. Yer best waitin' till morn lest ye find yerself filled with buckshot. He ain't especial neighbourly after dark and nor in the daytime.'

'What about Jennifer Mills? I've heard she's in town?'

'Her hut's up ahead, but I wouldn't go callin' on her after dark neither.'

'Problems with bushrangers, is it?'

Clements spits. 'I'd hardly call 'em that. Bunch o' Norfolk Island loafers and layabouts is what they are, won't lift a finger except in raisin' a mug to their lips. This district has the best farmin' land ye'll ever see and most of it layin' fallow for the want of labour.'

By the dim dusklight, I see we have reached the edge of the settlement. Here the river branches into the South Esk and Lake River, the latter home to the bulk of the settlers. 'The place makes Launceston look like Sydney,' I say.

'Don't let the locals hear ye sayin' it. Ye'll find neither inn nor church nor schoolhouse, just wretched farms choked with every kind of noxious weed. Ye're welcome to bed down in the coachman's quarters for a modest fee, by and by.'

'Is that why we were so late in leaving, so you could do a little side business upon our arrival?'

'That was on account of my poor, sore head. Luckily for me I know just the remedy.'

I help Clements stable his horses, agreeing to further assist him in the morning with the retrieval of his cart as recompense for tonight's accommodation. It is only once I set eyes on the dirty straw pallet that I realise I've been had.

'Call this the coachman's quarters, do you? Unfit for sows is this.'

'Yer more'n welcome to try yer luck elsewhere, chum, though as I said people don't take kindly to doorknockin' after dark. Don't go near no chicken coops is my advice.'

'And I don't suppose there'll be any supper?'

'Got me a nice pock hock and a bottle o' rum. Ye're entitled to a share.'

I loosen up after a couple of drinks but not so much that I forget about the coinpurse on my hip. Clements seems a decent sort but I reckon he'd gut and pickle me for even a fraction of that sum. 'What d'ye want with Widow Mills anyways?' he says. 'Poor woman's at her wit's end. Reckon she could find use for another husband, if that's what ye're thinkin'.'

'I knew her husband once. Thomas Tombs said I might call on her.'

'Tombs? Reckon he's called on her himself if that's what ye want to go callin' it. Now there's a fellow too filthy even for Norfolk Plains, not that the old harbourmaster was very much tidier.'

'You're not wrong there. I've sailed with them both, though not together. There's no getting to know a man like being stuck on a boat with him for weeks on end.'

'Worse even than sharin' a mucky pallet unfit for sows?'

'Worse even than that.'

◆

JENNIFER MILLS' cottage is no different from the rest, its crooked roof thatched with bundles of reeds, smoke rising from its narrow chimney. The coachman's infernal liquor has left a foul taste in my mouth, but the morn is come and I have not been robbed. It is no more than an hour past dawn and the river lays shrouded in morning mist.

A tired-looking woman hunches over a tub of washing at the bench in front of her cottage. 'Who's this a'visitin'? Ain't seen your mug before, Ginger.'

'I'm George Baggs. I knew your husband.'

'Then you knew him a sight better'n I ever did.'

She is a thin-faced woman with a fierce countenance, her hands bright red from the pail of freezing water. I hear the muffled sounds of children playing inside.

'I know little of what happened to your husband,' I say. 'Drowned en route to Hobart Town, did he?'

'I took you for a whaling man wearin' that coat. What's it to you?'

'I thought maybe you were in want of something.'

Her mouth smiles but her eyes do not. 'Heard I was short a feller, did you? Reckon I'll go and put the billy on. You come and sit awhile.'

A rough-hewn table, two wood blocks for seats, three dirty children playing on the mucky floor. 'Outside the lot of you or else it's a beatin'!' she says, and they are gone before she can match words to deeds. She stands at the stove preparing tea.

'What are their names?' I say.

'What's that?'

'Your children, what are their names?'

'You ain't their father, are you? Eldest's John, named after me dad. Next one's Charles and the girl's Eliza.'

'Your father's Captain Brabyn?'

'He is, but he's gone up to Sydney and a fat lot of good he does me there. Meanwhile the children ain't got one pair of shoes between the three.' She puts a mug of steaming tea in front of me. 'Now what is it? I ain't got all day.'

'I'd like to know what happened to your husband.'

'You ain't from the company, are you? About time I was compensated.'

'I don't even know which company you mean.'

'Of course you don't. Sailed out of Hobart Town on *Adamant* and it went straight to the bottom.'

'I'm sorry to hear it.'

'No worse a provider now he's three years in his grave, is Peter. How's the tea?'

'Fine, thank you.'

'You ain't a bad sort, Ginger, calling on a poor widow just out of the goodness of your heart.'

'Thomas Tombs mentioned you to me.'

'It's coming out, ain't it? Been more'n once has Tombs, when he ain't upcountry with his dogs.'

'I'm not here for that.'

'Just thought to pass the time o' day with Widow Mills, did you?'

I withdraw a dollar from my pocket and place it on the table before us. She looks at it and snatches it up. 'My daughter's about the same age as your eldest and living with the Garretts,' I say.

'That native lass Daisy?'

'That's her. I've come to take her home to her mother.'

'Working as a servant girl, ain't she?'

'I believe it is something of that nature. I remember your husband telling me you were a friend of Mrs Garrett. I thought I might persuade you to intercede on my behalf.'

'Old Bridget? That bottle's her only confidant now. She doesn't give a hoot for a blessed thing. They've taken badly to the drink the pair o' them, though I don't reckon it to be on account of any conscience they might have had.'

'What do you mean, Jennifer?'

'It's on Garrett's account my Peter was labelled a bush-ranger. Maybe he pinched a sheep or two but he weren't alone in that and the Governor had him sacked. Only reason he signed up on that whaler is so we'd have something to put in our children's mouths.'

'And you blame Garrett for this?'

'We used to be invited to their dinners up in Launceston. Governors, reverends, everyone who mattered. Ain't heard a peep since our Peter died. Of course the Garretts have fallen on hard times. Bowman's running rings around them now. To see them cryin' poor … '

'Perhaps if they're that hard up, I could offer to purchase the girl back? She is after all my daughter.'

'Depends how many o' them Sydney dollars you've got stashed away in your kitbag, Ginger.'

'Never you mind about that. Who's Bowman?'

'Font of all knowledge, am I? Reckon your dollar just ran out.'

I place a second coin on the table and it goes the way of the first.

'You ain't from around here, or else you'd know all there is to know about Timothy Bowman.'

'I may have heard the name. New commissary up in Launceston?'

'Too right, and now he's bought up half the district with all the capital he says he has. Used to be Garrett pulling tricks like that. Now Bowman's magistrate and coroner, all Garrett's old titles.'

'What went wrong for Garrett?'

'You'll have to ask 'im yourself, but it might have something to do with all the knives he went around putting in people's backs. Life has a way of evenin' the score on such folk. Wish it would hurry along and even the score on me.'

'I predict you'll be waiting a good while longer, Jennifer.'

'Cheery fellow, ain't you? But generous with your money. Now let's put our heads together in figurin' how best to extricate that girl o' yours.'

Before long it is myself who needs extricating for I have given Widow Mills the idea she is to be paid by the word. She expounds on the subject of the many ills wrought her and her heart purely seethes with revenge. Not so many years ago she was one of the eligible lasses of the colony and now at twenty-four she is a penniless widow. Recently she made representation to the Commandant regarding what might be done for her children. He labelled her an impertinent hussy and said if she bothered him again he would put an iron collar around her neck and have her paraded around town. Now she is on the lookout for a husband and it is a position to which I am encouraged to apply. Four holey dollars is all she'll receive from me and, as I am at pains to explain, that is an entire pound.

'Reckon I'd sooner have a proper supper than blow it all on shoes for the littluns,' she says. 'They've tough feet anyhow.'

'I'm sure you know what's best.'

The morning mist has lifted and there are folk about, many of them eying the stranger in their midst. Not a word do I offer in passing for the merest offhand comment might invite a barrage of unwanted questioning. *Is he armed?* is the first and more importantly *Has he a coin for the giving?* To these unspoken enquiries the answers are yes and no. It won't be long before news of the stranger and his holey dollars spreads, and I wouldn't be at all surprised to encounter a highwayman on the road ahead. Pray then I do not for I have taken an oath never to fire on woman or man. I have seen more corpses than I care to and I sleep uneasy at the thought. This policy has served me well although I am no Quaker nor a churchgoing man. If I am lucky then Widow Mills will hold her tongue the whole day through, but if I am unlucky injurious forces move against me even now.

The coachman said it was a halfmile to the doctor's bend but I must have covered that distance and with no such bend in sight. It is a district given over to the raising of wheat and it must be nearly harvest time.

'You lost, mister?'

I turn and see a scamp of eight or nine. He has a mop of dirty hair the colour of straw and his bare feet are caked with mud.

'Are you following me, boy?'

'Only as you're goin' the wrong way. All this is Bowman's, dintcha know?'

We walk in step. 'Maybe I'm visiting the esteemed Mr Bowman. Could be I'm after a job.'

'Naw, you're not after no job. You're after Garrett's but you ain't even on the right river.'

'You're Jennifer Mills' eldest, aren't you? I never got a proper look at you.'

'John Mills, that's me.'

'And you must have been listening outside while I was visiting with your mam.'

'Just makin' sure she comes to no harm.'

'Well I never laid a finger on her, did I?'

'No, you din't. Wanted to know which way to Garrett's.'

'And now you say I'm following the wrong river.'

'It's the South Esk you're wantin' and this here's the Lake River. Now you've two rivers for the crossin'.'

'But you'll show me the best place for crossing, won't you John?'

'I'll take you to Garrett's for the price of a dollar. You won't even wet your feet.'

'And what will you do with such money?'

'Get the littluns fed.'

This might be a ruse, an ambush in the offing, but I think it more likely Jennifer sent him after me in the hope of further payment. I could probably find Garrett's myself now that I know I'm on the wrong river but there might be a beating in it for the boy.

'Daisy's known to you, is she?' I say. 'Reckon you're the same age.'

'Daisy Garrett, aye. I sometimes see her around.'

'Well, she's my daughter.'

The boy has me trespassing through Bowman's fields before doubling back along the river. The water is slack but I reckon plenty deep in the middle. On the nearest bank an old punt wallows in mud so thick that we have a devil of a time getting it out. The opposite bank is no less muddy and by the time I'm across I'm filthy. 'What do you say to this?' I say. 'Reckon it might be grounds for forfeiture on our deal.'

'Nearly there, mister.'

The second crossing is not much easier, the boat in question even more aged than the first, but finally I am on the necessary bank of the appropriate river. I will need to wash and dry my clothes before calling on Garrett, however. 'Cheer up John, you've earned your pay. That's Garrett's up there, is it?' All I see is a hut I take to be the servant's quarters, the main house hidden from view.

'Aye.'

I show him the coin I mean to give him but he seems not to notice it. 'What ails you, lad?' I say.

'Knew my father, did you?'

'Peter Mills? Strong as an ox and wilier than a fox, harbourmaster for all the district.'

'Mam don't remember him kindly oftentimes, says it's him made us destitute.'

'We'll all have our doings judged but I reckon a man is poorly placed for judging his own. Your dad did the best he could and you ought to be proud of him.'

'It's all Garrett's fault what happened to us.'

'Your mother said the same thing in as many words. Comes a time when a man has to answer for himself, John.'

'You've come to shoot old Garrett, haven't you?'

'Pistol's likely jammed from the wet even if I did have murdering intentions. No, I won't fire on the man. I said something similar to your old dad one time. Stake your life on never firing is what I said.'

'That don't make proper sense, mister. What's the use in totin' a gun if you won't ever fire it?'

'It's for defending yourself like a bee with its sting. And if circumstances should demand it, wait until the last possible moment before firing and pray to God your powder's dry.'

I hand him the coin.

'I hope you get to see your daughter, mister.'

◆

IT IS a two-roomed cottage not appreciably different from a hundred like it and it takes me a while to realise that these are no servant quarters but the dwelling itself. Garrett used to own the finest farmhouse in the district but now I think it has been forfeited to Bowman. Sturdier than some but more rickety than others, the cottage is perched on muddy ground not far from the gurgling river. The day is warmer than it has been and I am drier than I was but on neither score would I count myself satisfied. There is scant evidence of any labour done hereabouts for the weeds run riot.

When I place my knock upon the door there is no answer. No smoke from the chimney nor sound from within. Perhaps they have gone away and if so my endeavours shall count for nothing. I knock more boldly and I think there is someone hiding behind the door for I can hear their breathing. I raise my hand a third time intent on raising a din to wake the dead, but before such blows can land the door opens and I see a girl standing there in the gloom.

'Daisy? It's you, isn't it?'

'Ssshhh, you'll wake the master and mistress.'

'Come outside, girl. Don't you recognise your own flesh and blood? For pity's sake, I'm your father.'

On the threshold she studies me and I her and the intervening years have made the other strange. The girl is dressed in an old pinafore, her hair tied up in a bun. She was a youngling when last I saw her and now she is fast approaching womanhood.

'What is your name if you claim to be my father?'

I tell her and it grieves me so, and in that moment under the child's disbelieving eyes I am dumbstruck by a hard-won and unasked for truth. Though my heart still beats and my lungs draw breath, I know in my marrow that I am already dead. The girl stares through me as if it were only the wind come a'knocking and in that look I feel my soul shrivel up and shiver in a searing cold. No more than an echo of a bell rung long ago am I, no more a man than the ghost of one. If she will not answer then I shall fly from this earth for the world has no home it means for me to find.

'I dreamed you were coming, father.'

Simple words but they mean the world to me. 'And here I am, Dais. I mean to take you back home to your mother.'

'Take me home?'

'Home to Longtartennerner and the islands where you were born. I know your mother would give anything to see you again. Are your master and mistress still abed at this late hour? Come quickly if so.'

She is neither in nor out, half of her going and the other half staying, when there comes a hectoring from the interior room. It is Garrett past noon awoken and she rushes to his side. Too long did I dither at the riverbank and thus the opportunity for spiriting my daughter away is passed. From my place on the doorstep I hear a rustling and the tinkling of a chamberpot. At length the inner door opens and Garrett shambles out with Daisy in tow, the latter busying herself with the makings of his breakfast.

'Come and sit, Baggs,' he says, and I do just that. His hair is lank and greasy and his jacket soiled, one of the sleeves pinned down where an arm used to be.

'It's good to see you again, Jacob.'

He drinks from a mug of beer and wipes his mouth. 'I see that the sea is yet to claim you, George. Don't tell me you've come looking for a job for I've nothing for you now.'

Daisy places his breakfast down but he barely takes a mouthful before pushing it away. She refills his empty mug.

'I see my Daisy's been looking after you,' I say.

'Not much good with one arm, am I? Not much work for a one-armed surgeon. Can't even cut up my own meat.'

'How did you come to lose the other?'

'Same way as everything else, had it stolen up in Sydney.'

'Someone stole your arm?'

'Near enough. I was waiting for my trial and they had me performing surgeries and amputations for my keep. One day I nicked my hand with the bonesaw and I thought nothing of it until one of my fingers went black. By the time I had it looked at the bones in the forefinger had started separating and the whole hand had swollen up purple. The surgeon Arnold asked me what I'd been sawing that day. Limbs, I told him, diseases and maladies of the skin. At first the blunderer wanted to take off just the hand but by the time he was done it was the whole bloody arm. And then the trial itself was a farce.'

'You were acquitted?'

'Acquitted but with my name besmirched. It is a grave injustice and one for which I am made to serve undue penance.

I hold Mills accountable although he did not live long enough to taste the fruit of his bitter harvest.'

'And yet Widow Mills would hold you responsible for her husband's death.'

He does not speak, he spits: 'Dark agents and instruments of spite and slander. This place is befouled by a cabal of the ill-bred and the illiterate, men so ignorant they wallow in the mire of their own excretions and call it their high society. I am a long way above such rakers of muck and peddlers of filth. Leave them to their schemes and machinations and it will not be long before they turn on one another and are in turn devoured.'

'You mustn't remain silent, Jacob.'

'Indeed I mustn't, but to whom would you have me direct my appeal? I've written to Macquarie and Lord Bathurst and have had no suitable answer. All I asked was to be given leave to retire on a pension and even that was denied. I find myself hounded and ensnarled by creditors and questioned at length over the muddled state of the hospital stores. Bowman is the commissary now so let him be the one to answer to it. Now he profits on every count whereas I am left to the ruins of what I might have had. If only it were still 1803 .... '

'You were the one who told me those times wouldn't be coming again. Grab some land, you said.'

'And did you heed my counsel?'

'I did not.'

'I'll carve it on your tombstone, George: *Nothing Ventured.* That is if you merit one at all.'

'Better men have none. How is it you suppose you'll be remembered, Jacob?'

A pause. 'They'll number me the first, as is my due. First surgeon, first magistrate of the north. First gentleman to feel the ground beneath him robbed.'

'You're quite sure you weren't the first robber too?'

'Whatever can you mean, first robber? I had a grant for every God-given acre.'

'There were folk here prior to that. Surely the land belonged to them even if they didn't have a paper saying it was theirs.'

'You speak of clansmen? I stole their birthright, so says you?'

'I do.'

'And who are you to stand in judgement? The nonentity George Baggs.'

'And yet I do judge you, Jacob.'

'Every inch of land I called my own was properly granted by government. It is to the Governor and the King you must direct your ire if you think the land improperly taken.'

'I am the illiterate of whom you spoke before. I couldn't even sign my own name.'

'Then you shall have no answer but the one I deign to provide you. By your reasoning it is Britain itself which erred.'

'A French surveyor told me that as long ago as 1802. Said the scale of my country's invasion was stupendous.'

'Sour grapes to the French, then as now. They were bested here just as they were bested at Waterloo. Do not imagine a *Terre de Diemen* an earthly paradise.'

'I've been meaning to ask whatever became of the native boy you had with you in Launceston. Cleveland I believe you called him?'

'I must confess to vague recollection, but I daresay Bridget will recall the particulars.'

'He'd ought to be nearly grown.'

'Known to you, this lad?'

'No, I was only curious. Seems the clansmen have a habit of vanishing.'

'Such I believe to be their custom.'

'You were at Risdon with Lieutenant Moore, weren't you? All those years ago.'

'It is a matter of public knowledge that I was.'

'That day the clans came down, I've heard it said it was you who ordered the carronade fired. Or is that a slander also?'

'What business is it of yours if I did or didn't?'

'James Kelly told me a native boy was taken that day and that the Reverend Knopwood baptised him. Recall that child, do you?'

'I recall his name, Robert Hobart May. *Robert* after the Reverend, *Hobart* after the town, and *May* for the month.'

'Where is that child now? Has he vanished too?'

'You'd have to ask old Knopwood.'

'I will if I ever see him. He baptised my daughter, although I was not there to see it done. Did you include the month she was taken in her name too?'

The child is there as she has been all this time. Not a sound has she made, and she makes none now.

'Your name and mine has she,' Garrett says.

'Your name and mine, although she was not taken in an affray and both her parents are alive. Will she be made to vanish too?'

He laughs curtly. 'George Baggs, Inquisitor. Is this the reason for your visit? Pour your father a drink, girl.'

Daisy places a mug of beer before me and withdraws as far as the confines of the room will allow.

'You see my right hand?' Garrett says, holding it palm up as though swearing on his bible.

'Of course.'

He puts the hand down. 'Now see the other.'

'It isn't there.'

'But it is. I feel it still, and it itches damnably. I raise this hand before you in swearing my oath.'

'To whom do you swear? God Almighty?'

'No, I swear my oath to the vanished and the vanquished. Let them speak now every one.'

His eyes bore into me, this near corpse with spittle flecking its lips, and I am assailed by the knowledge that it is myself who will vanish.

'There is no law,' the wraith before me says, 'not British law nor any other. There is only taking or being taken. Think yourself apart from this?'

'I do not.'

'A thousand seals took you, a hundred thousand. Where are those seals? Where are their pups?'

'Vanished.'

'Vanished, and yet you wear their furs even now. And why?'

'For warmth.'

'One pelt for warmth, but what about the rest?'

'I took them for selling.'

'For profit, same as I took the land. And why did you take their flesh?'

'For eating, or for trading with clansmen.'

'And what did you take from the clansmen in exchange?'

'I took that which was freely given.'

Warrander molookener kartummeter loonner, Laman said. *I always went with you before –*

'I took what I wanted,' I say. 'I took whatever could be had.'

'Schemer, opportunist – *you took whatever could be had.* You are unfit to judge me for we are plunderers both.'

'Who shall absolve us?'

'No one. Last season we reaped a rich harvest and now it is gone to smuts. Today our fields lie fallow and tomorrow we shall find ourselves gobbled up by our competitors. Only then shall we cry injustice.'

'It is a dark scene you draw, Jacob. Some would describe it otherwise.'

'Dark scenes? You wanted to know about Risdon. The truth is you shall never know what happened that day. I could give my account and Moore his and already these are two in divergence. I could say I gave no order for the carronade to be fired and you would either believe or disbelieve me as per your inclination. I might call Moore a fool and a drunkard and he might term me a liar and a brigand. Some would say the clans came down the hill with warlike intentions and others that they came in peace, but come they did and then there was firing aplenty. Moore's men were a rascally bunch who served without distinction and were soon disbanded thereafter.'

'But you saw it fired, this carronade?'

'Certainly I saw it fired. Impossible to aim such a gun at anything smaller than a ship but it does fearful damage at close range. That was the gun off Flinders' ship, *Investigator*. Eighteen months charting the country and it sailed into Sydney Cove no better than a wreck the day before we sailed for Risdon. Now tell me why you are really here, Baggs.'

'I came for my daughter, Jacob. I mean to take her home.'

'Indeed, but what makes you think I shall consent to it? The girl performs an invaluable function.'

'I have the means by which to pay you.'

'Good that you do for the girl is my property and I shall not acquiesce without satisfactory recompense. Shall we call it fifty pounds? It will cost me all of that to source another.'

'Truly you have fallen on hard times if you would sink so low as to fleece a man trying to take his child home to its mother. I could not hope to meet so extortionate a price.'

'I cannot do without the girl. No, she stays here.'

'Then I shall take her for nothing. No magistrate would convict me of such a crime.'

'It is my property and I call you a thief. Freely you gave the girl and in doing so forfeited your fictive claim. Begone now and do not think to darken these walls again lest I fire upon you as a bandit.'

'Speak not of banditry for there is but one bandit here, Jacob. Now name your proper price.'

'I will accept forty pounds and not a shilling less.'

'My offer is ten percent of that.'

'Four pounds! Leave now and spare yourself further embarrassment.'

'Eight then, paid in full.' I reach into my jacket.

'Twenty pounds.'

'Ten and not a penny higher. Do not test me or else it is the pistol I withdraw next.'

'A poor sum this and a fraction of fair value. It grieves my heart but I will accept fifteen, albeit with the greatest reluctance.'

'Damn you forever for the pauper you have made me. Twelve pounds leaves me destitute and I shall barely be able to afford the cart back to Launceston.'

I put the purse on the table and commence my count. Garrett watches silently as I count the dollars off in fours to show their value. When I am done the table is covered in coins and my purse is nearly empty. I did well to siphon off a portion into a second purse which stays hidden.

'Twelve pounds won't restore my fortune but I'll take it even so,' he says, examining each coin for sign of forgery, a process which takes considerably longer with only one hand. 'Although I despair of getting decent help around here.'

'What about young John Mills? He seems an able lad.'

'I'll offer no kindness to that son of a whore, besides which a girl is better to my liking.'

'I believe there's a daughter also.'

'There is nothing but enmity between houses Mills and Garrett. I wish Peter lived longer but only so that I might throttle him myself. I ought not to let your daughter go for Bridget will cry afoul.'

'Then we shall take our leave. You can see that the coins are good and proper.'

He exhales, this ruin in the place where a man once sat. 'No satisfaction have I. But yes, you may consider our business done.' He addresses Daisy: 'Girl, you're to gather your things without disturbing the mistress.'

The girl says nothing and her step is not much louder. The mistress snores on.

'That's everything?' I say to her as she closes the inner door. She nods in assent. 'Then I bid you a good day, Garrett.'

But he is in a stupor and will not raise his head. His mug is empty, the bottle on the sideboard expended.

◆

NOW WE are homeward bound, myself and a child who says little unless spoken to and barely even then. No comment on my dealings in Norfolk Plains does she offer, no sign of her pleasure or otherwise. That she does not much remember me need not be said, for to her I am only another master even if I go by the name of father. What dreams she has beyond the prophecy of my coming I would not hazard to guess.

I will not attempt another river crossing today, instead judging Garrett fairly compensated for the loan of his boat. Even accounting for the bend in the river it is not far to the coachman's. If we are lucky he will be heading back to Launceston this afternoon and if not I daresay my coin will persuade him otherwise. I tell Daisy the plan and her only response is to ask whether she will be obliged to row. I tell her that it will not be necessary. She consents to me lifting her into the boat to avoiding getting muddy and it is the first time I have held her since she was four. A sharp peal of grief like a sudden squall shudders through me and I try to quell it rather than explain how I feel. She is my blood and there are others no better known to me than this.

Upon our arrival at the town jetty, it hardly escapes the townsfolk's attention that the stranger has returned with a native girl in tow. If before they were only mildly hostile, now their malevolence is more sharply defined. I would keep rowing all the way to Launceston but then I will be judged a thief. We will do well to get shot of this place and quickly.

In the sullen mob there is but one face it is my pleasure to see and that is of the boy John Mills. With a firm grasp of Daisy's hand, I push through the throng toward him.

'Here you are again, John,' I say, pressing another coin into his hand without making a show of it. 'Know you if the coach goes back to Launceston today?'

'I couldn't say. I see you've found your daughter.'

I have him lead the way, my attention on a group of surly men by the river. It may be that news of my earnings has reached their ears and if so I pray the coachman can be quickly roused. As we round the corner, I see his horses in their stable and the man himself on the front step.

'Decided me lodgings weren't half bad, did ye?' he says. 'Ye were supposed to help me retrieve the cart this morn. Lucky for ye I had some lads fetch it for me after ye'd snuck out.'

'It completely escaped my mind, Clements. I was very much hoping you'd take us back to Launceston today.'

'Ye've shit for brains if ye were very much hopin' that. Tuesday and Friday I come, Thursday and Saturday I go. Today's Wednesday unless I'm very much mistaken, and ye know what that means?'

'Tell me what it means, Clements.'

'It's me bleedin' rest day. Speakin' of which, it's time for a drink.'

'I'll pay you double to go back today. Double for me, double for the girl. That's four fares.'

'That's mighty generous but it don't pique my interest even so.'

'Double it again then.'

He thinks about it. 'It's too late this aft for settin' out. Wait until tomorrer and I'll drink the rest o' ye money tonight, seein' as how it's burnin' such a bloody great hole in yer britches.'

'You were the one warned me about loafers and layabouts. If you'll cast your eyes yonder you'll see a few of them now.'

He looks. 'Aye.'

'And I'll not wait to see how things play out after dark.'

'My word no, something's got their goat. Spoke out of turn, did ye?'

'Someone surely did. Word gets around quick, doesn't it John?'

'Begging your pardon, mister?'

'It isn't everyday a stranger comes to town flinging his coin about. How many dollars have I given you now?'

'I swear I never said nowt.'

'In that case it must've been your mother. Now run along, there's a lad.'

'Ye're in a pickle,' Clements says when the boy is gone. 'What d'ye think'll happen when I start tackin' up the horses?'

'I'll go speak to those men if you think it will help.'

'Ye'll do no such thing. Now give me a coin or two and I'll go pay 'em off.'

Another two dollars down and no lusty sailor ever blew his earnings faster. It won't be long until every last penny is spent. The coachman shuffles down the street and after a while he shuffles back. Daisy says nothing but I find I grow accustomed to her silences.

◆

NIGHTFALL FINDS us some miles short of Launceston but I am untroubled on this account. Too long have I wallowed in the roil and strife and I have found myself pining for the sea and the islands. It is my belief that Daisy feels the same for it is in her marrow same as mine. I have busied myself in the task of her retrieval and now that it is done there looms a vast nothing in its place. It is myself who is leaving this realm and in my passing I shall not unduly trouble the child. Merely to see mother and daughter reunited is all I ask.

No one is coming, not from Launceston ahead nor Norfolk Plains behind. The men who would do us ill are all abed. Clements' horses are hobbled and his cart unhitched. Before us is the prospect of supper and a bottle of rum. Clements is satisfied to find himself so handsomely paid but to his credit he does not find cause to bleat about it.

And we drink, my thoughts gone a'hazy in their swaddling of rum.

'There is a ship!' cries Daisy.

'Will ye let me live or no?' says Halfpenny.

'Don't go thinkin' I did that for ye,' says Jimmy.

'You ain't takin' my girl!' cries Moe.

I would reply to each of them but they whip away on the wind, all four.

In my dream I am myself the coachman, but I must be the poorest one imaginable for luggage is falling off the cart all the while. My passengers do not seem to notice as I bounce the carriage over the deepest ruts and let their luggage slide down into the mud. With each creaking turn of the wheels the load is lightened and my heart is glad in the knowledge that I shall soon be unburdened entirely.

When I look back again there is but one passenger and it is Daisy. She opens her mouth as if to speak.

◆

THOUGH IT is the best part of twenty years since I saw him, I often find myself thinking on the words of Pierre Faure. I am older now than he was then and yet in my mind I am still a boy and he a man. *I make maps, George,* he said. *First it is a map*, Robbins replied. There was a time when George Town was naught but a sign on a post and before that presumably only scratchings on Flinders' map, but now there is a proper settlement where Governor Macquarie always wanted one put. The road from Launceston is no good but then there is a map for that. There is a proper wharf and a battery in case the French should ever return. Colonel Cimitiere's regiment is stationed here for such a purpose and in the meantime they are tasked with policing troubledoers.

It is December 1ˢᵗ, dawn of another summer, and there is the taste of smoke in the air. The muddy streets crawl with ruddy redcoats and convicts and the sun beats down on them every one. I spy a familiar face down at dockside and to my surprise it is Henry Barrett, the York Town gardener, clad in the raiment of a constable.

'What ho, Henry,' I say. 'You'll recall my daughter Daisy?'

'My how the lass has grown! I believe this calls for an article of refreshment.'

We repair to the public house and there drink our fill. Daisy consents to being given a small mug of beer. It is pleasant to be in good company and I tell Henry so. We speak of those

who have made names for themselves and of others who went
to water, Garrett and Mills the latter.

'A rottener pair of criminals you would not want to find,'
Henry says. 'Reckon I warned you.'

'I must say I never imagined you a public officer, Henry.
I'd have judged you altogether too honest.'

'Needs must, George. I'm not above firin' on outlaws nor
pilferin' the public purse. You look like a man come into money
yourself.'

I tell him of the debt to Nichols forgiven and of what has
recently become of that sum.

'Nichols, now there's a name I've heard just lately.
Postmaster up in Sydney, wasn't he?'

'Still is, although when I saw him he was laid up in bed.'

'He's gone and carked it, George. Says so in the *Gazette*
fresh off the Sydney packet.' Henry calls for a newspaper and
reads from the obituary notices.

> *'On Monday last, at his house in George Street, after*
> *a long illness, Mr Isaac Nichols, Postmaster, leaving*
> *a widow and three sons to lament his death.'*

'It can't be. What's that edition dated?'

'November 13. That's after you sailed, is it?'

'By a week it is.'

'Then I reckon yours is the touch of death, George.
Perhaps it's me who ought to be watching his step.'

But I am not listening to Henry's jests. Like the clansmen,
I burn my way across this land and am in doing so burned.
Daisy knows it and says nothing, she sees and will not tell. Her
father is karpennooyouhener, tainted, herself daughter to the
damned.

'You look to've seen a ghost, George,' Henry says. 'Who
else crossed your path and wound up dead?'

Tom Stepney, Joseph Halfpenny, to name just two.

We're all of us dead, Henry, I say without speaking. *All of us dead and swept away.* A moment from now he will ask me where I'm headed and I shall tell him we go looking for Moe, and then he will tell me of his Mary back in York Town. Of her future burning to death in that same hut he will say not a word, and nor shall he speak of their adult son falling into a trypot full of boiling oil years from now. There is a time coming and it shan't be mine to tell, a world where I am gone as though I never was. Daisy will be there and all she will say is she had a father and his name was George Baggs. Today the dead do not speak but tomorrow they surely will.

Then we are out into the hot, bright day and I am bidding my friend goodbye. He is a man not given to outbursts of emotion and nor am I and here we are parting in the manner of old friends, embracing and slapping one another on the back. I shake his hand and wish good health to his family.

In the street a crowd has gathered to watch a man being flogged at the triangles and the commissariat store stands empty as a consequence. The commissary has one eye on me and the other on the grisly business unfolding outside. I will not bear witness to such cruel sport but I cannot help but hear the cracking of the cat and the unfortunate man's accompanying shrieks.

'Hundred'll do for 'im, I reckon,' the commissary says. 'They say a lash from Taylor's worth two.'

I look up. 'Private Taylor, is it? Used to be in Launceston?'

'Corporal Taylor now.'

'How many is the criminal due?'

'Another fifty, but he won't last half that.'

'And what was his crime?'

'Actin' with insubordination.'

From where I stand I could not see the man being punished even if I wanted to, such is the press of the throng.

I hurry about my business, burning through the last of my dollars except those I have set aside for our passage. Before long I am very nearly skint but in possession of a musket as well as an old bronze spyglass. Foolish is he who walks through town with only a pistol let alone goes gallivanting around the countryside. In this regard each year is wretcheder than the last and it won't be long before all Van Diemen's Land is swarming with gun toting halfwits.

Pushing through the crowd, I catch an unwanted glimpse of the convict's red-ribboned back and sniff the tang of his blood. His head is slumped forward and he barely raises a whimper in response to the singing of the whip. The attendant doctor is poised to halt proceedings and thus the flagellator approaches each action as though it might be his last.

We are halfway up the street before I hear the whip crack again.

◆

IN A brig like *Glory* it would not be more than a day's sailing to Longtartennerner, but there is no such brig standing on the George Town wharf that means to try the Furneaux this season. There are several ragtag whaleboats, however, most poorly crewed and improperly outfitted, and it is no trouble negotiating passage on one in exchange for my labour. My agreement is with Jamie Canning, the man I judge least likely to slit my throat and make off with my daughter. Some years older than me and with a tangle of black hair streaked with grey, Canning is said to have a clanwife who has borne him a daughter of his own.

'I'll take you to Clarke Island if I can,' he says, 'although we're bound for the northside of Cape Barren and not the south.'

I ask him what his interest in the region is.

'I don't mind telling you I've been mining crystals at a place near Rooks River. I could use a man who can be trusted.'

Rooks River, William Bastard Rook.

I tell Canning I've no particular interest in taking up the pickaxe and that I can think of nothing further than getting Daisy home to her mother.

'Moe's your wife, is she? I thought she was Brown's. But then I didn't mean to make it any business of mine.'

I mull over his words as we get underway. Though I am required at the oar I make sure to keep Daisy close for the other men look a villainous bunch. It is the best part of a year since I last laid eyes on my wife and all the while I left her with Brown. Could it be that he considers her his property in my absence? As we battle the heavy riptide, I try to drive such speculation from my mind for if I do not trust Brown then I trust no man. Thus springs the seed of doubt.

Once we are clear of the heads it is a good run with a fresh nor'wester and I hold the girl close. Canning means to make it to Waterhouse Island today but it is a distance of some forty miles and I think him a trifle optimistic. In mid-afternoon we sight a rock called the Barrenjoey and it is a place I sealed myself in the dim mist of a vanished history. I begin to tell the story but not even Canning is interested as it is only a jagged outcropping where life is absent. Brown saw this coming a decade ago and today his prophecy stands fulfilled.

Late in the day we are still miles short of Waterhouse and thus Canning has us haul up on Ninth Island, a lonely windswept place albeit one favoured by muttonbirds. Nothing could be easier than wringing their scrawny necks although there is always the risk of being snakebitten. A fire and a feast are soon to follow. Daisy remains leery but at least she has the good sense not to stray from my sight. There is rum aplenty and the cooing birds all round.

'Our daughters are about the same age, I reckon,' Canning says. 'Mine I named Maria after the island. You know it?'

'Only a little. Where do your wife and child reside, Jamie?'

'They are on the Derwent with the South Arm clan. Must be five years ago I brought in a bunch because Tom Davey wanted to speak with them. So many crammed onto my boat they very nearly sank it, my wife the only one who spoke a word of English. You should have seen their faces when they saw Hobart Town.'

'It must have seemed a different world. You judge them safe at South Arm?'

'At least until the Pittwater settlers think to let their stock roam that region.'

'And when they do, Jamie?'

'Then I shall take my family further afield, perhaps to Bruny Island.'

'They won't be safe on Bruny now that James Kelly has opened his whaling station.'

'Then I shall send them still further afield. I would not imagine your own wife any safer, George.'

'What makes you say that?'

'You've been away a good while, haven't you?'

'Not more than a year.'

'A year's a long time in the Furneaux Isles. There's bad folk around. Mark well these words for it is our children's very lives.'

'What'll we do, Jamie?'

'Get your kin clear is my advice.'

Daisy says nothing but I feel her stiffen.

◆

I AWAKE to a night as dark as any I have known. Not a single star, each one hidden behind an invisible wall of cloud. No wind nor rain and with the sea becalmed it is so quiet that all I can hear is my daughter's snores. Lying there awhile, I begin to discern the scratching and shuffling of the muttonbirds in their burrows. I get up as quietly as I can, standing rigid to see if I have disturbed anyone's sleep. It is only fifteen or twenty paces to water's edge and I stand there a long time adjusting to the gloom.

I walk to where the beach gives out and sit on a rock with my feet in the water. It is not what I shall do that occupies my mind but that which I have already done. I would seek forgiveness, not from a distant God, but those I have walked among. Some of them are dead.

The more time passes, the more I find my thoughts turning back to New Year Island and Pierre Faure. I would have gone with him on his longboat if only he'd allowed it. I might have seen France or died a youthful death. But it was my fate to come to Van Diemen's Land and thereupon to linger. I shall not be leaving this place again.

Come morning the country is revealed, Double Sandy Point across the water and Waterhouse Island at a distance of fifteen or twenty miles. Beyond that is the dim outline of the Furneaux's jagged peaks. My arms are sore from yesterday's labour, long experience having taught me that today will be more onerous. We will not make Longtartennerner today but in all likelihood we will reach the country Chief Laman favours.

Throughout the morning I watch the coast for fires and initially there are none. Nor are there signs of the English this far from Launceston. After two or three hours' exertion we attain the passage between Waterhouse Island and the main, the course taking us near the grey cliffs of the larger island's southwest point. Here tide turns crosswise to our purposes, but eventually we escape into the island's lee and haul up on the beach. It is every bit as hot as I thought it might be. After a lunch of pork and yesterday's muttonbirds, Canning and his men doze while I sit on the beach with Daisy. Before us is the wide expanse of Ringarooma Bay, her grandfather's country.

'See that smudge of fire across the bay?' I say. 'That'll have been set by your mother's people.'

'Is she there?'

'She was on Longtartennerner with your uncle but that was months ago.' I point across the water in the direction of the distant hills. 'Those are the Furneaux Isles. Longtartennerner's the nearest of them.'

'Mother's there?'

'I don't know, Daisy, but I promise you we'll find her.'

I have an inkling that this wisp of a closemouthed child, neither black nor white, is the very future. With her matted hair and her forlorn expression, she is in a place I cannot reach. What words she will utter and what deeds enact are beyond my reckoning. Not a word more does she offer but I know she is thinking and watching the water.

'Ten years ago I first set eyes on this place,' I say. 'Your grandfather could have slain me if he'd wanted to and then you'd have never been born. But he didn't and he sent his daughter a'sealing with me. He's a wise man, Laman.'

'I go to grandfather.'

I unfurl the spyglass and hold it up to my eye, but I cannot make anything out at this distance. But the place is right and the season and so I pray it is Laman's people setting those fires.

When Canning rises I tell him of my change of plan.

'You want settin' down there instead of Clarke?'

'I reckon that fire along the coast will be from the girl's grandfather. He'll know whether my wife's over on Clarke or not.'

'All the same I'll not spend days waitin' around.'

'I'm not asking you to, just set us down there at Tomahawk River. Surely you don't mean to try Banks Strait this aft?'

'I haven't decided,' Canning says, consulting the western sky.

'I'd wait till tomorrow if I were you. She's prone to turning dangerous.'

'Don't I know it, George. All right, it's Tomahawk tonight and tomorrow we'll go our separate ways.'

In the afternoon the wind turns to our disadvantage and we make hard work of the remaining miles, but the burning in my arms does not sadden me for this labour shall soon be done. As we approach the mainland I see that the country is blackened for miles around as per the custom of the season. When we are near Tomahawk, Canning offers to spell me and I look through the spyglass, but of clansmen and sealers I see not a one. It is as good and as open a country as exists in all Van Diemen's Land and one abounding with every kind of game. There is a rocky island at Tomahawk River separated from the main by a shallow channel and it is here at the rivermouth that I have us land. The cove on the island's eastern side commands an impressive view of Cape Portland and the Furneaux. Today the bay stands calm, hundreds of cormorants sunning themselves on the smooth offshore rocks. The beach is smooth and flat and silent. Canning's men go about making camp and I tell them they might as well have a campfire for Laman's men will have seen the whaleboat. I think the clans have learned not to walk on the beach the way they used to for fear of karpennooyouhener.

'Ain't like it was even three or four years ago,' Canning says. 'These days those bastards snatch girls as young as yours and mine from their campfires. Clansmen slain, wives and daughters taken to the islands.'

'Which islands?' I say. 'Not Clarke?'

'Not Clarke as far as I know. There's a bunch of miscreants who make their base on Gun Carriage Island, but they're not the only ones. Furneaux's crawlin' with rum folk and freebooters. It isn't safe for your missus and for Heaven's sake not your little girl.'

Where is Daisy safe if not in her grandfather's country? It is a bewildering question and one without answer. Many are the men who would seek to ill-use Daisy and to whom might she appeal if they did? Certainly not the new Lieutenant-Governor, Sorell. It is a cruel life she is born into and one crueller in the offing.

◆

I AM awake in the earliest light. None shall disturb me and thus my heart revels in the rapture of its being. I know not the precise date but it is December 1819 and I am nigh on twenty years in this land. I am drawn to light as a moth to flame and it has me poised to wade over from Tomahawk Island to the main. I could not bring my musket even if I wanted to and nor should I wish to ruin my boots, so I make a pile of such items at the back of the dunes. The water is deeper than I imagined and I soon lose my footing, and then I am swimming or rather thrashing about. I will never swim as elegantly as my wife but nor shall I drown in waters barely higher than my head.

Once across, I stand on the edge of a field of rounded shale replete with rockpools and their attendant crabs. My eyes sting from the salt and my clothes are sopping wet but I shall not be dissuaded. Looking back, I see a wisp of smoke but the campsite itself is hidden. Skirting the shale as best I can, I arrive at a stretch of beach leading south to the outlet of the river. With each step the morn grows brighter and my sense of rapture fades. I am wet through and my thighs are chafing. Before long I have divested myself of both jacket and trousers.

They are watching me as I knew they would, three huntsmen at the place where the beach turns to scrub. I carry my clothes in a bundle and they their spears and it seems I must go to them for they have not moved a muscle. I hold up my hand in greeting but they offer no acknowledgement and when I am within fifty yards they raise their spears to a throwing position.

'I'm unarmed,' I say, raising my hands. 'Yah peulinghenar.'

The sky explodes and I writhe around with a mouthful of sand. A spear has caught the fleshy part of my thigh, the wound barely a graze and yet the pain is intense. The clansmen stand over me, blocking the sun.

'I'm George Baggs,' I say, holding my thigh with both hands. 'Take me to Laman Bunganna.'

The men say nothing and one of them bends to retrieve his spear. The men are unknown to me and painted for war but it is no accident that I am only lightly injured. 'I've brought his granddaughter,' I say. 'Moe's child Daisy.'

One of them is older and stouter than the others, his chest and legs heavily scarred, and he offers me his hand. He hauls me grimacing to my feet. The younger men eye my wound with a professional interest and I think their discussion centres on the grazing shot one of them has struck. The younger men assist me in walking while the other carries my clothes. I can see their camp and their cooking fires in a grove by the river.

The sun is high and the day advanced and I am fretting about Daisy. I meant to make my reconnaissance quickly and now I find myself an invalid and a prisoner. Canning will be awake soon if he is not already and no doubt a'puzzling my whereabouts. I do not think him one to make off with my girl but then I know the man but slightly and he has already expressed his eagerness to get over to the Furneaux.

'Yah peulinghenar, Baggs.'

It is Chief Laman, as ever painted red. He does not smile but invites me to sit by the fire.

'It's good to see you again, Laman Bunganna. I've brought your granddaughter Daisy. She's over on Tomahawk Island with some sealers.'

He frowns on hearing the last word and repeats it aloud. 'Karpennooyouhener,' he adds. 'You are a bad devil, Baggs.'

He says more I fail to understand but I catch his drift that it is better the devil you know. I try to explain that I believe Jamie Canning to be a good man but that I am eager to retrieve Daisy. I do not think I can walk far on this leg and nor is it wise to send Laman's huntsmen without me for fear they will be fired upon. Laman goes into a long discourse and I think he is telling me about various skirmishes he has had up and down this coast. 'Kartummeter parkutetennar,' he says. 'Kartummeter lillerclapperlar, kartummeter karpennooyouhener.'

'How many whaleboats?' I say. 'How many lillerclapperlar?'

He holds up three fingers, then thinks about it and adds a fourth and a fifth.

'Five whaleboats. Do they all come from the islands?'

He shakes his head no, pointing every which way. Some come from the islands, some from the Eddystone in the east, some from the west as I have done. And what do these men want now that all the seals have been slaughtered? They come for women and they take whatever can be had. Laman shows me a scar on his leg from where he has been shot and another below his ribcage. These days the straitsmen do not even attempt to parley, instead firing on any clansmen they see. Once taken aboard the boats, most of the women are never seen by their families again. And it is a harsh life on the islands. In response

to these attacks, Laman's men have taken to spearing any
Englishmen they find. He explains that the only reason I got off
lightly was because I came naked and an ordinary straitsman
would never do that.

'And where is my wife?' I say her proper name. 'Is she still
over on Longtartennerner?'

Laman looks surprised and shakes his head no. I look
behind me to where he is pointing. I am being watched by a
group of women and one of them is Moe. I try to stand but my
leg is throbbing and the wound oozing blood. I sit back down
and Moe comes flanked by her younger sisters.

'I had no idea you were here, Moe,' I say.

She nods but it is as though we are barely acquainted.
'Good to see you,' she says.

The women chatter away on the subject of my injury. I
am woozy and lightheaded, my thoughts confused. Is she my
wife or not, and where are my trousers? There they are drying
by the fire.

'I thought you were over on Longtartennerner,' I say.

It is like she doesn't understand, but I know she does.

'With Jimmy,' I add.

She scowls. 'No more with Jimmy Brown.'

'What happened?'

But she will not say, not in her father's company and
perhaps not at all.

'I brought Daisy home,' I say. 'She's over on Tomahawk
Island.'

That changes everything, as I knew it would. 'Ningher?
You brought my Daisy?'

'If you'll help me up I'll get her back from those straitsmen.'

No one seems inclined to assist me or to dress my wound
and so I sit up and reach for my trousers. I must finish what
I set out to accomplish even if I should be obliged to do so on

one leg. Flies are harassing me and the sting of wet salt is unpleasant but I get the trousers on and my jacket too.

Laman and his huntsmen follow me down to the beach, the women not far behind. No doubt they anticipate treachery and it grieves me to think that the understanding between our peoples has been destroyed. Already at the edge of my vision there is an encroaching darkness and each step only serves to further darken this visage. I am very thirsty and there is naught on offer except the sea and I am not yet mad enough for that.

And there is a sail!

It is a vision which cannot be blinked away, a whaleboat running along the coast. As the boat draws closer, I see it is Canning and crew with Daisy on the thwart and my God the man has come good in the hour of my greatest need. Seeing Laman and his men, Canning stands the boat offshore and I am obliged to swim out as best I can. I strip down to my bare arse. It isn't far and they haul me up, wretched creature that I am.

'You're bleeding,' Canning says. 'Did they spear you?'

'Not gravely.'

'It looks it to me.' He hands me a blanket and I sit next to Daisy and point out her mother on the beach.

'Haul away, boys,' Canning says.

'Wait, I'll have you set us down. I've a few coins left in my kitbag if you'll take them as fair payment.'

'Have your wife swim out and I'll get both mother and child to South Arm.'

'This is their country as South Arm is to your wife,' I say. 'We'll make our stand here. There's the best part of two pounds in that bag and it is yours if you'll kindly set us down. Now that they've seen their kin, they won't harm a hair on your head.'

'A madman's promise and one not long for this world,' he says, but he steers us around.

'I pray you've a bottle of rum to give for I am in agony,' I say. 'I'll be needing my musket too. A pound and fifteen shillings I think it is.'

'The madman shall have his rum but I won't take a penny of his money.'

We haul up under the eyes of the huntsmen and I lift Daisy out. A thunderbolt of pain shoots through me but it is of little consequence for I watch as mother and child run to one another.

'Take the money for I shall not have need of it,' I say to Canning, calf deep in the sea with the bloodstained blanket across my shoulder. 'Just hand me my musket and a bottle if you will.' I carry these items beyond the tideline in two trips and by the time I am finished the pain has settled to a dull stinging. Perhaps the saltwater is of some assistance for the bleeding has lessened, but the sky is brighter and my thoughts wracked with fever. I call out to Canning but he is gone, the whaleboat set for the islands.

And I am a burning man.

◆

MOE SHAKES me awake. 'Pernickerter, George! Lillerclapperlar.'

'It'll just be Canning again. Probably he couldn't get across.'

'Pernickerter!'

I see a whaleboat but could not say if it is Canning or no for I have mislaid my spyglass. 'Where are my trousers, Moe? And my jacket?'

On my feet and in my clothes, I am dizzy and my leg is hot to touch. She is a fine woman, Moe, even if it is her preference not to see me again. I see that Daisy has thrown away her English attire.

I stand on the beach with my musket primed, Laman and his huntsmen readying their spears. There is a tingling in my fingers and a skittering in my heart for it is not Canning making landfall but another crew entirely. The boatsteerer is a man unknown to me but it is Jimmy Brown at the starboard oar. Five men with muskets to my one.

'Reckoned ye were dead, George,' Jimmy says as they clamber out. He holds out his hand for me to shake and I will not shake it.

'Then you reckoned wrong, Jimmy.'

'Not far wrong by the looks. Found Moe, did ye?'

'Looks like she ran off from you but then women were always doing that.'

'Ye ought've stayed in Sydney, George. Far safer for ye there. Reckon ye saved me life but then I've long since paid it back.'

'You'll cut me down, will you? You used to say we were brothers.'

'That were years ago, George. Now stand aside.'

'You'll threaten me no further, Jimmy. What business have your men here?'

'Ain't my men, George. Don't reckon ye've met Duncan McMillan?'

McMillan is the tall one with the scarred hands. 'This here's my crew,' he says. 'Who are you and what business is it of yours what I do?'

'My name is George Baggs and it is everything to me.'

'Never heard of you, George. Now stand aside, I hear there's womenfolk about.'

'Well you've heard of me now and I shall not stand aside. You might think yourself five to my one but we'll find out how well you fight with a spear running through you fore-and-aft.'

'Don't think him afraid to fire upon ye, George,' Brown says. 'Wouldn't be first man he's found cause for cuttin' down.'

'Then let it rain red, fellows, for I shall not tarry a moment longer.'

And I fire.

◆

SUNSET COMES like a blessing. Brown lays facedown where I felled him although the tide is coming for us both. I am myself shot through but in surprisingly little discomfort. One of Laman's huntsmen is slain with a second badly wounded but the whaleboat is gone and today's raid has been repelled. I saw a spear protruding from McMillan's shoulder as he ran.

They are watching from the dunes, Laman and his men. I feel their eyes. No words have they and I do not begrudge them for I am very nearly at a place beyond words myself. It must be an hour since Moe and Daisy came down. It was my heart's wish to see them one last time.

Wollighererperarner, George, I heard Moe say.

◆

IT IS later and I am disorderly,

two decades in a burning land, supping my rum like water.

My mind a'racing,

our island by the name of New Year, each one scrawnier than the last. What tomorrow will bring, two blind eyes for the turning, roguery beyond all calculation. What mockery is this, a flag used for straining water, such a paper exists on our corvette. I must get off this island, what remains of the *George, but what about the oil*? The foot of the crumbling cliff, untouched by Europe's designs, and it is a killing drop.

As we slide past the perilous cape,

we have outstayed our welcome, *there go yer eighty skins.* A man sunk so low, he means to repay in blood, more to bein' a sealer than just sealin'. Them traps are right intricate, it has given us a terrible flux, sweet little doxy at the back of the tavern. Men can sleep anywhere, a bucket of yesterday's shite, how long was your sentence? Haunted by such a vision, I'd ask you to look in the mirror, his lips are almost black.

To confirm I am a man and not some unwanted vision,

I'll dc as birds do, in a state of frankest nudity. She is slender and beautiful, he speaks in a commanding tone, they have slain two kangaroos. Yet there is a thing like language, my arms windmilling without effect, and this is our courtship dance. Place fairly swarming with soldiers, the ink symbols marked upon them, the guard's gone on a jag. A clanswoman waving a musket, from a hiding place in the reeds, I espy no lick of flame. In an affray not far from here, my mother and the manner of my siring, you admit of your suspicions. Purely a matter of business, a darkling land this England, and I know not where it ends.

The cleverman contorts his body,

the rest of us only riding on his coattails, *do not think I shall absolve you yet.* When you wanted women, to fight other clans, Yah peulinghenar Baggs. To hurl abuse across the water, a curse upon my head, ye can't give back what ain't yers to give. I take ye for a bolter, she speaks of karpennooyouhener, I do not fail to recognise my own name.

If I am moved by such tales most often it is,

to slit men's throats whilst they sleep, course then I battered its brains out. I am barely listening to these braggarts, the seventeen pounds meant for Nichols, a cruel town Sydney as I have often said. The cart sinks wheel-deep in mud, others see death well enough, albeit for a modest fee. Let them speak now every one, it were only the wind come a'knocking, will she be made to vanish too? I grow accustomed to her silences, such history best left forgotten, a bloody great hole in yer britches. A man being flogged at the triangles, that man might be you yourself, *a widow and three sons to lament his death.*

Shuffling of the muttonbirds in their burrows, a devil wills it so, our children's very lives.

◆

IT IS a darkness enveloping me and swallowing me entire.

◆

AM I dreaming still? I am a half-frozen boy telling tales from the doorway as a way of being admitted to the fireside. In my mind I am on an evening beach looking out over the water at the islands from whence I sprang.

Those unearthly blue hills tug at me. By Christ I shall scale them yet.

In my dream, myself and everyone I'd ever known were stood together on a beach no different than this. Thousands of them, clansmen and the English and even my dear old mam. From the sea an enormous wave was set to crash upon them and I thought *My God we are swept away like Tom Stepney from his rock.*

And I am gone.

APPENDICES

APPENDIX A

NORTHEAST CLAN WORD LIST USED IN *DIEMENS*

◆

My gratitude to Aunty Patsy Cameron, who provided this word list and her support and expertise in its usage in *Diemens*.

LOCATIONS

Kunermurlukeker	Tamar River
Larener	George Rocks
Larerpoonne	Bay of Fires
Leengteenner	Tomahawk River
Longtartennerner	Clarke Island
Ringarooma	Ringarooma River
Tangumronener	Eddystone Point
Tebrakunna	Cape Portland

PEOPLE

Bunganna	leader
Kannowner	free white man
Karpennooyouhener	bad person
Loonner	black woman
Luewottenner	child/infant
Meena	I or me/mine
Pannerkarner	black man
Parkutetennar	soldier
Perringye	bushranger
Pleengenner	white man
Tyereelore	island woman/wife
Warrander	we

THINGS/OTHER WORDS

Beege	oar*
Crackena	sit down†
Kartummeter	many/several
Kueberrenner	seal
Larngerner	look and track
Legana	water
Lillerclapperlar	whaleboat
Marebrunner	smoke
Molookener	hunt
Myhena	body†
Nartick	hot
Nummerwar	no
Oongurlerpooler	cut
Pargonee	pull
Parhamoeniyack	tired
Partrollarne	musket
Partroller	fire
Parwarlar	yes
Pernickerter	quickly/make haste
Plentenner	snake
Tangehaller	burnt forest
Teewoorer	sun/warm
Tunnack	cold
Wollighererperarner	goodbye
Wongherne	stay
Yah peulinghenar	hello, greetings
Yarnenner	swimming

* South East language
† Oyster Bay language

SOURCES

Plomley, N. J. B. (1976). *A Word-List of the Tasmanian Aboriginal Languages*. Launceston: N. J. B. Plomley in association with the Government of Tasmania.

_______. (1992). Tasmanian Aboriginal Place Names, Occasional Paper No. 3. Launceston: Queen Victoria Museum and Art Gallery.

Roth, H. L. (1970). *The Aborigines of Tasmania*. Hobart: Fullers Bookshop Pty Ltd.

APPENDIX B

'PARDONED TO SERVE HIS MAJESTY BY SEA' THE LIFE OF GEORGE BRIGGS

◆

I FIRST encountered the name of sealer George Briggs in James Boyce's peerless history *Van Diemen's Land*. Employed by Captain James Kelly on a whaleboat circumnavigating Tasmania in 1815–16, Briggs is said to have been the key negotiator between Kelly's crew and the Aboriginal Tasmanians they met during the journey.[1] KM Bowden provides a fuller account based on the writings of Kelly himself: 'At noon [we] landed at Ringarooma Point. Here we suddenly fell in with a large "mob" of natives, who, upon their first appearance seemed hostile, but on seeing Briggs, who they knew particularly well [...] seemed delighted.'[2] Briggs is said to have 'left two wives and five children upon the islands', one of the wives being 'a daughter of the chief Lamanbunganah.'[3] When Lamanbunganah asked for assistance in fighting another chief, his brother Tolobunganah, Briggs declined. 'At this Laman seemed greatly dissatisfied, and told Briggs, in a very hostile tone, that he had often before gone with him to fight other tribes when he (Briggs) wanted women.'[4] Briggs, we are told, managed to dodge this responsibility without being drawn into conflict and the whaleboat voyage continued unimpeded.

In their histories, Boyce and Bowden have drawn upon a narrative by James Kelly published in 1854 as 'Some unrecorded passages in the history of Van Diemen's Land.

(From a very old stager.)' Kelly's account offers a fascinating insight into an important chapter in Tasmanian history, but it is also problematic. Kelly was hardly a disinterested observer and likely shaped his work to present himself and his crew in a favourable light. Famed for his exaggerations and tall tales later in life, Kelly 'once won a bet that his trousers would hold five bushels of wheat'.[5] Kelly's claim to have measured the length of a man's leap at 11 yards is absurd,[6] and his description of George Town seems dubious. He describes visiting the government cottage, barracks and storehouse at George Town in January 1816,[7] in contrast to Governor Macquarie's lament of more than a year later that the works had 'made very slow progress'.[8] In June 1817, Lieutenant-Governor Sorell reported to Macquarie that there is 'no Building erected [at George Town] but a temporary Store and a Lime Hut',[9] casting doubt on the veracity of Kelly's narrative.

Despite these reservations, I was nevertheless intrigued about George Briggs and wanted to know more. Websites such as *Trove* and *FamilySearch* aggregate a wealth of material unavailable to previous generations of researchers, and thus we discover that George William Christopher Lamuel Briggs was born in the town of Dunstable in England in June 1787.[10] His parents were William Briggs and Mary Jane Simms and he was baptised on December 31, 1788, the eldest of nine children.[11] On July 12, 1800, shortly after his thirteenth birthday, Briggs was convicted in London at Newgate Prison on a charge of piracy. Instead of facing execution, George (listed here as Geo Briggs) was instead 'Pardoned to serve His Majesty by sea'.[12]

We can only surmise how this might have happened. It is not specified where Briggs was arrested, but it was probably in London and not Dunstable, his piratical deeds on the muddy banks of the Thames. David Wells explains that, at this time, '[c]rime on the river was rife [as] one third of the people employed in dock labour were engaged in some form of criminal activity'.[13] The lowest rung on the criminal ladder was the mudlark, usually a small boy whose task it was to linger in the mud at low tide and retrieve goods thrown down from nearby ships. These thefts cost merchants an estimated £500,000 per year (£53,000,000 in today's money).[14] In 1798, London magistrates established the Marine Police to curb such piracy, and the scheme proved so successful that founder Patrick Colquhoun was able to boast a saving of £122,000 in the first year.[15] Young George Briggs may well have run afoul of the world's first police force.

Historians Brian Plomley and Kristen Anne Henley contend that Briggs was born in England and 'arrived at Port Jackson on the *Harrington* on March 4, 1805'.[16] This is in contradiction to Bowden, who describes Briggs as 'native born', that is born in the New South Wales colony.[17] *Harrington* was a 150 or 180-ton brig with a complicated history, captured by the French and returned to the British in time to sail from Madras in 1801 under the command of William Campbell.[18] When *Harrington* arrived in Sydney that June, Governor King refused to allow its cargo of 4,000 gallons of spirits to be landed.[19] Over the next year, *Harrington* was engaged in sealing activity in Bass Strait, Norfolk Island and King Island, landing a party of 12 Englishmen on New Year Island off King Island.[20] By the time the French corvettes *Le Géographe* and *Le Naturaliste* arrived at King Island in December 1802, the *Harrington* sealers had been there 13 months. Is it possible that George Briggs was among them, and that Plomley and Henley were mistaken in believing him to have arrived in Australia in 1805?

Sent in a longboat to circumnavigate King Island, French surveyor Pierre Faure spent three days in the company of the *Harrington* sealers.[21] If Briggs was among them, then he was present at a remarkable event and one that played a critical part in the subsequent colonisation of Tasmania. Governor King sent Lieutenant Charles Robbins to intercept the French at King Island, where Robbins infamously (and presumably accidentally) flew the Union Jack upside down over the French tents as a means of pressing the British claim over Van Diemen's Land.[22] Within two years, the British had established colonies on the Derwent in the south and the Tamar in the north of the island.

There was also money to be made. It is a little-known fact that Australia's first export commodity was sealskins. After the wreck of the *Sydney Cove* on Preservation Island in 1797, salvage efforts were made not only to rescue the sailors languishing there, but to retrieve the ship's valuable cargo of rum. Explorer Matthew Flinders was aboard one such voyage and discovered 'the great seal rookeries of the Furneaux, and other groups lying in the eastern end of Bass Strait'.[23] The following year, Captain Bishop of the *Nautilus* led a sealing venture to nearby Cape Barren Island, yielding '9000 seal skins of the first quality and several tons of oil', a cargo which eventually sold for $14,000 in Canton.[24] Such skins were durable and waterproof, making excellent caps, capes and stoles, and were highly sought after on the Chinese and London markets where they sold for upward of a pound apiece. *Harrington* brought 3,000 sealskins to Sydney in December 1801 and a further 5,200 the following June. By December 1804, Sydney firm Kable & Underwood had brought in 32,000 skins and, along with William Campbell, were said to employ 180 sealers in Bass Strait.[25] By October 1805, 216 men were working as sealers, a figure which constituted 10–15 per cent of the free men in the colony.[26]

But while profits for the sealing masters were considerable, working conditions for sealers were often hellish.

It is difficult to appreciate the demands, physical and emotional, of the roller-coaster ride that was primitive Georgian sealing. Approaching coasts we wouldn't venture near today in much more buoyant craft, these men, many of whom couldn't swim, pulled oars on heavy, timber boats, stormed ashore on the crest of a wave, stood backs to an often-treacherous sea, clubbing and stabbing in bawling frenzy, while angry, frightened, biting animals tried to stampede past, throwing hundreds of pounds of blubber and teeth behind a headlong rush to the ocean. Even success meant long hours of stench and butchery, risky clambering with heavy pelts over unforgiving, slippery stone, loading tossing, perilous, egg-shell casks into pitching, foundering clinker boats.[27]

Worse, sealers were often paid by a 'lay' system whereby they would receive a percentage of the skins taken over the course of a voyage in lieu of wages. A 1/100th lay was common. Deducted from this were expenses incurred for items such as food, clothing and tobacco, and thus it was not uncommon for sealers to become heavily indebted to their masters despite their months-long labour.[28]

Once the seals had been slain, 'a hooked device would drag the carcase before the skin was removed, usually in one piece (feet, snout and eyeholes intact), and then pegged out to dry and treated with salt'.[29] Seal oil was a valuable commodity, procured by melting blubber in a cast iron trypot and then draining the oil into casks. Elephant seals were especially prized for their oil, three gallons of which might fetch a pound at market. As an adult bull yielded as much as 17 gallons, this was a lucrative albeit short-lived business.[30]

The short-sightedness of the English sealers was apparent to the French as early as 1802, Commandant Baudin observing that '[t]here is every sign that in a short while your fishermen will have drained [King Island] of its resources through the hunting of the fur seals and the sea elephants [...] in a little while you will hear it said that they have entirely disappeared.'[31] By 1810, the elephant seals of King Island had been hunted near to extinction and the rookeries of the Furneaux lay devastated.

Whether George Briggs was a party to this wholesale slaughter is not known, but fragments of his later career can be assembled by way of the shipping notices in the *Sydney Gazette and New South Wales Advertiser*, especially if we accept that George Briggs, George Buggs and George Baggs were the same man.[32] Thus we discover a George Buggs departing Sydney aboard the schooner *Governor Hunter* on April 14, 1805.[33] On December 8, of that year, *Governor Hunter* is again 'ready to proceed to Bass's Straits' with George Baggs among its crew.[34] In the New South Wales General Muster of 1806, Briggs is listed as 'Sealing' in 'Kable employ' in the category 'E. C.' (Emancipated Convict).[35] 'Kable employ' refers to Henry Kable, a renowned Sydney businessman and ex-convict who had partnered with boatbuilder James Underwood in forming a successful trading enterprise.

Briggs might have continued sealing for the Sydney traders for many years, except for an event that was to alter the course of his life. Listed under his correct name, Briggs is named as departing Sydney aboard *Governor Hunter* on November 6, 1808.[36] On July 30, 1809, the *Gazette* reported that the *Governor Hunter* had run aground on Badger Island, off north-east Tasmania, on April 1.[37] Owner Isaac Nichols purchased another ship to sail to the rescue and *Governor Hunter* was refloated and returned to Sydney in April 1810 after an absence of nearly 18 months.[38] This gives rise to a simple question: did Briggs take this opportunity to flee his sealing masters and make a life for himself in Van Diemen's Land?

It is at this point that Briggs is said to have been the first sealer to make his home on Longtartennerner (Clarke Island), less than 20 kilometres from where *Governor Hunter* ran aground.[39] Briggs is thought to have been in contact with the pairrebeenne clan of the tebrakunna (Cape Portland) region of north-east Tasmania.[40] The chief of this clan, Mannalargenna, is said to have given his daughter Woretemoeteyenner to Briggs in marriage, suggesting that Mannalargenna is the chieftain named Lamanbunganah in Kelly's narrative. The nature of this marriage is disputed, however. As Plomley and Henley would have it, Briggs abducted his bride (whom they name Waremodeenner), sired several children by her, and then sold her to another sealer, John Thomas, for a guinea sometime after 1820.[41] Surely this is the 'African slave trade in miniature' that George Robinson railed against two decades later.[42] Perhaps not, as Walter and Daniels explain: 'Given that George Briggs learned Woretemoeteyenner's language and was on good terms with her father for many years, it was likely an arrangement rather than a direct abduction.'[43] Woretemoeteyenner's life proved even more remarkable, and some of the couple's children led incredible lives in their own right.[44] 'Dolly' Dalrymple was born in 1812, Eliza in 1817, Mary in 1818, and John in 1820. Another was fated to die in childhood, however:

> One of these women, who had been for many years
> attached to a sailor, a young man of respectable
> connections, but of a wild and volatile disposition,
> one evening wandered from her sealing party
> with a young child at her breast, and accidentally

> falling in with a band of natives, was immediately
> attacked, and threatened to be severely punished;
> her infant was snatched from her, and thrown into
> a large fire [... the woman] plucked her child from
> the devouring element and ran off with it into the
> woods [...] making her escape [and] before morning
> reached the town of Launceston, a distance of about
> 10 miles, where she once more found a comfortable
> home at the residence of a gentleman of that place.
> This gentleman and his lady, greatly to their credit,
> had previously taken under their protection, the
> eldest child of this woman, now a fine girl about
> 11 years old, and the first child born by a native
> woman to a white man in Van Diemen's Land. She
> is called Miss Dalrymple.[45]

Historian Lynette Russell explores the nature of the relationship between English sealers and Tasmanian Aboriginal women in *Roving Mariners*, arguing that she is 'seeking an alternative view of this past that disrupts the idea that it can be easily and unproblematically divided into simple dichotomies and binaries of colonizer and colonized'.[46] While George Robinson saw only slavery for Tasmanian Aboriginal women, Russell asserts that these women 'lived complex lives that shifted and altered over time, sometimes even morphing from captive to partner and wife, all the while maintaining their cultural sense of themselves'.[47]

We do not know to what extent Briggs and Woretemoeteyenner considered themselves husband and wife, but uncomfortable facts remain. 'Dolly' was baptised Dalrymple Mountgarrett Briggs in Launceston by Reverend Knopwood in 1814,[48] at which time Dolly was not living with her parents but with surgeon Jacob Mountgarrett and his wife Bridget. Briggs' second wife, whom Plomley and Henley call 'Meetoneyernanner' or 'Dumpe', later lived with another sealer, Tom Tucker.[49] Robinson wrote in his journal that 'Dumpe [was] living with Tucker and by whom she has a child living, has killed two children, a boy and a girl, directly after they were born, and [Tucker] beat her plenty with a stick or club'.[50] Meanwhile, Woretemoeteyenner was sold to John Thomas for the price of one guinea. While it is difficult to imagine this as anything other than slavery, it is worth noting that it was not only women of Aboriginal descent who were bought and sold in Van Diemen's Land. Alison Alexander points to an incident in 1816 in which a man 'brought his wife to hammer' after which 'she was sold and delivered to a settler for one gallon of rum and 20 ewes.'[51] In Van Diemen's Land, women were often seen as commodities and were frequently treated in a manner we would consider barbaric.

Briggs fades into obscurity after 1816. On June 19, 1819, the pages of the *Hobart Town Gazette* report that 'Mr Charles Read proceeding on the Schooner *Sindbad* from Port Dalrymple, requests all claims against him may be presented for payment. – Also George Briggs, servant.'[52] In October of that same year, we see Briggs departing Sydney aboard Glory,[53] and in June 1823 he is aboard Nereus, its muster offering our only physical description of the man. Briggs is described as having 'hazel eyes, light red hair, fair ruddy complexion and freckles; from Dunstable (Bedfordshire)', later finding work as a 'seaman on Griffiths' schooner (June 1831).'[54] *Geneanet* lists Briggs' death as July 11, 1837, and his burial place as Kingston,[55] the latter of which seems unlikely as Kingston, then known as Browns River, was nothing more than a hamlet in 1837. *FamilySearch* would have it that Briggs was buried at Cornelian Bay in Hobart,[56] but this is also unlikely as it did not open until 1872, although some remains from older cemeteries were relocated there. It seems more likely that Briggs' final resting place was in Launceston, although no record has ever been found.

I am a Briggs too, albeit one descended from a different George Briggs. My great-grandmother Mary Ann Briggs was born in Grimsby, Lincolnshire in 1884. Her parents were Thomas and Mary Codd Briggs, born in Lincolnshire in 1843 and 1844. Thomas' parents were George and Catherine Rose Briggs, born in Lincolnshire in 1800 and 1803. My most distant recorded Briggs ancestor is John Briggs, born in 1754. Fourteen years later, George William Christopher Lamuel Briggs' father William was born in Austerfield, South Yorkshire, no more than forty miles from the birthplace of my ancestors. This is not surprising as roughly halfway between Austerfield and Grimsby lies the village of Brigg, ancestral home of the Briggs clan.

Julie Gough, Tasmanian artist and descendent of Woretemoeteyenner and George Briggs, explores the lives of her ancestors in her artwork. Gough's 2007 piece representing the trauma of Woretemoeteyenner's sale consists of a 'book sealed shut with a funereal black beaded cover'.[57] Gough writes that, '[t]his artwork is about the frustration, anxiety and anger that I carry about those times. I am like this closed book; this story is in me, but it is hard to fathom.'[58] As difficult and as traumatic as opening this book might be, it is the story of our shared history and one we must call our own.

NOTES

1 James Boyce, *Van Diemen's Land* (Melbourne: Black Inc., 2008), 96.

2 KM Bowden, *Captain James Kelly of Hobart Town* (Adelaide: The Griffiths Press, 1964), 36.

3 Ibid.

4 Ibid.

5 ER Pretyman, 'Some Notes on the Life and Times of Captain James Kelly,' *Papers & Proceedings of the Royal Society of Tasmania*, 1970, Vol. 105, 111.

6 Bowden, *Captain James Kelly*, 31.

7 Ibid., 35.

8 *Historical Records of Australia, Series 3 Vol. 2.* (Sydney: Government Printer, 1921), 192.

9 Ibid., 252.

10 'England Births and Christenings, 1538–1975 Database', FamilySearch, accessed July 13, 2022, https://familysearch.org/ark:/61903/1:1:JMG1-N52

11 FamilySearch, accessed July 13, 2022, https://www.familysearch.org/tree/person/details/L6N1-P2W.

12 'UK, Prison Commission Records, 1770–1951', Ancestry, accessed July 13, 2022, https://www.ancestry.com.au/imageviewer/collections/61810/images/61810_pcom2_180-00233?treeid=&personid=&hintid=&queryId=79a0c0eb2a794e3d54926e5528d6af04&usePUB=true&_phsrc=AvW2981&_phstart=successSource&usePUBJs=true&_ga=2.206240342.419159320.1617527302-1279535119.1546417886&_gac=1.21017289.1614477214.Cj0KCQiA-OeBBhDiARIsADyBcE6_PrAQq5ILUVXzoRsTMMrXVeRpJKQ5bMdyYg_mY_VLEdMcsj9FEAkaAhjJEALw_wcB&pId=626307&lang=en-AU.

13 David Wells, *The Thames River Police* (London: West India Committee, 2017), 12.

14 Ibid.

15 Ibid., 18.

16 NJB Plomley and K. Henley, 'The Sealers of Bass Strait and the Cape Barren Island Community', *Tasmanian Historical Research Association*, 1990, Vol. 37, 54.

17 Bowden, *Captain James Kelly of Hobart Town*, 23.

18 'Harrington (1796 ship)', Wikipedia, accessed July 13, 2022, https://en.wikipedia.org/wiki/Harrington_(1796_ship)

19 *Historical Records of New South Wales, Vol. 4* (Sydney: Government Printer, 1895), 410.

20 Francois Péron, *King Island and the Sealing Trade 1802* (Canberra: Roebuck Society, 1971), 16.

21 Ibid., 16.

22 Ibid., 8.

23 JCH Gill, 'Notes on the Sealing Industry of Early Australia', *Journal of the Royal Historical Society of Queensland*, 1967, Vol. 8, 223.

24 Ibid., 225.

25 Ibid.

26 DR Hainsworth, 'Iron Men in Wooden Ships: the Sydney Sealers 1800–1820', *Australian Society for the Study of Labour History*, 1967, Vol. 13, 19.

27 Peter Entwisle, *Taka: A Vignette Life of William Tucker 1784–1817* (Dunedin: Port Daniel Press, 2005), 37.

28 Hainsworth, 'Iron Men in Wooden Ships', 20.

29 Lynette Russell, *Roving Mariners: Australian Aboriginal Whalers and Sealers in the Southern Oceans, 1790–1870* (Albany: State University of New York Press, 2012), 95.

30 Ibid.

31 Péron, *King Island and the Sealing Trade 1802*, 44.

32 Plomley and Henley, 'The Sealers of Bass Strait and the Cape Barren Island Community', 54.

33 *The Sydney Gazette and New South Wales Advertiser*, April 14, 1805, 1.

34 *The Sydney Gazette and New South Wales Advertiser*, December 8, 1805, 2.

35 'New South Wales and Tasmania, Australia Convict Musters, 1806–1849', Ancestry, accessed July 13, 2022, https://www. ancestry.com.au/discoveryui-content/view/308609:1185?ti d=&pid=&queryId=1e4bdc96a0835cceaf2e976f972907f3&_ phsrc=Kaa8&_phstart=successSource

36 *The Sydney Gazette and New South Wales Advertiser*, November 6, 1808, 2.

37 *The Sydney Gazette and New South Wales Advertiser*, July 30, 1809, 1.

38 *The Sydney Gazette and New South Wales Advertiser*, April 7, 1810, 1.

39 Patsy Cameron, *Grease and Ochre: the Blending of Two Cultures at the Colonial Sea Frontier* (Hobart: Fullers Bookshop Pty Ltd, 2011), 74.

40 Ibid.

41 Plomley and Henley, 'The Sealers of Bass Strait and the Cape Barren Island Community', 74.

42 NJB Plomley, *Friendly Mission: the Tasmanian Journals and Papers of George Augustus Robinson 1829–34* (Hobart: Quintus Publishing, 2008), 91.

43 Maggie Walter and Louise Daniels, 'Personalising the History Wars: Woretemoeteyenner's story', *International Journal of Critical Indigenous Studies*, 2008, Vol.1, 37.

44 Ibid.

45 Charles Jeffreys, *Van Diemen's Land: Geographical and Descriptive Delineations of the Island of Van Diemen's Land* (London: JM Richardson, 1820), 120.

46 Russell, *Roving Mariners,* 17–18.

47 Ibid., 19.

48 Walter and Daniels, 'Personalising the History Wars', 37.

49 Plomley, *Friendly Mission,* 327.

50 Ibid.

51 Alison Alexander, *Corruption and Skullduggery: Edward Lord, Maria Riseley and Hobart's Tempestuous Beginnings* (Dynnyrne: Pillinger Press, 2015), 133.

52 *Hobart Town Gazette and Southern Reporter,* July 19, 1819, 1.

53 *The Sydney Gazette and New South Wales Advertiser,* October 2, 1819, 3.

54 Plomley and Henley, 'The Sealers of Bass Strait and the Cape Barren Island Community', 74.

55 Geneanet, accessed July 13, 2022, https://gw.geneanet.org/alisontassie?lang=en&p=george+william+christopher+lamuel&n=briggs

56 FamilySearch, accessed July 13, 2022, https://www.familysearch.org/tree/person/details/L6N1-P2W.

57 Julie Gough, *Fugitive History: The Art of Julie Gough* (Perth: UWAP, 2018), 15.

58 Ibid., 266.

ACKNOWLEDGEMENTS

I am deeply indebted to Aunty Patsy Cameron for her boundless generosity and invaluable advice in the representation of Tasmanian northeast clan language in *Diemens*. Aunty Patsy is a tireless advocate for the language and culture of her people and working with her was an incredible experience.

Many friends and family members read drafts of *Diemens* over the years, assisting and encouraging me with their advice. Thank you to Amanda Fiore, Alan Fyfe, Anthony Phillips, Cat Sparks, Marty Young and, most importantly, my mother Diane Drury.

I would like to thank Dr David Whish-Wilson and Dr Anne Ryden at Curtin University for their expertise and kind words of support in guiding me through my research journey. While writing *Diemens*, I had the opportunity to travel to Tasmania several times and to meet many people who helped me in various ways. My thanks to Raymond Arnold, David Fitzpatrick, Rick Snell, as well as Ivy and the rest of the volunteers at the Bass & Flinders Maritime Museum. Thank you also to Dr Rayne Allinson, Kent Whitmore and Lucinda Sharp at Forty South Publishing for assisting with the publication of this work.

On p198, news of Napoleon's defeat comes from p1 of the *London Gazette*, 12 June 1815. On p222 is an excerpt from p2 of the *Sydney Gazette*, 17 October 1818. On p257 is an excerpt from p3 of the *Sydney Gazette*, 13 November 1819.

The Davy Lowston song on pp186-7 is traditional and of unknown origin.

ABOUT THE AUTHOR

GUY SALVIDGE is a writer and English teacher who is currently in the final stages of completing a PhD in Creative Writing at Curtin University. His fiction has been awarded the City of Rockingham, Joe O'Sullivan and IP Picks prizes. Guy is the author of the novels *Yellowcake Springs*, *Yellowcake Summer* and *Complicity City*. He lives in rural Western Australia with his wife and children but he hopes someday to live in lutruwita/ Tasmania.

www.ingramcontent.com/pod-product-compliance
Lightning Source LLC
Chambersburg PA
CBHW030804210726
48290CB00002B/419